Kim,

Thanks for your support!

Sawyer Bennett

Sawyer Bennett

Legal Affairs Boxed Set
Volumes 1 – 6
Objection
Stipulation
Violation
Mitigation
Reparation
Affirmation

By Sawyer Bennett

All Rights Reserved.
Copyright © 2014 by Sawyer Bennett
Published by Big Dog Books

This book is a work of fiction. Names, characters, places and incidents either are products of the author's imagination or are used fictitiously. Any resemblance to actual events, locales or persons, living or dead, is entirely coincidental.

No part of this book can be reproduced in any form or by electronic or mechanical means including information storage and retrieval systems, without the express written permission of the author. The only exception is by a reviewer who may quote short excerpts in a review.

ISBN: 978-1-940883-18-2

Find Sawyer on the web!
www.sawyerbennett.com
www.twitter.com/bennettbooks
www.facebook.com/bennettbooks

Contents

OBJECTION

Chapter One	.....	5
Chapter Two	.....	10
Chapter Three	.....	16
Chapter Four	.....	21
Chapter Five	.....	26
Chapter Six	.....	32
Chapter Seven	.....	38
Chapter Eight	.....	45
Chapter Nine	.....	51
Chapter Ten	.....	57
Chapter Eleven	.....	63
Chapter Twelve	.....	69

STIPULATION

Chapter One	.....	79
Chapter Two	.....	85
Chapter Three	.....	91
Chapter Four	.....	97
Chapter Five	.....	102
Chapter Six	.....	108
Chapter Seven	.....	114
Chapter Eight	.....	120
Chapter Nine	.....	125
Chapter Ten	.....	131

VIOLATION

Chapter One	.....	141
Chapter Two	.....	147
Chapter Three	.....	153
Chapter Four	.....	159
Chapter Five	.....	165
Chapter Six	.....	173
Chapter Seven	.....	178
Chapter Eight	.....	184
Chapter Nine	.....	189
Chapter Ten	.....	195
Chapter Eleven	.....	201

MITIGATION

Chapter One	.....	211
Chapter Two	.....	216
Chapter Three	.....	221
Chapter Four	.....	227
Chapter Five	.....	232
Chapter Six	.....	239
Chapter Seven	.....	244
Chapter Eight	.....	251
Chapter Nine	.....	256
Chapter Ten	.....	261
Chapter Eleven	.....	267

REPARATION

Chapter One	.....	279
Chapter Two	.....	284
Chapter Three	.....	290
Chapter Four	.....	297

Chapter Five	.....	303
Chapter Six	.....	308
Chapter Seven	.....	313
Chapter Eight	.....	320
Chapter Nine	.....	326
Chapter Ten	.....	333

AFFIRMATION

Chapter One	.....	345
Chapter Two	.....	351
Chapter Three	.....	357
Chapter Four	.....	363
Chapter Five	.....	368
Chapter Six	.....	374
Chapter Seven	.....	381
Chapter Eight	.....	388
Chapter Nine	.....	394
Chapter Ten	.....	400
Chapter Eleven	.....	406
Chapter Twelve	.....	412
Chapter Thirteen	.....	418
Chapter Fourteen	.....	423
Epilogue	.....	428

Thank you for reading!

Books by Sawyer Bennett

About the Author

OBJECTION

Sawyer Bennett

LEGAL AFFAIRS
Vol. 1 - Objection

By Sawyer Bennett

All Rights Reserved.
Copyright © 2013 by Sawyer Bennett
Published by Big Dog Books

This book is a work of fiction. Names, characters, places and incidents either are products of the author's imagination or are used fictitiously. Any resemblance to actual events, locales or persons, living or dead, is entirely coincidental.

No part of this book can be reproduced in any form or by electronic or mechanical means including information storage and retrieval systems, without the express written permission of the author. The only exception is by a reviewer who may quote short excerpts in a review.

Chapter One

Looking in the mirror, I tug on the tight, red mini dress that I'm wearing. It's hugging my hips like a glove, and my breasts are practically spilling out. The only good thing is that the color goes wonderfully with my raven-colored hair and green eyes.

"I look like a slut," I complain to Macy.

She comes to stand behind me, perusing my appearance. "Exactly! That's just what I was going for."

Turning to her with pleading eyes, I say, "I can't go through with this. I was drunk when I agreed to it."

Macy's blue eyes alight with mischief as she takes me by the shoulders, turning me back around to the mirror. She looks at me in the reflection. "Yet you agreed all the same, McKayla, and you only have five minutes left before you have to leave to meet your date. Now, go put on that sexy red lipstick to match your dress."

Date.

Funny word for what this is.

Two weeks ago, in a moment of drunken despair over losing my boyfriend of three years, Macy talked me into trying this exclusive and discreet service that she was a member of. It was called One Night Only, and it catered to the rich and sexually depraved of New York's finest. Macy had been a proud member for the past two years and swore by it.

But then again, Macy is... well, Macy. She is my dearest friend in the world, my roommate for the past six years, and perhaps the weirdest, most ostentatious, and most deviant socialite that New York has ever seen. She graduated from Columbia with me, earning a political science degree that she had no intention of ever using. While I went on to schlep my way through Columbia's law school program over the next three years, Macy was on the hunt for the future Mr. Macy Carrington.

That's right... she expects her husband to take

her name and refer to himself that way. Her qualifications are clear. He has to be equally as rich as her, wouldn't mind her taking the occasional lover, and would need to treat her like the queen she believes herself to be.

Until that time, she is happy spending her nights partying and getting her rocks off—her words, not mine—through One Night Only.

Back to that.

It's a service that is highly secretive, but in major demand. It caters to those people that are looking for one-night stands with a partner who is matched to their specifications and guaranteed disease free. Macy pays an exorbitant amount of her inheritance each month for club benefits, which usually means she's going on a different "date" at least four times a week.

That puts her square in the category of skankerific, but I still love her more than I love the air I breathe. Macy and I have been together through thick and thin, ups and downs, love and betrayal. She's stood by me when no one else would, and I give her the love and acceptance she's never had from her emotionally cold, but uber wealthy parents.

Macy has her quirks—her deviant behavior, for one—but there has never been a more loyal person to me in the world. Besides that, she's let me live in her Manhattan penthouse apartment dirt cheap for the last six years because I was a poor and impoverished undergrad, and now I'm a poor and impoverished attorney. I graduated from law school a year ago with a crappy job that keeps me busy eighty hours a week and a $120,000 in law school loans that will take me until I am seventy to pay off.

Taking the lipstick from my makeup drawer, I coat my lips with the Hooker Red stain and brush some gloss over them. Even though I'm having major second thoughts about what I'm getting ready to do, there's also a part of me—deep down—that is thrilled to be doing something so far out of my comfort zone…

Having a one-night stand.

I wouldn't be in this position had my boyfriend, Pete—aka the Douche—not ripped my heart out six months ago. Over what was, I thought, a romantic dinner that would result in a marriage proposal, he ended up telling me that he wanted to break up. Something about wanting to travel the world as a wildlife photographer and not wanting to be pinned down. I thought that was weird… seeing as how I don't even think he owned a camera.

So I said goodbye to the Douche, immersed myself in misery and work, and yes, in a night of complete drunkenness, agreed to Macy's idea that I join One Night Only… at her expense, of course.

By the time I woke up the next morning, with a raging headache and puke in my throat, Macy had me signed up. A simple physical and blood test later, and I was a full-fledged member.

Now I have a date with Number 134—a tall, gorgeous hunk of a man that is supposedly going to put my battery-operated boyfriend to shame tonight. I made sure my application said I was only interested in vanilla sex, and I apparently was matched to someone with the same tastes.

Smacking my lips together, I turn to Macy once more for her final assessment. She gives me the critical eye, running her eyes over me slowly while she taps her finger to her chin. "You are definitely one-hundred percent, perfectly fuckable."

Rolling my eyes at her, I pick up my clutch purse and double check my contents. Credit card, iPhone, lip gloss, and Mace.

All a girl could ever wish for on a date.

Date.

Funny word.

CHAPTER Two

Holy shit!
This is it.
No turning back.

I walk into Sullivan's, a swanky bar on the Upper East Side, where Number 134 suggested we meet. Our communications so far have been limited to one encrypted, anonymous email from Number 134 (him) to Number 3498 (me) setting the date, time, and place. If our membership numbers have been assigned chronologically, then he's clearly been in the system for a while. He said he'd arrange for the hotel so I didn't have to worry about it.

As pre-arranged, I went up to the bar and took a seat, ordering a white wine from the bartender. I arrived almost half an hour early, hoping to get one drink under my belt to calm the nerves that were jangling around inside of me.

I want to do this. Despite my hesitations, I really, really want to do this. But it still doesn't stop me from being nervous over meeting Number 134.

He told me to call him Mike, but that's not really his name. Everything is about the anonymity, and I told him my name was Stella. I doubt we'd even use the fake names we gave each other. It's not like we'd be having any deep conversation tonight, and I have no plans to reveal any more identifying information about myself.

As soon as the bartender sets my wine in front of me, I hear, "I'll pay for that."

It's on my lips to decline... to say that I'm waiting on someone, but when I turn to the voice, I'm assaulted by the decadence that is none other than Number 134 himself.

He's even more beautiful than his picture, radiating pure magnetism and sex appeal. He's tall, which is good, because I am, too. But I can tell he'll tower over my five-nine frame by several inches.

Dark brown hair cropped in a fashionable, yet short style, along with an elegant, dark gray suit. I peg him as a banker or financier. His eyes are golden-brown, more golden than anything. He's smiling at me in a completely relaxed, but I'm here to fuck you senseless, kind of way, and it manages to show the two dimples he sports on either side of his full lips.

If what's in his pants is as magnificent as what's on the outside, I'm going to go to sleep a very happy girl tonight. He's utterly perfect. Exactly what I need.

Number 134... I mean Mike... hands over his credit card to the bartender, telling him that he'll have a Jameson neat. I'm surprised, because I didn't think we'd be staying here long. Idle chitchat, schmoozing, or wooing is not required tonight. Us sleeping together is pretty much a done deal.

Turning to me, Mike sticks out his hand. "Mike... Number 134 at your service, Stella."

Giving a light laugh, I place my palm against his to shake, but he lifts my hand to his lips to brush a light kiss there. In any other circumstances, it would have been a completely cheesy move, but somehow... Mike owns it, as evidenced by the chills that break out on my arm.

He releases his hold on me, and I rest my arms on the bar. Mike takes the seat next to me, propping one arm on the bar and another on the back of my barstool. Again, under ordinary circumstances, this move would have seemed a little too proprietary for two people that had just met. But given the fact we would be getting vertical—or maybe it would be horizontal, who knows—it seems like a natural move.

"So, what's a guy like you doing in a place like this?" I quip.

Mike chuckles and it's rich and warm, causing me to immediately lose some of my nervousness. "Well," he says conspiratorially as he leans in toward me, "I heard there was going to be a stunningly ravishing woman at this bar tonight, and I simply had to come out and try to win her."

I laugh and take a sip of wine. "I heard about this woman. They say she's kind of a sure bet, so I don't think you have anything to worry about."

Grinning at me, Mike reaches a finger out to tuck a lock of my hair behind my ear. It's an intimate move and one that I find myself very much enjoying. He looks at me, his lips pursed in amusement. "I have to say. I'm beyond pleased with our match. Your picture had me entranced, but it really didn't do you justice."

"You did hear the part where I said I was a sure bet, right? No need to spout compliments. I'm sleeping with you tonight," I tell him with a return grin.

"Yet, I felt compelled to give it to you all the same. I'm the kind of man that sort of just speaks his mind."

"I like that. In fact," I say, my voice just a tad lower as I lean in toward him, "what exactly is on your mind for tonight?"

It's so weird how odd this conversation is, yet how natural it feels at the same time. It's almost liberating... knowing exactly how the night is going to end and doing away with all pretense. I've never been a sexually overt person, but tonight—dolled up in my sluttiest dress, with a tiny scrap of lace covering my goods below—knowing that Mike will have his hands all over me soon... Well, it sort of brings out my inner sex kitten.

Mike's eye's flare wide over my question, and his smile takes on a more carnal look. He takes the hand that is resting on my barstool and brings it behind my neck, cupping me firmly. Pulling me closer, he leans in, running his lips lightly along my jaw until they are hovering near my ear.

"You want to know what's on my mind?" he growls, and I nod helplessly.

He places a light kiss below my ear and says, "I'm trying to decide if I want to fuck you in the elevator or wait until we get in the room. Then I'm trying to figure out if I should fuck you missionary or from behind... probably both, and only after I've gone down on you. Then it's always open for debate whether I take you out on the balcony. It's been a fantasy of mine, you see, and I made sure to reserve a room with a gorgeous view over Central Park tonight."

My mouth goes dry, and my tongue slips out to swipe at my lips. Mike pulls back and his eyes are burning with lust, causing my skin to tighten and my legs to involuntarily press tightly together. Turning to the bartender, I hold up my hand, signaling that we're ready for our check, even though Mike hasn't even received his drink yet.

CHAPTER Three

I'm in the Twilight Zone.

That must be the reason.

Otherwise, there is no plausible or sane explanation for the wanton behavior that I'm exhibiting right this very moment.

Me... an upstanding member of this community and member of the New York State Bar. A reputable young woman who now stands in an elevator with Mike's lips roaming my neck and his finger sunk deep inside of me.

He wasted no time as he pushed the button to our floor and the doors closed. He stalked toward me, cupping my head to bring my mouth to his, and his other hand going directly between my legs.

It was a thrilling turn on, causing waves of pleasure to pulse through me, while his tongue dominated mine in the most searing, sexually explosive kiss I had ever been given. His expert hand softly fondled me for a moment, and then he was inside of me, curling his finger in a way that had my knees buckling. He immediately saved the day by pushing one of his legs in between mine to hold me steady.

When the elevator starts to slow near our floor, Mike calmly removes his hand, smoothes my dress down, and gives me a light kiss on my nose. I manage to drag my glazed eyes up to his and mumble a word of "Thanks", to which he smirks, "Any time."

When we get into the room, which is fabulously gorgeous and does indeed have a huge balcony overlooking Central Park, Mike asks, "Do you want another drink?"

Away from the sexy foreplay in the elevator and now faced with a man who seems super composed and calm, I'm suddenly very shy. I shake my head no, however, because I want to get this moving... back to the land of sex and lust, where I can get lost and forget about my heartaches.

Smiling, Mike crooks a finger at me, and I walk

up to him. When I'm within reaching distance, he takes my hand, softly rubbing the back with his thumb.

"So, how often have you done this... used One Night Only?"

"This is my first time," I tell him, red staining my cheeks.

"Really?" he asks in surprise. "You seem so confident... at least, downstairs you did. Now I'm seeing it though... a touch of shyness."

"Don't worry," I assure him. "I'm not getting cold feet. I'm going through with this."

"Damn right, you're going through with it," he says with a confidence that is slightly menacing, but strangely sexy. "I felt enough of your response in the elevator to know that. But don't worry... tonight—I'll lead."

Just like that, my nerves quiet and a sense of bold confidence takes root. Taking a step back from him, I reach to the side of my dress and drag my zipper down. "You can lead. But I'll start."

Mike's eyes go darkly intense, cutting deep into me. "By all means," he murmurs.

Peeling my dress off, I let it slip to the floor and step out of it. I chose my lingerie carefully tonight, opting for a black lace bra that made my B puppies look like Cs and a matching lace G-string that tied at my hips. I leave on my four-inch black Louboutins—

compliments of Macy—knowing they add to my overall sex appeal.

Now that I am virtually naked in front of him, and taking note of the way his eyes roam hungrily over my body, and yeah... now noticing the impressive erection that is tenting his dress pants, I have another case of shyness overtake me.

"It's your turn to take over," I tell him, hoping he'll become the leader he promised me he'd be.

Mike steps up close to me and grazes his knuckles over the swell of my breasts. My body shivers, and he gives a rumble of appreciation deep in his throat.

"Standing up or lying down? Bed or balcony? Missionary or doggie style? Any preference?"

His voice is low, gravely, filled with sex and lust, and my mind swims with the possibilities. Swallowing hard, I say, "I don't care... as long as there's an orgasm involved."

Chuckling, Mike sweeps me up in his arms and starts carrying me to the bed. "I guarantee you two... to start out with."

Oh, please, yes!

When I'm laid out and on full display before him, Mike steps back and quickly sheds his clothes. I watch him... holding my breath as he reveals himself to me. His chest, his abs. All rock hard and chiseled muscle that clearly shows he works out—a lot. I follow the dark brown trail of hair that starts right below his belly button and watch as he takes his pants off, revealing a massive erection that looks to be blessed from the Heavens above.

God, I hope that's going to fit, or I'm going to be walking funny for some time to come.

But it would be so worth it, I bet.

My eyes widen as Mike takes himself in his hand and starts to stroke. He grows unfathomably larger before my eyes, and I swallow hard.

I can't help myself when I giggle and voice my inner thoughts. "I hope that will fit."

A blinding smile peels across his face, and he laughs. "You're funny. But no worries… I'm going to have you so wet, I'll slide right home. Trust me."

And I do for some reason. Because he is standing before me, radiating sexual charm and a confidence that is unmatched. Besides… he's Number 134. He's been around the block a time or two.

I guarantee he knows what he's doing, and that's good enough by me.

Chapter Four

My bedroom door flies open and Macy comes barreling in, launching herself on top of me.

"Tell me, tell me, tell me! I want details. I was too tired and couldn't stay awake for you to tell me last night when you got home."

Snickering, I think to myself, That's because I didn't come home last night.

I had gotten in around 5:30 AM and, as I glance over at the clock, I see it's only a little after eight. Mike and I had stayed up all night and into the wee hours of the morning. I don't even remember the amount of times we had sex… or in between having sex, fooled around. It was a cornucopia of kisses, licks, touches, thrusts, and oh, shit… just thinking about it now makes my girlie parts start to wake up on overdrive.

I snuggle back down into my blankets as a smile plays across my face, thinking about last night.

Mike had indeed given me two orgasms to start out with. He had stripped my bra and panties off, leaving the Louboutins on because he said they were "sexy as fuck". Pulling my legs apart and crawling in between, he'd proceeded to show me that, with his mouth alone, I could come twice in under five minutes.

Taking the lead as he promised, he chose missionary to start out, granting me another quick orgasm as his hand worked me and his hips pumped hard. He then flipped me over on my hands and knees and brought me to the promised land once again. Only then, did he finally come for the first time.

He didn't need long to recover and, in between, we shared a bottle of water and talked about mundane stuff, neither one of us willing to reveal what we did for a living. We talked about movies and the arts, and then, all of a sudden, Mike picked me up off the bed and carried me out onto the balcony. It was dark and we were sheltered, but New York buzzed below us. He took me from behind again while I gazed out over Central Park and tried not to scream too loudly when nirvana struck me.

I blush when I remember that Mike took me straight from the balcony into the shower, equipped with no less than eight water nozzles. He slowly washed me, and then himself, and when he was done, he pushed me gently down to my knees and said, "Let's see how fast you can get me back into the game."

That thought alone starts my blood flowing because it was incredibly domineering, but also incredibly hot. Plus, I had been imagining doing that to him anyway, so it was with a happy smile on my face that I took him into my mouth. I was never very good at giving a blow job—I think because I just didn't enjoy doing it. But for some reason… with Mike… it was an almost divine experience for me. I knew he was exhausted, and he had just come supremely hard not ten minutes before, but I immediately wrought out strained groans and hip flexes with my touch, and yeah… it didn't take him that long at all to get back into the game again.

Then it was on for some all-out, slippery good shower sex.

Finally, we crashed on the bed, spooning and dozing for a few hours, his arms wrapped tightly around me. I woke to him poking me from behind as his hand went between my legs again. Within moments, I was ready for him, and he had lifted my leg to enter me from behind.

Finally, yes... finally, because dayum... I was getting a little sore, Mike told me he wanted to give me a big send off. He crawled back between my legs once more, putting that gorgeous face and those sinful lips against me, and made me come one last time. I'll have to say, he had to work for it that time, because I was beyond exhausted. I had even pushed his head away at one point, telling him to forget about it... I didn't think I had another orgasm in me, but he merely swatted my hands away while growling and doubled up on his efforts. It took him thirty minutes, but he got the job done, and I'm proud to say that last time he made me come was the strongest of them all.

Then... it was over.

We got dressed, walked down to the lobby together, and Mike waited for me to get a cab. He gave me a soft kiss on my lips and whispered, "That may have been the best night of my life. I shit you not!"

I snickered on the inside, because... come on... seriously? A guy like Mike has some major experience, and I'm betting he's had many nights like that. But for me... I won't lie... it was absolutely the best freakin' sex I'd ever had in my life, and I'm pretty sure it can't be topped.

"Are you going to give me the juicy details or not?" Macy complains.

"Or not," I grumble, trying to burrow deeper into my covers. It's Sunday, and I plan to sleep most of it away.

"Fine," she huffs. "Just tell me... on a scale of one to ten—"

"Eleven," I cut her off before she can even finish.

"Eleven?" she asks, stunned.

"Solid eleven," I assure her.

That satisfies her for now and she jumps off my bed, yelling that she's going to make us breakfast, but already my eyes are starting to close from fatigue. No sooner do they shut though, than my phone starts ringing. Grabbing it from the nightstand, I see it's from my boss, Lorraine Cummings. It's not a call I can ignore. It doesn't matter what I'm doing, or what time of the day or night, she always expects me to answer.

Clearing my throat, I try to sound chipper when I say, "Good morning, Lorraine. What can I do for you?"

"I have some important news, McKayla. I need you to get down to the office right now."

CHAPTER Five

Un-fucking-believable.

It's my first day on my new job, and Monday is as craptastic as ever. I'm running fifteen minutes late.

And yes, a new job.

Just Friday… when I had left the office, I worked for Lorraine Cummings, a ferocious bulldog of an attorney who has made my life a living hell. She demanded no less than eighty-hour work weeks, and she liked to think I was her own personal, verbal punching bag. She demanded, never said thank you, and usually yelled at me fifty percent of the time I was in her near vicinity.

When I dragged my tired ass into the office on Sunday morning following her call, she advised me that the Law Firm of Lorraine Cummings had been "acquired" by the firm of Connover and Crown, LLP and starting the very next day, I would report to work at their offices on West 56th.

I loved how she said the word "acquired," as if she was some sort of conglomeration that was just ripe for the picking. Truth be told, I knew Lorraine had been struggling for months with the bills because I had missed a paycheck or two. She always promised me she'd catch me up but so far, I've not seen a cent of it.

I've thought... no dreamed, of finding another job, and I even have feelers out. But this economy is tough, and there's a glut of fresh-faced, new attorneys out there all battling for the same measly job on the bottom of the totem pole. Unless you graduated first in your class, you were on a one-way ticket to probably nowhere. And sadly, I'd graduated at the top of the bottom third in my class.

Lorraine assured me I had a job at Connover and Crown, basically due to a whole lot of begging she did on my behalf, and that she and I would embark on a new and glorious adventure together.

I had to bite down hard on my tongue not to laugh at that. You see, I may not have been a bright, shining star in my law school class, but I wasn't stupid either. I'm going to Connover and Crown not because Lorraine had to beg on my behalf but rather because I have a case. No, not just a case... an immensely fucking great case. A case that is worth millions, along with a client that thinks the sun rises and sets upon me. Lorraine can't kick me to the curb because the case will go with me, and frankly... I'm betting that one case is why I'm employed at Connover and Crown.

I'm thankful to have a job, and I'll have to see how these circumstances pan out. But for now, I am extremely late thanks to hitting my snooze button five times in a row this morning. After my meeting with Lorraine, I came back to the apartment and crawled into bed, sleeping the rest of the day and night away. I barely had time this morning to wrap my wet hair in a severe bun and Google the directions to my new place of employment.

As soon as the elevator opens on the twenty-first floor, I practically run into the lobby, causing my heels to skid to an ungraceful stop in front of the receptionist. The platinum-blonde ice princess behind the mahogany desk gives me a snotty once over, and says, "Your shirt is buttoned up wrong."

Looking down, I say, "Oh shit," and hastily refasten my blouse, thankful that no one else is in the lobby.

When I'm presentable, she says, "You must be McKayla Dawson. The meeting is already underway. Mr. Connover is not going to be happy you're late. He's a perfectionist when it comes to that stuff."

As if to accentuate her message, she snaps her chewing gum in her mouth and flattens her lips in a disdainful grimace.

I don't have time for this shit, I'm already irritated I'm late, and it's completely my fault. So, of course, I take it out on her. "Look, Blondie. I'm not one to take shit from anyone, especially not a rude, gum-smacking receptionist. Have a care you don't cross me."

Blondie's eyes go wide and moisten, a fresh sheen of tears pooling.

Oh, fuck. I made her cry, and now I feel like crap. This day could not get any worse.

"Look... I'm sorry," I tell her sincerely, because I have never been able to carry off rude and mean before. "I'm having a bad morning, and I took it out on you. I'm really, really sorry."

I expect her to dash the tears away and sneer at my regretfulness, but instead, she gives me a small smile. "No, I'm sorry. I was rude and well... I don't even have an excuse. You called me on it. Good for you."

Cocking my head at her in curiosity, I stick out

my hand. "What's your name? You already know I'm McKayla, but my friends call me Mac."

She shakes my hand and says, "I'm Bea. Now, hurry down that hall there and take the third door on the right. Oh, and tell Mr. Connover that the train was running late, and you'll be just fine."

Giving her a grin, I head down the hall. "Thanks," I call out as an afterthought, and she shoots me a wave.

When I reach the door she directed me to, I hitch my briefcase satchel over my shoulder and smooth down my skirt. Taking a deep breath, I give a light knock and then open the conference room door.

My eyes immediately lock with Lorraine's, who is sitting on one side of the long, oval table. She glares at me in anger due to my tardiness.

"I'm so sorry I'm late," I apologize. "I—the train was running late this morning. Always seems to happen on Monday."

Lorraine's anger doesn't diminish, and it is with a clipped tone that she says, "Then may I suggest you leave earlier on Mondays. McKayla… this is your new boss, Matthew Connover."

Not needing another second of Lorraine's vicious gaze, I pull my eyes up to the man sitting at the end of the table.

Brown hair… golden eyes… sensuous lips that deliver orgasms upon contact, now set in a surprised grimace on his face.

Holy fuck!

It's Number 134.

CHAPTER *Six*

Matt rises from the conference room table and steps toward me, his hand stretched out. "Miss Dawson... it's lovely to meet you. Lorraine has told me a lot about you."

I'm sure!

Although his words are welcoming, his gaze is frosty as he shakes my hand. He then immediately drops it like I'm diseased.

"Pleased to meet you, Mr. Connover," I manage to choke out, my heart beating like the hooves of a Kentucky Derby winner.

"Call me Matt," he says, and there is no

mistaking his tone of extreme displeasure over me being here. I'm really not getting why he's pissed. It's not like I planned this out. So I do the only thing I know how to do when I'm being attacked for no apparent reason—I stick my chin out and notch my pride up just a little more.

"You can call me McKayla... or Mac."

He inclines his head slightly in acknowledgement and sits back down, indicating the chair to Lorraine's left is where I should sit.

Matt introduces me to a man on the other side of the table. He's about fifty, balding, and looks incredibly worn out. "Mac... this is my partner, William Crown."

He gives me a wan smile and mumbles, "It's Bill, actually. Nice to meet you."

I shoot him a return smile, feeling sorry for his overall beat-down nature. It must be hell to work here or something, and that makes my stomach roll just a little.

"I wanted to have this meeting with you and Lorraine to welcome you to Connover and Crown this morning. We're excited to have you both here." His lack of enthusiasm couldn't be more obvious, but Lorraine pays it no mind. I'm sure she's just happy not to be a struggling business owner now, knowing that she'll get her full paycheck each month.

Lorraine leans over, exposing her deep cleavage, and lays a well-manicured hand on Matt's arm, simpering, "Matt... I know I speak for both McKayla and me when I tell you we are just overjoyed to be part of your team. You can count on us to get the job done."

I want to roll my eyes over her flirtatious gesture, because Lorraine is nothing short of a man-eater. I'm surprised she's not humping his leg as we speak. I have to suppress a giggle though, when Matt's eyes narrow at her overtness and he pulls his arm away.

"Thank you for that sentiment, Lorraine. I'm sure you'll do just fine here."

"More than just fine," she gushes.

Matt doesn't respond but hands Lorraine and me each a folder. "Here are the necessary forms you'll need to fill out for human resources. Lorraine... you'll be direct reporting to Bill, and McKayla... you'll be reporting to me."

Lorraine issues a small cough, and everyone turns their eyes to her. "I thought McKayla would still report to me. I'm very familiar with her work and have the necessary skills to manage her."

Her voice is strong, assured, and I'm betting she thinks Matt will concede. Instead, he just gives her the barest of glances as he stands up from the table. "That's not how we do things here. Your expertise is in corporate work, which falls squarely under Bill's department. McKayla does litigation, which is under my authority. But there will be a few cases that you will work on together and, in those instances, you will be her direct supervisor. Now, after you ladies fill those papers out, I'll have our head of resources, Krystal Anders, come in, get you set up, and introduce you around."

Matt gives a nod to Lorraine, but doesn't spare a glance at me, as he starts to walk out the door. However, I have questions that need answered before I start my career at Connover and Crown.

"Excuse me, Matt… but I have a few questions I need answered."

He turns around with surprise on his face and, yes, a flash of irritation. "I'm sure Miss Anders can answer whatever questions you have."

Matt turns away again, but I stop him. "Actually, I doubt she can. This question is specifically for you."

When he turns back my way, the irritation is still there… but I see something else.

Respect?

Before Matt can answer, Lorraine jumps up from the table. "I apologize, Matt. Our little McKayla here doesn't understand the etiquette of how a high-powered firm works. I'm sure Miss Anders can help her out."

I turn to Lorraine and speak as pleasantly as

possible. "And I'm sure Mr. Connover needs to answer this question."

Lorraine starts to huff, and I can tell she's going to lay into me the way she normally does, but I turn away to look at Matt. He gives me a small smile and says, "By all means... how can I help you?"

"Well, I'm assuming when you 'acquired' Lorraine's firm," and yes, I made air-quotes with my fingers, "you took on all of her assets as well as her debts?"

Matt nods but doesn't say anything.

"I'd like to know if you intend to honor the firm's debt to me of a few missed paychecks I went without when we had some leaner times?"

Matt's eyebrows shoot up in surprise, and then his gaze flicks to Lorraine in question. She starts a flurry of apologies for forgetting about that detail, but Matt just holds up his hand to stop her. Returning his stare to me, he says, "While your question was important, Miss Anders could have indeed handled that. Regardless, I'll ensure your past paychecks are caught up before the end of the day. Now, if you'll excuse me, I have a meeting to attend. I'm sure Miss Anders can handle your other questions."

Lorraine tries to apologize one more time, but he's already opening the door and walking through it. Just before he leaves, he turns to me, "McKayla...

let's plan on meeting at 4:30 PM to go over your new duties in the litigation department."

He doesn't even wait for my response before he's gone, Bill following on his heels.

I stare at the door, lost in thought, my memories of my sex-athon with Matt competing with the cold businessman I just met.

"How could you?" Lorraine hisses at me. "I would have handled those paychecks. You didn't need to bring Matt into it. He must think I'm an idiot."

Or a liar, I think to myself, because I'm sure she left that detail out on purpose, not ever thinking in a million years I'd bring it up.

"Sorry, Lorraine," I say with as much sincerity I can muster. "I'm sure you would have handled it fine."

Turning away from her, I sit back down at the table and prepare to fill out the forms that will now tie me to Matt Connover—extraordinary, one-time lover... and now my boss.

CHAPTER Seven

At promptly 4:30 PM, I present myself to Matt's office. I practically had to have a map drawn to it because his firm is so large. I found out during my initiation tour that Connover and Crown employs thirty-eight lawyers and fifty-two staff persons. Its main practice areas are corporate and civil litigation, although there are also smaller practice areas like elder law, criminal law and the such.

Apparently, Matt built the firm from the ground up, starting it just a mere ten years ago when he had graduated law school. Miss Anders hinted that Matt was the majority owner, and Bill was more or less an original investor, who was sort of just hanging on to a nominal amount of ownership interest at this point.

Knocking, I hear him say, "Come in," and I steel myself to just about anything. When I open the door, I see he's still on the phone, but he waves me in and points to a chair across from him. I settle in and gaze around while he talks.

I take in the understated elegance of his office decor. Browns, tans, and grays seem to be his color preference, and his taste in furniture leans toward the contemporary. Spying his degrees on the wall, I see he did his undergraduate at Stanford and got his law degree at Harvard.

Freakin' smarty pants.

Not that Columbia was anything to sneeze at.

"No, we're not settling for that amount. Twenty-five is our bottom line. You have until close of business tomorrow to decide and let me remind you... I not only represent Mrs. Sanderson, but I also represent each of her three children, and if you don't pay the twenty-five, then I'll be filing Mrs. Sanderson's suit only. And after I've dragged your company through the shit-storm that is our legal system for the next three years, I'll file the first child's suit... and I'll drag your ass through the same shit-storm for the three years after that. Then the next child's, and then the next. I'll have you tied up in litigation long after you're ready to retire from the practice of law, and get this... I could give a fuck if I win even one of those cases. The mere fact I'll drown you in legal expenses makes me go all tingly inside. So do yourself a favor, pay the twenty-five and save yourself the heartburn."

Matt listens for just a few seconds, and then he says, "Very good. I expect the check tomorrow by noon."

He hangs up the phone without a good-bye and immediately types a few notes on his computer. While his long fingers work the keyboard over, I ruminate on that conversation.

Damn, that was some hot legal talk. I have no clue if his case had merit or not, but I would have paid whatever he was telling me to pay after hearing that.

When Matt finally stops typing and swivels his chair to face me, I say, "So... sounds like you just settled a case for $25,000. Congrats."

His face remains impassive, not even a hint of a smile. He says, "Try twenty-five million."

"Excuse me?" I say, stunned, because I surely misheard him.

"Twenty-five million," he reiterates, calm as day.

Clearing my throat and trying to calculate what

one-third of twenty-five million would be, because... holy shit, that's a huge legal fee, I ask, "May I inquire as to what type of case?"

Standing from his computer, Matt walks over to a mini-fridge and pulls out a bottled water. He holds one up to me, but I shake my head no.

"Train accident," he says matter-of-factly. "Mrs. Sanderson and her kids were on a train. They were all killed when a truck driver who was drunk off his ass got his rig stuck on the tracks. Train couldn't stop. Kids and mom died a fiery death."

"Oh," I say quietly. "That's terrible. But hey... you should be happy. What a settlement!"

"It was worth more," he says in disdain, but he doesn't elucidate. However, as an attorney, my interest is peaked way too greatly to let it go at that.

"Then why didn't you settle for more? Seems like you had the upper hand."

With a pained sigh, Matt sits down behind his desk again, taking a sip of his water. "Mrs. Sanderson's husband doesn't want to go to court. At all. He says he just doesn't have it in him to relive the pain of what happened. So he gave me the authority to take the one million they were offering today and told me to make the case go away."

"So you were bluffing just then?"

"That I was," he confirms, sounding neither

proud nor victorious.

I'm impressed with Matt. His overt confidence was a key element in getting Mr. Sanderson justice, but I'd also learned from Miss Anders that Matt has an incredible reputation in the courtroom. He has a track record to back up his bluff, and that was probably the key to getting the case settled.

"I'm not happy about you working here," he says without preamble.

"I gathered that by your icy welcome this morning. I get that you're mad about it. I guess I just can't figure out why?"

His eyebrows raise, and he looks at me, stunned. "You can't figure out why I'm mad? How about because I had my tongue between your legs two days ago, or the fact we both almost overdosed on orgasms, or maybe it's because I got a fucking hard on the minute you walked in that conference room door? Take your pick... there are a variety of reasons why I'm mad."

His words are gritted out, but they have a sexy quality to them as well, and oh my God... the fact he got a hard on from looking at me?

Wow.

Pleasure zings through my body, with the knowledge that I still affect him that way. However, it's with a measured, logical tone, I say, "I'm not sure why this is a problem? We spent a night together. It's over. We forget about it, and we go on."

Matt rolls his eyes at me as if I just said the dumbest thing in the world. "I don't need this shit in my business. I don't need you walking around all doe-eyed at me, hoping for something more."

"What?" I practically shriek at him, anger now surging hot in my veins. "What makes you think I'll be doing that?"

Egotistical moron!

He looks at me like he can't even believe I'd find fault with his reasoning. "I'm just anticipating it. It's a woman thing."

Okay, now I'm beyond pissed. Standing up from my chair, I walk up to the edge of his desk and slap my palms on it. I lean forward and glare at him as if laser beams are shooting from my eyes. The fact that this man is my boss and holds my future employment in his hands does nothing to diminish the nuclear blast of an ass-chewing I'm getting ready to hand out.

"Listen, you jackass," I sneer at him, not caring one whit if this gets me fired. "I can conduct myself in a businesslike manner, and yeah… you got me to scream a few times the other night. But I can guarantee you—you're not the only man in New York that can accomplish that feat. I'm certainly not in any danger of walking around all… What did you call it?

'Doe-eyed?' I'm not even sure what the fuck that is."

My breath is coming out harshly, and I'm daring him to argue with me. He returns my look with a wary gaze, and he chooses to hold his tongue.

Wise man.

"One last thing," I continue. "I'll do my job, and I'll do it well. But if you so much as try to fire me or treat me any differently because of our little encounter, I'll sue you for discrimination faster than you can blink. Are we clear?"

Matt stares at me for a few seconds, his jaw popping back and forth. He's angry, but he finally grits out, "Crystal clear."

I turn on my heel and walk out his door.

CHAPTER Eight

I don't see Matt for the next two days at work, but the office calendar said he was in Atlanta for a court hearing. I took the time to acclimate myself to my office, meet as many of the other firm members as I could, and work on the one, single case that I had to my name.

Most of my work as an associate attorney with Lorraine was to basically do the grunt work on her cases. I had one true case that was mine alone, and that's because Lorraine told me she wouldn't touch it with a ten-foot pole. Miss "I Only Represent Corporate America" couldn't bother herself to touch a regular old personal injury case. In fact, she actually sneered at me when I told her I had taken the case of one Mr. Larry Jackson.

I pretty much worked the case myself, trying to figure things out as I went along. Luckily, I had a Torts professor at Columbia that gladly dispensed out advice to me as I needed it. One day... I'm assuming out of sheer boredom, Lorraine asked me about the case. When I told her my client had a rather severe brain injury and the economist I hired had projected his medical and earning losses into the millions, her face did take on a rather orgasmic look and, since then, she didn't think the case was all that stupid anymore.

You may wonder how I ended up with such a delectable case being only one year out of law school.

Well, it was pretty easy.

Apparently, it's not that great of a case. My client claims a dump truck turned left in front of him, and he had no time to stop. The dump truck driver insists my client was speeding and didn't have his headlights on, even though it was almost half an hour before dawn, when headlights would have been required.

The insurance company even took great pride in showing me pictures of my client's speedometer showing the needle stuck at sixty-six miles per hour when he was in a fifty-five mile per hour zone.

So, yeah… I landed this case because seven other attorneys had turned it down. They all said it was a dog… said there was no chance at victory, which is depressing to say the least. But I am not ready to give up.

I admit the speedometer is an issue, and I haven't quite figured that out yet, but I did blow their claim clear out of the water that the headlights weren't on. I hired an expert that studied my client's headlights. He said the bulbs unequivocally proved the lights were on because the filaments were bent, indicating there was a heat source on at the time of impact. Had the lights been off and thus cold, the filaments wouldn't be so 'bendy'—my words, not the expert's—and would have shattered instead.

Score one for the recent law school grad who has only one case to her name and plenty of time on her hands to try to figure this shit out.

On my third day at my new law firm, I have a lovely conversation with my client's wife, Miranda, and tell her about my move to Connover and Crown. I usually talk to Miranda because with Larry's head injury, he can't remember three-quarters of the stuff I tell him anyway. It's a tragic side effect, and one that cost him his job as an electrical engineer, which he had worked at for thirteen years. We chat for quite awhile and then I sign off, promising to call her the following week with an update.

Putting Larry's case aside, I pull out a thick stack of files that Lorraine wants me to review for her—back to the grunt work. It's at times like this I could kick myself in the ass for ever wanting to be a lawyer.

I get immersed into the scintillating world of corporate finance—aka drool-inducing law—and am just considering a break for a cup of coffee when someone knocks on my door. I don't even look up from the arbitration clause I'm reviewing for like the hundredth time because it's so boring and merely say, "Come in."

"Got a minute?" Matt says.

My head snaps up and I put on my mental boxing gloves, prepared for him to jab me with a scathing remark, or God forbid, call me doe-eyed. Which, if he does that, may cause me to need my literal boxing gloves.

I don't respond, just look at him in question with my head tilted slightly.

He takes my silence as acquiescence, and let's face it... he's the boss so he can come and go in my office as he pleases. When he takes a seat opposite my desk, I take a moment—just a few seconds really—to appreciate the hotness of Lawyer Matthew. He looks utterly resplendent in his dark gray suit that is perfectly tailored to fit his frame, and he's rocking a buttery yellow tie with gray striping. His hair is perfectly styled, but there is a tiny hint of stubble on his chin. He appraises me with his golden eyes, and I wait patiently to see what he wants.

After glancing around my office and taking note of my bare walls, he says, "Aren't you going to decorate in here?"

Shrugging my shoulders, I say, "Sure... one day."

He's quiet for another few moments, and then his eyes finally settle on mine with a look of frustration. "Look... I want to apologize for what I said the other day. I was more than a little unsettled when you walked in, and it had nothing to do with that bullshit about you being 'doe-eyed'. In fact, I'm not even sure what the hell that means myself."

I snicker to myself but don't let him see anything more than genuine interest on my face. It certainly will not help my boss to know I find him adorable in a weird sort of way.

"It's important to me that my business stay business, and my personal remain personal. Understand?"

"Totally," I say in firm agreement.

"I mean... the other night, we were explosive," he adds.

"To the moon," I supply.

"And that has no business in this office."

"No place at all."

"No matter how hot that experience was."

"It's not even an issue."

"So... we're in agreement?"

"I have no clue," I say sincerely, only because I really have no idea what he's getting at. "But if what you're trying to say is that what we had was amazing, but that it is over and done with, then I'm in full agreement."

Matt stands up. "Then we can put that in the past and never think about it again?"

"It's already gone from my mind," I say with resolve.

"Good," Matt says emphatically, although his face still carries a touch of worry.

Or is that regret?

I don't want there to be any animosity between my boss and me, and while yeah... I'm still going to continue to think about that amazing night because—BEST SEX EVER—it was never meant to be anything more than a one-night stand, and our time has indeed passed.

"Thanks for the apology, Matt, and I'm really looking forward to working for you."

He gives me a smile, and his two dimples pop out. "Yeah, me too."

When he walks out and the door closes behind him, I let my forehead thunk down on my desk and groan.

It's so weird that I know what my boss looks like naked.

CHAPTER Nine

"Personally, I suggest you keep your lips sealed and let me do the talking," Lorraine growls at me as we walk toward Matt's office. She still hasn't forgiven me for asking about my missed paychecks, convinced I'm trying to sabotage her.

Perhaps the greatest thing about this new employment with Connover and Crown is that Lorraine is no longer the boss of me. I mean... sure, she has supervisory authority over me on some of the cases, but Matt is my boss, and she can no longer threaten to fire me every other day. It makes me want to just stop in my tracks, put my thumbs in my ears, stick my tongue out while waggling my fingers at her, and say, "Neener, neener, neener".

Childish, I know, which is why that particular fantasy will just reside in my head. Along with all my hot fantasies of my night with my boss, Number 134.

Matt quickly waves us into his office and motions us over to a large worktable that takes up one corner of his office. We take a seat and wait for him to finish his phone call. I busy myself flipping through a few files but when I take a peek up every now and then, I catch Lorraine staring hungrily at Matt.

I wish I could tell her about my night with him and mock her with my "neener, neener, neener" move. That would knock that lustful gaze right off her face.

Oh well.

When Matt hangs up and stands up from his desk, Lorraine's head snaps down to a file in front of her, and she hastily opens it up. I mentally roll my eyes over her pathetic attempt to cover up the fact she was checking him out. Matt seems oblivious though, as he walks over and takes a seat between the two of us.

"Okay, so I want to go through your entire case list, figure out if you're comfortable handling them on your own, or if you need help, and sort of set a review schedule so I can stay in the loop with things."

I nod at Matt in understanding, but Lorraine just can't help herself. She does that little maneuver where she reaches out to touch his arm and says, "I have a good handle on my cases, Matt. I don't think you need to waste your time with them. I mean... I've been practicing for twelve years now."

Nope... I can't help the smug satisfaction I get when he pulls his arm away from her touch.

I could have told her that Matt is definitely all business when he's inside this building. It's equally as satisfying when Lorraine's face goes red when he says, "I appreciate that, Lorraine, but I have my fingers in all the cases in this firm. I like to know what's going on and ensure the cases are being worked well. And while you'll be reporting to Bill, I want to use today for me to get familiar with what you have."

With that, Matt starts having Lorraine go through each case where she gives him a summary, he gives a few recommendations if necessary, and they move on to the next case. Lorraine's mouth is set into a grim line by the time they are finished, although she does get a tiny bit cheerful when he points out the cases that I'm to work on underneath her. It's apparently a happy day for her that she will still have a little bit of control over me.

"Lorraine... you can go ahead and get back to work while I talk to McKayla about her brain injury case."

Lorraine opens her mouth to say something, but she can tell by the look on Matt's face that her time in his presence today is at an end. She grabs her files and leaves.

Matt pinches the bridge of his nose with a sigh. "Is she always like that?"

"Yeah," I say with a heavy heart.

"Well, if you have any problems with her, just let me know."

"Not going to happen," I tell him assuredly.

His eyebrows raise, and his lips quirk at me. "Excuse me?"

"I can handle Lorraine on my own. I won't be running to you if I have an issue."

Matt opens his mouth to argue, I can just tell, but I stare at him with a look that says the subject isn't open for discussion. His mouth snaps shut, and he shrugs his shoulders. "Suit yourself."

He then proceeds to grill me about my case, but I know it forward and backward. I can't tell if he's impressed or not when I tell him about how I proved the headlights were on. He merely grunts and nods his head, but I imagine compliments don't come often from someone like Matt.

After I finish, he says, "You know this case is a major uphill battle."

"Yeah… I sort of figured that out when seven other law firms turned it down."

"Then why did you take it?"

I hate to admit this, especially to a high-powered lawyer like Matt, but no sense in hiding it. "I just really liked Miranda and Larry Jackson. I felt sorry for them, and they remind me of my parents. Strong, hardworking… they didn't deserve this, and their life has been ruined because of it. I know those are stupid reasons to take a case."

Matt stares at me for a moment, his face unreadable. He'd make a great poker player. But I also remember him that night we were together and all of the emotions I read across his face. Desire, passion, lust. He wasn't masking anything then.

Finally, he says, "Those are stupid reasons to take a case. For you to even have a chance, you'll have to hire a really good accident reconstructionist, and you'll need to have expert medical witnesses, plus a biomechanical engineer. This case will probably cost a good fifty grand just to get it in the courtroom."

A biomechanical engineer? An accident reconstructionist? I have no clue what he's talking about, and I'm so out of my league here.

My heart sinks, because I doubt there's any way in hell that Matt will agree to front that type of money on what is probably a loser case. Yet I don't know what I'll do if he tries to make me get rid of it. I suppose I could leave, and go out on my own... get a loan or something to fund the case.

Matt interrupts my thoughts. "Those reasons may be stupid, but it doesn't mean they aren't the right reasons. Sometimes you take stupid risks in this business, just because you happen to really like the client."

"So we can keep the case?" I ask, hope coursing through me.

Matt can hear it in my voice, and he can't help but to smile fully at me. "Yeah. I'll fund this case. But it's going to be a monster. You're going to need me to help you with it."

"Absolutely," I say with excitement, having to restrain myself from running around the room in a victory lap.

I'm even betting now that I have the Great Litigator God, Matt Connover, on this case, the insurance company will start quaking in their boots. I can't wait to tell Larry and Miranda, although sadly, Larry will just forget.

Matt goes over a few more things that I need to do to get the ball rolling on the expert witnesses we'll need, and then he sends me packing so he can take another call.

CHAPTER Ten

It's Saturday, and just because I had a change in my employer and work address, it didn't equal a change in my work habits. I work every Saturday, come rain or shine. Lorraine demanded it of me when I first went to work for her after I passed the Bar, and I hated the hours. Then, when Pete dumped me, I immersed myself in work so I could forget the pain of my heartbreak. Work became like a drug for me—I needed it to survive.

Now that I'm starting to move past the pain of Pete and emerge back into the real world, I'm here working on a Saturday mainly out of habit, because I have nothing better to do. I've been here for almost seven hours already, but I have another three in me I bet.

Matt's agreement to help me on the Jackson case has renewed my love of the law. After I finish getting some urgent things handled for Lorraine—because everything is always urgent with her, and yet I don't see her in here working on a Saturday—I tear the Jackson file apart and re-organize it. Putting it in binders, I create a perfect organizational layout of my one and only case. I fill my bookshelf with those binders, then sit back in my chair and admire my work for a moment, feeling empowered and hopeful that I can really make something of this case.

After that, I scour the internet for information on biomechanical engineering, because Matt said I'd need one for the Jackson case, and I have no clue what a biomechanical engineer does. It sounds immensely technical and overly dry, and I'm dreading what I might find. The internet does indeed cough up a wealth of information for me.

I am nose deep in an article that has words like "velocity" and "deceleration" and my eyes are practically rolling into the back of my head, when the hair rises up on my arms. Looking up into the doorway, I yelp in fright to find Matt standing there quietly watching me.

Placing my hand on my chest, I give a nervous laugh. "Geez... you about gave me a heart attack."

Giving me an apologetic smile, he walks into my office and sits down across from my desk. "Sorry. I was walking by and saw you... thought I'd say hello."

I shoot him a jaunty wave. "Hello."

His eyes crinkle, and he rewards me with a dimpled smile. "So... how are you settling in?"

"Good. Everyone's been really nice and helpful." I hold up the article I'm reading. "I decided to figure out what the hell a biomechanical engineer is... a little light Saturday reading."

Amusement is all over his face when he nods at me. "I have some good articles for you to read. I'll email them over to you."

"Great," I say enthusiastically, but the thought of reading more about it makes my stomach hurt. I suck at this sort of stuff.

"How long have you been here?"

Glancing at my watch, I tell him, "Oh... only a little over seven hours. How about you?"

"A few hours. I have depositions next week in Chicago in a complex litigation case I have to get ready for."

I sigh... because I wish I were the type of lawyer that could have cases where I had to prep for depositions. Instead, I fall under Lorraine's whip to do her shit work and spend the remainder of my time pondering the merits of the Jackson case, without having the slightest idea of how to even make said case meritorious.

"What's with the long-suffering sigh?" Matt asks.

"Nothing," I say, my voice slightly gloomy as I fiddle with the papers on my desk. "I just can't wait for the day when I can be a real litigator and handle depositions, go to court hearings, and make arguments to a jury."

"That takes time," Matt says with a serious voice. "But... how about you sit in on these depositions with me next week, watch how they're handled, and I'll have you handle some smaller ones for me after that?"

My head snaps up. "Really? I mean, you don't even know what type of lawyer I am."

"True enough," he says. "But there's only one way to find out."

I'm giddy with excitement as I lean forward in my chair. "Thank you, Mr. Connover... I mean, Matt. Or Mr. Connover if that works for you. But just... thank you!"

Matt stands from his chair, walks to the door, and grimaces at me. "It's just Matt, okay? God knows I know you well enough for us to be on a first-name basis."

I go still all over because this is the first mention of our intimate knowledge of each other... since Matt made it clear the other day that it was something we should forget. I know I haven't forgotten. In fact, those images in my mind of all the carnal things we did to each other, have kept me warm company during the nights.

Matt nods at me stiffly and quickly changes the subject. "Have you hired an accident reconstructionist on the speed issue in the Jackson case?"

"No. I wasn't sure where to start with that."

Glancing at his watch and furrowing his brows, Matt walks back to my desk. "I have to get back to work but show me the accident report really quick, and I'll direct you where to go."

Standing up from my desk, I walk to the opposite side so that I can grab one of the binders from my shelf. Matt's in the way, so I murmur an 'excuse me,' and he steps back to let me pass.

But apparently, not far enough.

As I try to slide by him, my butt grazes up against his crotch... just barely... really, just the tiniest whisper.

It's still enough of a touch that shock waves zing through my body and I hear Matt hiss under his breath, even as he takes a quick step back.

I turn quickly and blurt out, "I'm sorry. I didn't mean to do that."

Matt's lips are set in a distasteful line, and he's glaring daggers at me. I suppose in an effort to cool his anger, he closes his eyes briefly and takes a deep breath. As his warm breath blows out over those sexy lips of his, his eyes slowly open, and now the anger is gone.

Instead, there is nothing but molten heat and lust in his gaze, which promptly causes my knees to start to shake.

Matt takes one step closer to me, and a quick glance down shows me that both of his hands are curled into fists.

He's clearly fighting for control, but I'm thinking it's a losing battle.

"I thought I could work in close proximity to you and be able to keep my hands to myself," he muses as he pins me with the intensity of his eyes. "Guess I was fucking lying to myself."

Chapter Eleven

I'm frozen in place. I have no clue what to do.

Yes, I have hormones, pheromones, and even just good old, run-of-the-mill moans stuck in the back of my throat, which are on the verge of busting loose. My mind whirls... what did Matt mean by that statement?

Do I slap him or jump him?

We stare at each other... his eyes blazing an inferno of desire, mine probably reflecting the "deer in the headlights" look.

Swallowing hard, I say, "I think—"

Matt lunges at me, catching me with one arm

around my waist and the other swiping across my desk, sending binders, papers, folders, pens, a tape dispenser, a stapler, two legal pads and a box of paper clips flying to the floor. "Don't say a fucking word, McKayla. Just don't."

Pushing one of his rock hard thighs in between my legs, he bends me back onto my desk and settles against me, raising both hands now to cup my face. My heart is on the verge of exploding in my chest, and only two things fill my mind.

First, please, please, please kiss me, Matt.

Second, please, please, please don't let me have a heart attack before he does.

I'm saved on both concerns as Matt pours lust, desire, anger, and passion into a kiss that causes my toes to curl against the flip-flops, which are barely clinging to my feet after I was practically thrown onto my desk.

My tongue is shy at first, but it only takes Matt one tiny rock of his hips against mine, and then it's on.

We kiss like we never kissed on that one night we spent together. It is filled with not only yearning, but with a bit of frustration and shame that we have no control over our actions.

This is wrong... we both know it.

Yet he hums with approval when I reach my

hand down between us and give him a light stroke, and I practically convulse when one of his hands cup my breast.

For a brief moment, Matt seems to come to his senses and stills against me. He rises up from my mouth and stares at me deeply, worry creasing his forehead. He even curses just the way I've come to appreciate about him. "Fuck, fuck, fuck, fuck."

"We don't have to—" I start to say, but he growls at me so I snap my mouth shut.

He stares at me for just a moment more, and then he abruptly stands up. I think it's over, that reality has reappeared, and disappointment fills me.

That lasts just a flicker of a moment because fantasy land returns as Matt starts stripping me of my clothes.

In less than fifteen seconds, he has me completely naked and splayed out on my desk in front of him. He looks down at me, eyes roaming, and he actually licks his lips like he's getting ready to gorge himself.

Yes, I'm ringing the dinner bell... bring it on.

I expect Matt to undo his pants and mount up, but he surprises me when he pulls one of my chairs closer to the desk and sits down. He takes my legs, spreads them outward, and tugs me to the edge of the desk, throwing said legs rather haphazardly over his shoulders.

Pleasure and thrills blanket my body as I realize that he's settling in to do me right. His face dives down, and I actually grunt... yes, grunt... at first contact. I then bite down hard on my tongue so I'm not screaming the rafters down.

I'm delirious with pleasure as Matt works my body to his liking. He uses touch and sound to give me the ultimate experience. Touch meaning fingers and tongue, and yes, even his chin, which has me bucking off the desk. Sound meaning the dirty, dirty things he whispers to me as he causes a rollercoaster of an orgasm to go rushing up my spine. I have to slap my hand over my mouth not to scream, and Matt looks up at me with pure male satisfaction.

It took him just under two minutes to send me to Heaven.

He's just that fucking good.

Not wasting any time, Matt undoes his belt and practically rips his jeans open, revealing what I'm betting is his most prized possession, and if in another reality we were a real couple, it would definitely be my most prized possession. Stepping between my legs, he leans his body over me and, in one practiced and very sexy-suave move, slams his way home to the hilt. Thank goodness my hand is still clasped over my mouth, or I would have shouted Matt's name in reverence.

Hips pumping hard, my desk shaking, Matt looks up at me and slowly removes my hand from over my mouth.

"Need to kiss you," he groans after a particularly hard surge into me.

"Yes," I agree.

"So fucking sexy," he murmurs.

"You feel so good."

"Could do this all day... all night."

"Word," I sing out, and then let out a low moan when his pelvis grinds into mine.

His mouth finally slams onto my lips, and he's kissing me with confidence, mating his tongue with mine while he never loses a single beat on his strokes.

Higher and higher, Matt takes both of us. It's quick, hard, and rough, but the feelings he evokes inside of me are warm and soft, despite the frenzied nature of what we're doing.

I know I should be worried that someone will walk by, and I know I should fret over the fact that my boss is banging me on my desk, and yes, I should even have a slight bit of concern that this is opening up a whole can of worms that are going to leave a nasty, slimy trail all over my employment here.

But as my second orgasm builds, and Matt pulls away from my lips so he can stare at me while we both start to fracture, the only thing I can even care about right now is that yes... I'm so happy this happened.

Yes, my body has betrayed every shred of common sense I use to possess.

We both shudder hard, muscles tensing and relaxing. Our breathing starts to even out, and eventually Matt rises up and pulls out of me.

After tucking himself back in and zipping his pants, Matt gallantly grabs a box of tissues that are sitting on a small table and helps me to clean up. I get dressed, and the silence that fills the room is oppressive.

When I tuck my shirt back into my jeans, Matt reaches up and smoothes a hand over my hair. The touch is soft... intimate. It makes me want to curl up into him and purr.

Then he brings me back to reality.

"This was wrong, McKayla. It was my fault, and I won't let it happen again."

Chapter Twelve

Matt turns to walk out of my office, and I let him.

For only a second, and then I jump forward, grabbing his wrist. "Wait a minute. I don't understand."

He stops and turns toward me, looking down at my hand holding on to him. I release it and step back.

"What's to understand?" he asks in frustration. "This is wrong... I'm your boss."

"It's only wrong if the sex influences how you treat me," I point out.

"And what if I treat you like shit because it

makes me angry to have this attraction to you? What if I give you the shittiest cases, and I mock you in front of your colleagues?"

Grinning over the concept, I tell him, "Then I'll sue you for sexual harassment."

Apparently, I'm not as funny as I think I am because Matt's gaze takes on a hint of danger and he steps into me, practically touching his nose to mine. "I'd chew you up and spit you out, little girl. You'd never be a match for me in court."

He stares at me hard, and then steps back to give me space. "Besides," he says, while running a hand through his hair, "you just proved my point. This is sexual harassment at its finest. I'd be stupid to let this carry on."

I get what he's saying. He may know my body inside and out, but he has no clue about my integrity. As far as he knows, I'm a crazy psycho that will stalk him now that I've gotten a taste of the Connover Love Machine.

Still, I'm really not ready to let this go. I like Matt… I really do. His confidence, his healthy ego, his fantastically amazing body. I want to get to know him better, and surely, the little issue that I'm his employee shouldn't stand in the way. I'm sure there have been plenty of successful workplace romances in the history of the world. I mean, look at Cleopatra and Marc Antony.

"Matt... I would never hold something like that over your head, and you'll have to trust me on that. I bet we could make this work. I'm sure once you got to know me better—"

Holding his hand up, he cuts me off. His tone is steely when he says, "See, that's just it, McKayla. I don't want to get to know you. This was a fuck... pure and simple. I'm not looking for anything more than that. But it's out of my system now, and I'd appreciate it if we could just forget this happened."

"Ouch," I say, because that truly hurt.

"I think with my dick, McKayla... not with my heart. It serves me well."

"Well, I have to say your dick is the most pleasant thing about you," I say sweetly, but with a touch of sarcasm.

I'm rewarded with a narrowing of Matt's eyes, and I can tell he's not use to someone sticking up to him like that.

When it boils down to it, Matt and I have pure animal magnetism between us. We have sexual chemistry in spades, and our bodies make some beautiful magic together.

But that's all it is. Both of us were only looking for one-night stands, not the love of our lives. And while many people can make the whole "friends with benefits" thing work fine for them, there is no way that could ever fly between an employer and his employee. Because even though sex is just sex, there is also intimacy involved, and that brings about certain emotions. Those emotions can then cloud your judgment, and I get that Matt can't afford to have that happen.

Hell, I can't really afford to let that happen. I need this job.

Straightening my shoulders and sticking my chin out, I walk back behind my desk and sit down. Bending over, I start to pick up the items that Matt swept to the floor not ten minutes ago. He watches me, but makes no move to help.

"I understand," I tell him with resolve. "And you're right. This has disaster written all over it. I'll let it go."

He stares at me for a moment, and I hold his gaze. I mean it... I'm letting it go.

Apparently, he's satisfied with the truthfulness of my words. "I'm really sorry, McKayla."

I give him a small smile. "Sure. Another place, another time, we'd have been perfect for each other, right?"

He returns the smile, but it is sad... hopeless. "Wrong. I don't do relationships, and you deserve more than that. It would only ever be a fuck. In fact, I'll be hitting up One Night Only soon."

With that, he turns away and walks out of my office, closing the door softly behind him.

He's an asshole. There is no doubt about that. But I have a feeling he's a pathetically damaged asshole, and something has made him this way. That makes me feel sorry for him, even though his words cut pretty deep.

He may act like this is about nothing more than blowing a nut, but that is definitely where I catch him in a lie. There is more to him... I know it.

I know it because men that are just interested in banging out a quick orgasm don't take their time to go down on a woman. They do that because they want the woman to feel exquisite pleasure. That takes a certain level of caring.

Matt may pretend he's all hard-hearted, but there is something inside of him that glows warm.

Unfortunately, it's not up to me to be the one to fan that into something else. He's made it clear that I'm not what he wants or needs. He eloquently stated that when he told me he'd be hitting up One Night Only again.

The thought of Matt having sex with another woman causes jealousy to flare up inside of me, but I tamp it down. I have no claim to him, and it's time to put on my big girl panties and concentrate on my job.

From here on out, Matt and I will nurture a

strictly business, completely professional relationship. I will look to him to mentor me as a lawyer, and I will learn how to become the best litigator that I can be.

This will sustain me. I'll make sure of it.

Even as something deep inside me whispers, *This isn't over.*

STIPULATION

Sawyer Bennett

Legal Affairs
Vol. 2 - Stipulation
By Sawyer Bennett

All Rights Reserved.
Copyright © 2014 by Sawyer Bennett
Published by Big Dog Books

This book is a work of fiction. Names, characters, places and incidents either are products of the author's imagination or are used fictitiously. Any resemblance to actual events, locales or persons, living or dead, is entirely coincidental.

No part of this book can be reproduced in any form or by electronic or mechanical means including information storage and retrieval systems, without the express written permission of the author. The only exception is by a reviewer who may quote short excerpts in a review.

Chapter One

"Do you have your pajamas?"

"Yes," I say with a smile.

"And toothpaste?"

"Yup."

"And everything you need in your briefcase?"

"Double-checked."

"Finally... and most importantly, did you pack sexy lingerie?"

My eyebrows shoot upward at Macy while she gives me a lecherous grin. "There is no need for sexy lingerie," I admonish her. "It's a business trip, for goodness sake."

"Yeah, but an overnight business trip... two nights to be exact, with sexy, hot, and orgasm-inducing Number 134," Macy points out.

"He's not Number 134," I snap at her. "He's Matt Connover, my boss."

Macy sighs in pleasure, assuredly replaying all the sexy details of my encounters with Matt, which I ultimately told her about over two bottles of wine. "He'll always be Number 134 to me."

"You're demented," I tell her. "Demented and sad... but social."

Macy throws a pillow at me, catching me squarely in the face. "Stop quoting 80s' movies. It freaks me out when you do that."

"I did it just to get you to shut up about Matt. You skeeve me out when you start fantasizing about him based on my experiences."

Snickering, I bend over and zip up my suitcase. I have to meet Matt at the airport in an hour, so I need to get down and get a cab. Pulling out the handle on my overnight and snapping it in place, I start rolling toward the front door. "Will you miss me while I'm gone?"

"I will totally miss you while you're gone," Macy tells me. "You're my girl."

"I'll always be your girl," I tell her, and then amend. "That was Forrest Gump... definitely not an 80s' movie."

"Much more palatable," she commends me.

I give Macy a quick hug, tell her to not get into any trouble while I'm gone, and then head to the airport.

When I get there, I hustle my way through security and toward my gate. Even though JFK is crowded, I immediately spot Matt. He's reading a newspaper, a briefcase and carry-on suitcase beside him. He's wearing another perfectly tailored suit, that probably costs more than a month of my salary, and has one leg crossed over the other. He looks like the height of confidence and sophistication all rolled into one.

As if sensing I'm there, he lifts his face up and scans the crowd, coming to a firm rest on me. His whiskey eyes trail down me briefly, and then come back up. The look isn't sensual, but it isn't businesslike either. In fact, I might categorize it as wistful. Matt gives me a small smile in welcome as I approach.

I take a seat next to him and ask, "How was your weekend?"

I ask because I still can't help the inane jealousy that courses through me when I think about Matt hitting up One Night Only as he said he would. I also ask because I'm a glutton for punishment. Because not knowing is worse than knowing the absolute worst thing he could possibly say to me, which I realize is a confusing and spectacularly tongue-trippy sort of thought had I indeed actually voiced it, but since I used my inside voice, it's all good.

Matt doesn't disappoint. After staring hard at me for a moment, his lips curl up and he says, "I had an amazing weekend. One of the best ever."

Bitter acid swirls in my stomach. His comment is pointed, designed to hurt, and also to make sure I clearly remember what he told me. Our time is over, and he has moved on. He apparently had a great hookup with someone and just like that... I'm forgotten.

It makes me a little bitchy, so I say, "What a coincidence. Me too. Gotta love that One Night Only."

That tiny muscle in Matt's jaw pops back and forth as he stares at me, then he smiles at me. Almost evilly. "Definitely love it, although they should rename it Two Nights Only. It was that good of a weekend."

Oh, that pisses me off, and I'm pissed off at myself that it pisses me off. Score one for Matt Connover. That was like a punch in the gut and, even though I have no right to be, my feelings are hurt just a tiny bit.

Sometimes I hate being a woman and all the things that come with it that make me soft and mushy.

Pushing those thoughts aside, because they really have no room in my head, I ask Matt to tell me more about the case that is sending us all the way to Chicago for depositions. He makes a smooth transition from gloating over his weekend sexcapades, and spends the next twenty minutes until our flight is ready describing, with mind-numbing detail, about his lawsuit. It's against a major auto manufacturer that produced a vehicle where the seatbelts were faulty, causing their customers to be ejected from the vehicle during rollovers, or shot through the windshield in head-on collisions. Matt spoke with fervor and righteous indignation over the poor victims, practically sneering when he told me he had proof that they knew the seatbelts were faulty, but didn't want to spend the money to do a recall. Rather, they rolled the dice and hoped no one made a claim for compensation.

I have a feeling that they are going to be very sorry for crossing Matt Connover.

Apparently, we would be doing the depositions of some of the big wigs in the corporation, to see just how high up the ladder the conspiracy to keep the secrets of the faulty seatbelts went. My job would be to sit there and take tedious notes on every question and answer, making sure that I even paid attention to the deponents' facial reactions in case Matt stumbled on something that they really didn't want him to know about.

I'm excited to see Matt in action. Despite the rocky start to our working relationship, I am eager to learn from him. I did some of my own Googling of the illustrious Matt Connover, and found that he is well respected in the legal community. He's already made quite a name for himself after only ten years of practice.

I just need to remember to keep my libido in check, my heart on guard, and my work beyond impeccable, and all will be well in my life.

CHAPTER Two

The first day of depositions are over, and we've all met down in the hotel bar/restaurant for drinks, dinner, and then more drinks.

We're on the more drinks part now, and there is room to celebrate. Matt killed it today, and it was almost a surreal experience.

First, we were at the corporate defendant's law firm, a massive, steel-and-glass structure that dwarfed the rest of the Chicago skyline. The depositions took place in the largest conference room I've ever seen. The table was massive and could seat fifty people, although there were only about fifteen in attendance.

The lawsuit is complex, and there are multiple parties. There are five plaintiffs total, and all of their lawyers had flown in to hear the testimony. Matt had long ago been appointed lead counsel. He was the only one asking the questions—and the man was pure genius.

I thought the questioning would be contentious but quite the contrary... Matt took the 'good old boy' approach. He softened up each deponent with benign questions, carefully poking and prodding. Nodding in commiseration, he gave sympathetic looks over how hard their jobs were. At one point, during the first deposition, I even began to wonder if Matt's heart was really in it.

But then, just when he had them practically eating out of his hand, he attacked and went on the offensive. He caught them in lie after lie, and then pulled out reams of documents to shove under their noses, showing how he exposed their lies. I swear he even had one guy in tears after pointing out the multitude of untruths that had been captured by the court reporter, who was recording every single word with a smirk on her face.

Yes, tonight we are celebrating, even though we have another day's worth of depositions tomorrow. Matt told me it wouldn't be so easy during the next round. He told me that, rest assured, the defense would be up all night preparing their witnesses to try to withstand Matt's attacks the following day.

Still, I have an immense level of pride in Matt as I watch the other plaintiffs' lawyers slap him on the back and repeatedly shake his hand. They are all riding high on the fresh kills today, no doubt seeing the way paved clear for a successful outcome for the victims in this case. Matt is like a bright beacon among a sea of dull and boring people. Everyone wants to be around him, everyone wants to hear what nugget of wisdom or wit will come out of those sexy lips, and everyone wants a piece of him.

Including me.

We are into our third round of drinks following dinner, and I mentally tell myself that this is the last one. I need to get to bed and get some sleep, needing to keep my mental processes sharp tomorrow. Matt definitely relied on my notes, often stopping several times in the deposition to lean over and quietly ask me to clarify something that had been said.

Taking another sip of my wine, I watch Matt standing off to the side, deep in conversation with one of the other attorneys. It should be an absolute sin how good looking the man is, and another pang of longing and regret that we couldn't have something hits me deep in my chest.

Someone jostles my barstool, causing some of my wine to spill on my dress. I had changed from my plain black business suit to a jersey wraparound dress in navy blue for dinner, and grimaced when a large splash hit my lap. Turning around to glare, I come face to face with one of the other attorneys that was in the depositions. His name is Brian Something-Or-Other. When Matt introduced me to him earlier today, his eyes immediately dropped to my breasts and he looked at them continually throughout the day.

He pushes in toward the bar, knocking into me again. "Might want to have a little more care there," I tell him testily.

He turns to me with bleary eyes, and yup... he's drunk. Looking at me for a moment as if he doesn't recognize me, his eyes finally focus a bit and a sleazy smile takes over his face. Right on cue, his eyes drop to my cleavage, which is on half display in this dress, and then back up at me. He licks his lips and says, "Hey... you're Matt's paralegal, right? You were in the depositions today?"

And I sat across from you at dinner tonight for two hours, jerk. Good memory.

"I'm a lawyer," I tell him firmly.

"Right," he says, like a bell just went off in his head. He leans in toward me, wobbling slightly, and pretends that this is just our little secret. "You are one sexy fucking lawyer."

As if this couldn't get any worse, a little bit of spittle flies from his mouth and hits me on my chest. I look down in distaste, taking the napkin from under my wine glass and dabbing at my skin. This sudden movement apparently lures his gaze back down to my boobs, and he openly leers at them.

"They don't talk, you know," I tell him sarcastically, and he finally has the grace to look back up at me.

He's grinning when he says, "Yeah, but I bet I could make them sing if you gave me a go at them."

Okay, that's it. I'm calling it a night.

Dropping the napkin on the bar, I grab my purse and try to stand up from my barstool. Apparently, Brian doesn't understand that he's just royally pissed me off because he reaches a hand out, completely and utterly oblivious to the fact that he's in a public place, and actually squeezes my right boob. "Come on, baby… let's go back to my room and get it on."

Ew, that's just fucking gross. I'm momentarily shocked that he actually fondled me, but it lasts only a second. I knock his hand off and try to push my way past him, but he has the gall to reach back out and try to grab me again.

All out of patience, and apparently not

concerned myself with the fact that we are in a public place, I cock my arm back and get ready to punch him square in the snout. Before I can let my hand fly though, another hand reaches out and grabs Brian by the shoulder, slinging him away from me.

Brian is too drunk to fight against that kind of momentum and he goes sailing across the room, crashing into an empty table and chairs, where he falls to the floor.

And there's my knight in shining armor, standing over him with fists clenched and murder in his eyes.

Matt Connover.

Chapter Three

Matt reaches down and grabs Brian by the lapels of his jacket, hauling him off the floor. No one makes a move to intervene because Matt looks to be in control, although he seems to be vibrating with the need to do violence.

Putting his face in Brian's, he grits, "It will do me no good to beat your ass or tell you how reprehensible your conduct is, because you won't remember it in the morning. Rest assured... I'll be by your hotel room first thing in the morning, and then I'll decide which part of me you'll get."

Brian stares at Matt without any comprehension

of what he did... yes, he's that drunk. Matt is disgusted and he gives Brian a solid push while releasing his grip, causing Brian to stumble backward a few steps. He doesn't fall down only by the grace of a few of the other lawyers that catch him.

Spinning away, Matt walks past me out the bar, growling, "Let's go."

Grabbing my purse, I hurry to catch up to him.

Once the doors on the elevator shut, I have the nerve to look up to Matt. He's pissed, and I'm not sure if it's at Brian, me, or both of us.

"I'm sorry," I say, because the silence is awkward, and because I think that's what he's waiting for.

"For what?" he asks in surprise.

"I don't know," I offer lamely. "I thought you were pissed at me."

"Mac... you have nothing to be sorry for. That pig was drunk and inappropriate with you. He's lucky I didn't kill him."

"Well, that's a little overboard," I say with a laugh. "I'm sure he got the message how very wrong it was."

"No," Matt says, his voice icy. "He didn't get the message. But he will tomorrow morning when I pay him a visit."

"What will you do?" I ask, wondering if Matt would truly beat his ass. I don't want him to do that, but it sure would be awesome to know that someone wanted to do that on my behalf.

"He's off the case. I'm sending him packing."

"What?" I say, now feeling extreme guilt that Brian would lose his job. "You can't do that. He was just drunk."

Matt pushes away from the wall of the elevator where he'd been leaning, and stalks up to me. He gets all in my personal space, but I don't step back from it. Unfortunately, I'm a bad, bad girl, because damn it... I like him in my space.

Leaning down, Matt practically growls at me, "He had his fucking hands on your breast, Mac."

I wish I could tell you it was the violence in his voice, or even the absolute menace he was portraying, that got me excited, but it wasn't... it was the pure, flat-out jealousy that was practically dripping off his lips that got my motor running.

Matt-Fucking-Connover is jealous another man was touching me.

I'm so going to milk this for all it's worth.

"So what if he was touching me?" I whisper.

The golden tones in Matt's eyes turn a deep shade of amber, and he steps in even closer, now only a mere inch or so separating our bodies. "Because it should be my hands that are on your body... only mine."

I think the bells of Heaven have rung, but sadly, it's just the chime from our elevator that we've reached our floor. Matt steps back from me but grabs my hand as he exits. I have no choice but to follow along. He pulls me swiftly down the hallway, right to my hotel room door.

He doesn't even wait for me to get my key. Taking my purse from my hands, he roots around in there like a pig looking for a truffle. He pulls the key out, slips it in the reader, and opens my door. Then he's pushing me inside, his hand on my lower back. Following me right in, he propels me all the way into the center of the room, throwing my purse on the floor.

When I turn around to look at him, it's all over. The instant our eyes connect, an almost palpable spark leaps between us. In that instant, we launch ourselves at each other.

"Fuck, I can't believe I'm doing this again," Matt grumbles, just before his mouth starts to ravish mine. I groan instantly from the contact. We are so ferocious in our need to mate our tongues, our teeth clack together in an almost painful way. It doesn't stop us though... we keep kissing and kissing and kissing.

My hands immediately go to Matt's shirt, trying to swiftly undo the buttons, but making no headway whatsoever. Never one to be worried about finesse or decorum, I grip the material tightly in my hands and jerk as hard as I can, expecting buttons to spray all around us and his glorious chest to be exposed. In my mind, I even see it happening in slow motion, because yeah... that's how it would happen in those steamy, romance novels I like to read.

Instead, the buttons hold firm and my hands fly outward, holding nothing but air. Matt pulls away from my mouth to look down at me, taking note of the failed attempt to strip him bare... and I'm sure the way my mouth is hanging open in disbelief.

His eyes crinkle in amusement, and then he starts laughing.

Hard.

I mean gut-busting, belly-clenching, pee-your-pants hard. Pushing away from me, he actually has to put his hand down on the dresser to hold himself up while he laughs. "That was probably the funniest thing I've ever seen," he says between gasps, tears pooling in his eyes.

Glaring at him, I say, "Is your shirt made of like steel or something?"

And that causes him to succumb to fresh peals of laughter.

I merely cross my arms over my chest and rain down my most displeasing frown upon him. He finally gets control of himself, letting out a few stray snickers, and then he's standing straight in front of me. Holding his hands out in front of himself, he says, "I'm sorry... but that was funny."

"Yeah, not so much for me," I tell him. Walking to the door, I open it. "I'm sort of not in the mood now."

Matt's lips quirk at me, and he grins at me in sheer amusement. "I'm not going anywhere."

"I told you I'm not in the mood."

The irritating fool walks over and sits down on the edge of my bed. "Yes, you are. Now get over here," he says as he unbuckles his belt. "I'd kill for you to take me in your mouth right now."

CHAPTER Four

I'm weak. That's all there is to it. I close the door and walk back into the room, but I'm not convinced that this should evolve into sex.

"What are we doing, Matt?" I ask in a tired voice.

He gives me a devilish grin as he pulls his belt off, tossing it on the floor. "I'd say you're getting ready to give me a blow job, and then I'm going to make you come more times than you'll be able to remember tomorrow."

Well, oh shit... that practically just made me have an orgasm right there. Shaking my head to clear the sexual fuzziness away, I say more firmly, "I thought we both agreed this was wrong. Besides, you got your jollies off again at One Night Only this weekend and..."

I stop, because I almost admitted that his sleeping with someone else is a deal breaker for me. But is it? And do I really want him to know that knowledge affects me? He's been pretty clear about the fact that I'll only ever be a fuck for him, and I sure as hell don't want him having power over me... thinking that it hurts my feelings.

So I quickly say, "And besides... I slept with someone else, too, this weekend. Remember... most amazing weekend ever."

Matt pushes off from the bed and comes to stand in front of me. He takes his finger and thumb, gripping my chin so I have to meet his eyes. "I lied. I wasn't with anyone this weekend. And you lied for that matter, too. You didn't sleep with anyone else."

I start sputtering, jerking my chin away. "What makes you think I lied?"

He's having none of it. Drawing me into his arms, he wraps himself around me. He kisses me then, so very softly, and whispers. "I know you lied for the same reason I did. We don't want to admit this attraction, yet both of us are obsessed by it. You can't get me out of your mind, just as I can't get you out of my mine. I'm tired of fighting it, and I'm tired of jerking off when I'd rather be sunk deep inside of you. So I'm not fighting it anymore."

He kisses me again, just a light grazing of his lips against mine, and I sigh. While this relationship is still so very wrong, his words to me are so very, very right. I can handle that there will not be a relationship out of this, and that this will only ever be sex, because damn if it isn't the most powerful, fulfilling, and mind-blowing sex I've ever had. Yeah, I'm jumping in if he's on board.

I know this will come to bite me in the ass one day, but I'm still not able to walk away. I can foresee all types of problems cropping up just because I'm powerless to stop myself from banging my boss.

Pushing out of his arms, I drop to my knees in front of him and unzip his pants. I peek up at him, and he's staring down at me with dark eyes, his lower lip stuck between his teeth. He's holding his breath, watching to see what I do, and it makes me feel invincible.

He must see the power radiating off me, the quiet confidence I have in my stare, because he's compelled to say, even as he gently strokes my cheek, "This is just sex, McKayla... nothing more."

Taking him in my hand, I squeeze him gently, loving the way the air hisses out of his lungs. I lean forward and lick him from base to tip, looking up at him once more. "As long as it's nothing less."

"Fair enough," he grits out, before grasping my head and urging my face toward his dick.

I then proceed to give him, what I'm betting is, the best blow job he's ever had. Yeah, I know that sounds cocky, but the sounds he's emitting, the curse words he's dropping, and the way his body cannot seem to stay still under my ministrations... it's all adding up to be one hell of an inexplicably magical moment for the great Matt Connover.

"God... Mac... that feels good," he groans. I purr in approval, not wanting to remove my lips from him to thank him for his praise.

Intent on making him scream my name out, I pull him in deeper than ever, straight to the back of my throat, and give an extremely strong suck. His hands grip my hair, and he tries to pull me off. "Fuck... I'm going to come if you don't stop."

I think I snarled at him. I might have even released him long enough to gnash my teeth like a feral dog fighting over a bone, but it was enough that he released my head. I latch back on, intent on bringing Matt the same pleasure that he has doled out to me on more than occasion.

I pour my all into it, loving every time he trembles against me, loving when his words are harsh and dirty, but then sometimes reverent. I love the taste of him, and the reclamation of the power that I was holding earlier.

I'm loving all of it, but none of it compares to the feeling of when Matt finally orgasms so hard that his legs buckle and he falls to the bed, whispering over and over, "Mac... Mac... Mac..."

Matt chanting my name in reverence is much sexier than him screaming at the top of his lungs. This was indeed a job well done.

With a supremely satisfied smile on my face, I crawl up on the bed beside Matt and wait for him to recover.

Then it's my turn.

I can hardly wait.

Chapter Five

It's quitting time. The workweek is over, and a bunch of my colleagues invited me out for drinks with them. I declined, giving some lame-ass excuse that I already had plans, but truth be told, I don't feel like doing anything other than going home, eating a carton of Ben & Jerry, and falling into a coma-like sleep.

I'm exhausted, both mentally and physically.

Why you ask?

Well, I'll tell you.

I spent two days in Chicago with Matt, watching him depose witness after witness, while paying keen attention to his cat and mouse game so that I could take the best notes possible. At night, he kept me awake until the early morning hours, making love to me over and over and over again. He was insatiable. I was insatiable. We couldn't get enough of each other, but I drew the line when Matt wanted to pull me into the bathroom on the airplane so we could both join the Mile High Club.

When we got back late Wednesday night, he shared a cab with me, giving me a quick kiss goodnight when he dropped me off at my apartment. I was too tired to even cop a feel of his muscled body, merely mumbling a goodbye to him.

The rest of the week, I spent jumping to do Lorraine's every whim. Matt was off traveling again Thursday morning to Atlanta, and that seemed to give Lorraine a renewed sense of power over me. I swear, one day she even asked me to get a cup of coffee for her, but I faked a bout of diarrhea and told her I had to use the bathroom to get out of it. Every time after that, if she even looked like she was going to ask me to do something, I'd clutch at my stomach, hunch my body over, and moan with a pathetic look on my face. She'd wrinkle her nose in distaste and as soon as she was gone from my sight, I'd laugh out loud over my deviousness.

I haven't heard from Matt, not that I expected to.

On no less than three occasions after he brought me to a screaming orgasm, he didn't even wait for my heart rate to get back to normal before he would lean over me with a worried look in his eyes and say, "You know this is just sex, right?"

I'd dutifully say 'right,' and then gasp as he started kissing me again.

So, even though he was clear that it was just sex, and even though he made sure I understood that he wasn't relationship material, I still was sort of pining to hear from him. Yes, I know... it's sex... just sex. And great sex at that.

But I'm a woman. We get our feelings all mushed up in this stuff, and even though my brain rationally tells me not to let my heart get involved, it's kind of hard not to. I mean, there is more to Matt than just sex. He's an attorney I've come to respect a great deal in the short time I've known him. He's passionate about his work and is a champion for the underdog. He's a great employer, treating everyone fairly and equally. Also, he's funny as hell, and when he doesn't have me sobbing out in pleasure, he has me laughing so hard in bed that I'm terrified I'm going to make the faux pas of all faux pas. The dreaded fart while you're lying in your lover's arms.

Luckily, that hasn't happened... yet.

I finally broke down this morning and sent Matt

a short email, asking him when he got a chance if he could email those articles he mentioned on biomechanical engineering. I really didn't want them... actually wanted to puke from the thought of having to read them, but I wanted... no, needed, some type of contact from Matt.

After all, as a woman, I'm entitled to my period of insecurity and self-doubt that would assuredly overwhelm me at any minute and convince myself that Matt actually hates me and wants nothing to do with me.

When Matt replied to my email around lunchtime, I was so excited I choked on a piece of brown rice sushi that I was trying to swallow. After I hacked it up and spit it in the garbage, I opened the email, eager to suck down the details of some witty or flirty response he would send me.

Instead, he just responded: See attached articles.

Well, shit! What a letdown. I could literally feel my depression firing through my veins over the fact that what Matt had been telling me over and over again was true. I was really nothing more than great sex to him. He wasn't missing me, he wasn't pining after me, and he sure as hell didn't have time to flirt with me.

In fact, I'm betting he was already planning to hit One Night Only this upcoming weekend.

So, you see... that is why I'm too tired and depressed to do anything but head home and crawl into bed.

When I get to my apartment, I'm somewhat relieved that Macy is gone. She had left me a note that said:

Heading to the Hamptons to torture my parents for the weekend. See you Sunday.

Macy had invited me to go with her, but there was no way I was subjecting myself to that freak show. Macy and her parents despised each other, and they literally only got together to make each other suffer. It was sick and twisted, and so far out of the realm of my understanding. I lost my dad four years ago, and my mother and I were very close. We talked every day, by either phone or email, and there was nothing I couldn't talk to her about.

Well, except maybe Matt.

While I adore my Macy-girl, I'm glad she's gone because I don't feel like being around her natural effervescence tonight. She's like sunshine on a stick, and tonight I just feel like being depressed. I want to put on my stretchy pants and let my stomach hang out while I gorge on ice cream.

Which is exactly what I do. I put on my gray sweatpants, an old Columbia t-shirt, and my fuzzy slippers. I wash all of my makeup off, braid my hair into two pigtails, and curl myself up on the couch to watch a marathon of Law and Order: SVU with my two favorite men in the world... Ben and Jerry.

When I'm well into my third episode, and my ice cream carton is looking pathetically empty, the doorbell rings. Getting up from the couch, I shuffle to the door, intent on ignoring whoever is on the other side. When I put my eye up to the peephole, my skin gets all prickly with awareness.

Matt is standing there in a rumpled suit with his briefcase in one hand and his travel suitcase in the other.

CHAPTER Six

I take a moment before I open the door to do a mental checklist of how bad I look.

No makeup.

Check.

Bad hair.

Check.

Frumpy clothing with an ice cream stain on front.

Check.

Fuzzy slippers that look like something my grandma would wear.

Check.

Oh, hell... this is just sex, so let's see how bad Matt wants it.

I pull the door open and give him a smile, making sure he can get a good gander at the hot mess that is McKayla Dawson. "What are you doing here?"

In true Matt fashion, his eyes rake down my body slowly and back up again. When he meets my eyes, there's no mocking over how frightful I look. Instead, his eyes look fevered and his voice is husky when he says, "I've been fantasizing about you for two days. Why wouldn't I be here?"

He steps up to me and leans down to nuzzle my neck, his arms going around my waist. I push back at him, but he doesn't let me go.

"Matt... I look a mess. I wasn't expecting you."

"You look beautiful, and you're going to invite me in so I can fuck you senseless."

Yes, please... I'll take two!

I immediately step back when his grip loosens and motion for him to come in, closing the door behind him. He sets his briefcase down and removes his jacket to lay it over the back of the love seat. Perusing the large living room, he takes in the Brazilian hardwoods, the expensive leather furniture, and the custom drapery.

"How do you afford this place? I know I certainly don't pay you enough to live here."

"It is my roommate Macy's apartment. She's ungodly rich and apparently thinks I'm like her best friend or something, so she lets me live here for peanuts. I'm totally taking advantage of her," I quip.

"I seriously doubt you even know how to take advantage of someone," Matt murmurs as he lifts me up into his arms so that my legs go around his waist. "Enough talk, though. I need to be inside of you."

Wrapping my arms around his neck, I press against his lips, welcoming the feel of his tongue against mine. His palms grip my ass hard, pressing me down against his erection, which is already seeking release against his zipper. Pulling away slightly, I mumble against his lips, "Bedroom's down the hall."

Matt starts walking back toward my bedroom, rubbing his chin along my neck as we go. His five o'clock shadow abrades deliciously against my skin, causing me to shiver.

"I'd love to take a shower first," Matt says when I point out my bedroom door. "Will you join me?"

"Hmmmm," I muse. "You, me, hot, soapy shower… that sounds terrible."

Laughing, Matt follows my direction and carries me into my bathroom. While he strips both of us down, I ask, "So… how was Atlanta?"

"I'm exhausted, but it was a good trip. I got the case that we were mediating settled. Client's happy," he said, while trailing a finger up the outside of my leg and over my hipbone. His hand goes between my legs, so I barely can comprehend him when he asks, "How was the rest of your week?"

I think a garbled sound came out, followed by a low moan, and immediately finished by a breathy pant.

He grins at me. "That good, huh?"

I nod my head, and he pushes me into the shower. My hands start wandering, playing over the hard lines of his chest, digging into his shoulders. I let my fingertips gently bump along the marbled ridges of his stomach, and I playfully tug on his happy trail of hair. While Matt shampoos my hair, I take him in my hands and start stroking him to life, which doesn't take much effort on my part.

Batting my hands away, Matt says, "Let's finish this shower. I'm dying to get you in the bed."

"What's wrong with shower sex?" I ask, my lip sticking out in a full-blown pout that I'm hoping will earn a nibble from Matt.

Kissing me on the nose and sticking me under the water to rinse off, he says, "Nothing... I'm just so tired, I don't know if I can hold you up. Bed sex tonight. Shower sex in the morning after I've rested."

With that, Matt slaps me on the butt and hops out, wrapping a towel around his waist. "Hurry up... I'll be waiting."

He heads back into my bedroom, while I quickly slap some conditioner on my head and work it through my long locks. Rinsing it well, I turn the water off. I dry off as quickly as possible, but there's nothing worse than taking long, wet hair to bed. Quickly brushing the tangles out, I turn the hair dryer on, trying to get the majority of the dampness out of it.

But I think of Matt lying in my bed… naked… slightly moist… completely horny for me, and, after three minutes, I give up and turn the dryer off. We're just going to have to deal with wet pillows from my head.

Dropping my towel to the floor, I turn the bathroom light off and walk into the bedroom.

There is my hunk of burning love… my orgasm master, my energizer bunny, sprawled out waiting for me on the bed.

Fast asleep.

I can tell he tried to stay awake. He has one foot propped on the floor and the other on the bed; his legs are wide open with his package all squarely tucked in for a nice sleep. It's no longer standing at attention and seeking my interest the way it was five minutes ago.

Taking a moment, I gaze at Matt. He is an unbelievably sexy man, absolute perfection in my mind. He's strong, confident, and quick-witted—an alpha to the core.

But watching him lay on my bed, sound asleep, with his mouth slightly open and a soft snore emitting, he looks incredibly vulnerable to me right now.

The great sex god, Matt Connover, is too tired to make love to me tonight.

And there's something about it that touches my heart.

CHAPTER Seven

Yes, that is someone nibbling on my neck.
Not just someone... that's Matt nibbling on my neck.
As I start to wake fully up, other sensations assault me. Matt is pressed up against my back, my head resting on his arm, while the other is wrapped around my waist. His cock is pressed into my backside, and his lips are making a goose-bump trail along the skin of my neck.

I stretch my body and then, for good measure, push my butt into Matt Jr., who is insistently knocking on my back door. Matt Sr. groans in response, and the arm that was wrapped around my waist travels south, his fingers working their way between my legs.

Yup… that's on my list of best way ever to wake up!

"I can't believe you let me sleep last night," Matt chides as he sinks a finger into me. "You're a bad girl."

No words come out, just a breathy moan that causes Matt to chuckle, and he adds another finger. I feel compelled to converse with him… You know, show him that I can multitask while he wakes my body up.

"You looked so cute and vulnerable last night, I just couldn't do it," I tell him. Truth of the matter is, I crawled into bed next to him, pulled the covers over both of us, and watched him sleep. If he knew I had done that, I'm sure he would have labeled me a psycho, so I keep that knowledge to myself.

"Vulnerable?" Matt growls in my ear as he pushes his fingers into me extra deep. "Never call me that again. I'm the great and powerful Connover. Vulnerable has no business being anywhere in the vicinity of me."

Giggling, I reach my hand behind me and grab ahold of what has become my most prized possession.

Yes... mine!

I stroke him in time with the beat of his fingers, and we lay silently with nothing but moans and grunts echoing through my bedroom. After only a few minutes, Matt's voice is raspy and harsh when he says, "Playtime's over."

He pushes me onto my stomach, rolling over on top of me. Supporting his weight on his hands, he manages to kick my legs apart. I can feel him make a quick dip with his hips, and he's at my entrance. He's not seeking permission to come in either. He takes it upon himself with a few rough pushes and then he's all the way in, and God... it feels so fucking good.

Feels better and better every time.

To give himself better leverage, Matt grabs my hips and raises them off the bed, pulling out and slamming back into me. I let out a very unladylike ooph into the pillow, and then I just hang on for the ride.

And it's Matt-Fucking-Connover tunneling deep into me, so it's the ride of a lifetime. He alternates fast, then slow, hard, and then tender, hands gripping my hips or sneaking around to my front to rub me just right.

Long before he reaches the pinnacle, I'm already shaking, shuddering, and crying out words of praise for his performance. He soon follows me, again whispering my name in reverence as he comes.

Once we get our sea legs under us, we venture into the shower… where Round Two of the Mac and Matt Show takes place. We're not as graceful, and Matt even slips on the soapy tile once as he tries to pin me to the shower wall. He throws a hand out to make a grab at something—anything—to stop us falling and manages to grab onto my shampoo rack hanging around the showerhead. It slips off the metal pipe, catching the showerhead with such force that it rips away. It falls and hits Matt on the shoulder, for which he drops seven "F" bombs, and water starts pouring out of the bare pipe at an alarming rate.

Pride doesn't even do it justice when I think that Matt never even misses a beat. His feet gain purchase and he balances out, never missing a stroke inside of me. He pounds me into the tile wall until both of us are groaning in orgasm.

And being a true gentleman, he fixes my showerhead after we dry off.

Now I'm feeding him pancakes and sipping at my coffee, completely content with my morning sex-a-thon, the fact that Matt is sitting in my kitchen, and that we're talking about normal things. Oh, nothing too personal, but we're not talking about business. We found we have a mutual love affair for Criminal Minds and Family Guy, and that we are not in alignment on reality TV. I adore Big Brother and Survivor—he thinks those shows suck brain cells out of your head. I then point out that he's not getting any smarter by watching Family Guy.

Our banter is light and easy, and it's hard to remember that he's my boss and I'm his subordinate. It's even harder for me to remember that this is just sex, and our conversation is probably nothing more than the passing of time so that he can eat his breakfast.

When he finishes, he helps me with the dishes, bumping his shoulder companionably against mine. But then he says he needs to get home and take care of some things.

I wait for him to say he wants to see me tonight, but he busies himself with putting his jacket on and grabbing his briefcase. When he walks to my front door, I finally blurt, "So… what are you doing this weekend?"

God… did that sound pathetically hopeful?

Hopefully not.

He turns to look at me with a tight look on his face. "I have plans all weekend, so I'll see you in the office on Monday."

His words have a finality to them. He's not going to share what those plans are and, clearly, I'm not included. A deep pang of hurt hits me in the center of my chest, but I don't let him see it. I keep my smile bright when I tell him, "Cool. Have a great weekend, and I'll see you Monday."

Kissing me on the cheek, Matt says goodbye and leaves without a backward glance. He doesn't hold me in his arms and tell me he'll miss me.

He's already dismissed me from his mind.

Chapter Eight

My plans may not be with Matt this weekend—again, still smarting about that—but I do have plans. I'm in the law library at Columbia doing a huge research project on how to pierce the corporate veil for Lorraine that's due on Monday. Yes, I almost fell asleep just thinking those words.

Boring!

I could easily do the research at the office. Matt and Bill spared no expense on the online legal research software for Connover and Crown, but I love the law library at my alma mater. There's something about the dark cubbies and green banker's lamps on each table, emitting their soft glow, that makes me feel smarter. Like I can absorb the yawn-inducing material better. I'm always in my research zone here.

I've been at it for two hours, and I think I have most of my research collected. Now I settle in to read it in detail. I make frequent trips back and forth to the copier, and let my yellow highlighter mark the passages that apply to our case, or could poke a hole in our case.

That takes another three hours, and then I'm ready to begin typing a Memorandum that will summarize all of this work into an easy, twenty-minute read for Lorraine.

Yup... pisses me off that I'll have probably seven hours of work into a Memorandum that Lorraine will be able to read in twenty minutes and be well versed in the law. Such is the life of a lowly associate attorney fresh out of law school.

Once my Memorandum is finished, and I've proofed it three times—because if Lorraine catches a comma out of place, I'll get an ass-chewing—I print it and head to the copier for one last round of copies. One for Lorraine, one for me, and one for Matt, just because I know it will piss Lorraine off that I think I need to copy Matt on this.

As the papers are shooting out from the copier into the collection bin, my mind wanders. Of course, I think of Matt. I wonder what he has planned this weekend, and I'd be lying if I didn't say I was obsessing on the possible fact that he could be hooking up with someone else. Although we've been very clear and honest about giving into our attraction to each other, we never talked about us being monogamous. Matt has no need for loyalty to me because I've not asked for it, and my stomach churns over the fact that he might be screwing someone else tonight.

Someone prettier than me. Smarter than me. Sexier than me.

Sighing in longing and frustration, I don't notice the man standing next to the copier.

"Legal research gives me the same feeling," he says, assuming my sighs have more to do with the law than love.

Looking up, I see a very handsome man. He stands about six foot with dark blond hair and warm brown eyes. Dressed casually in jeans and a polo shirt, he leans one arm on the copier and pulls my copies out. Scanning it briefly, he says, "Piercing the corporate veil, huh? Dry stuff."

Nodding, I give him a smile in agreement. "Yup. Just spent a lovely seven hours on this puppy. I'm not entirely sure I'm not in a coma right now. Am I talking okay?"

Laughing, he hands me the copies and says, "You're talking just fine. I'm Cal Carson, by the way."

He sticks his hand out to me, and I give it a shake. "McKayla Dawson, first-year associate and relegated to the law library on weekends."

I take the copies from him and slip them in my briefcase. Standing up, I look back at Cal. "So, what type of law do you do?"

"Corporate and insurance defense," he says, with about as much enthusiasm as a man getting ready to have his teeth drilled. "But I'm thinking of a career change. You?"

"Oh, a little of this, a little of that. Whatever my boss tells me to do, actually."

"Been there, done that," he commiserates. "It will get better over time."

We both start walking out of the library together. "Didn't you have copies to make? I just assumed you were waiting for me to get done."

"Nah... I just saw you standing there and thought I'd introduce myself. Say... if you want me to read your memo, I'd be glad to. I just gave a symposium on this very subject."

"Really?" I ask, grateful to have another opinion. If I'm wrong about something, I can get it corrected and save myself from a Lorraine Special Tongue Lashing. "I don't want to bother you or anything."

"It's not a bother and certainly no hardship to help out a beautiful woman," he says, his eyes showing a tad bit warmer than they were before. I blush prettily because his words are nice, and I'm in a Matt funk.

"Okay... how about I buy you a cup of coffee across the street, and you can take a gander at it?"

Cal takes my elbow as we exit the law library. "I'll agree only if I buy the coffee."

"But that doesn't seem fair." I laugh. "You have to do work and pay for coffee."

"Trust me," Cal says. "Being able to spend half an hour in your presence is payment enough."

I look at Cal in a different light right now. He's clearly flirting with me, and I like it. It's been so very long since someone has done that. Not even Matt has taken the time, because he knows I'm a sure thing. He knows without a doubt that I'll drop trou when he crooks his finger at me.

But this is different. Since Pete, no one of the male persuasion has caused me to blush or made butterflies dance in my stomach.

Giving him a blinding smile, I say, "Okay... I accept your offer of coffee. Lead the way."

CHAPTER Nine

This day couldn't get any worse. It was a Monday after all, and it came on the heels of a craptastic weekend. I spent all weekend vacillating between working my ass off and moping over Matt.

I try to mentally kick my ass over and over again for getting feelings caught up in this strange 'thing' I have going on with Matt. It's a 'thing' because it's not a relationship. We don't really talk unless it's to murmur dirty words to each other. I mean, it's not like we're sharing our hopes and dreams with one another. In essence, other than giving me bone-melting orgasms, he doesn't really care for me.

Why is he plaguing my thoughts so much?

I figured coming into work might help me take my mind off things. I mean, I was met at my office door by Lorraine, who berated me for being five-minutes late, and for a solid thirty seconds... I didn't think of Matt.

No, I thought of putting my hands around Lorraine's scrawny neck and wringing the ever-fucking life out of her. But then she simmered down and asked to see the Memorandum I had drafted for her this weekend. She sat in her office, all prim and proper, and silently read my work.

The best possible scenario occurred, and she looked up at me with lips thinned flat and said, "I can use this. It's passable."

The vision of my fingers squeezing her throat pushed its way back in my mind, and I let myself succumb to the few seconds of bliss that it afforded me.

After Lorraine trounced out of my office, I spent my time reading the articles on biomechanical engineering that Matt had sent me. By the third one, I was starting to understand it a bit more and wasn't feeling nearly as stupid.

I took a quick lunch break and ran down the block to get a sub, eating it as I walked back to the office. I then immersed myself so deeply back into the world of biomechanics that I was surprised when I glanced at the clock to see that it was almost six PM.

Logging off my computer, I pack my briefcase up and head out. I stop by Lorraine's office before I leave, because she expects me to… just to make sure she doesn't have any other orders to parcel out. I stick my head in and say, "I'm heading out, Lorraine. Do you need anything?"

And I will punch you if you ask me to get you some coffee.

She looks up and gives me a cougar of a smile. "No. I'm just waiting on Matt to finish up with a mediation. He's taking me out to dinner tonight."

I truly hope it's not that apparent, but I know my face turns an angry red because I can feel it heat up like someone had stuck a hot iron on it.

The motherfucker lets me blow him and can't be bothered to buy me a meal, but he takes Lorraine "Skank" Cummings out for dinner?

I take a deep breath and hope my voice comes out in a neutrally calm way. "Dinner?"

"Yes," she gushes, reaching into her purse and swiping on some lipstick. I notice she gets a chunk on her right front tooth, but I don't point it out to her. Hope Matt finds that attractive. "He buzzed me this morning and asked if I had time for dinner tonight at seven. I knew it was just a matter of time."

My head is buzzing and I think I actually may take a step toward her to strangle her, but then I realize my anger is more for Matt than her. Though it's probably in everyone's best interest if I just call it a night and head home. In fact, I think it would behoove me to call in sick for a few days, because I really don't think I can handle this right now.

Turning around so she doesn't see the look on my face, I manage to grit out, "Well, have a nice time tonight."

She actually has the lame temerity to say, "Toodles."

I'm pissed, hurt, and really pissed. I stomp down the hall and, as I round the corner to the lobby, I'm brought up short by the surreal visage of seeing Matt standing with two other lawyers, talking quietly. And not just any lawyers… one of them is Cal Carson.

The conversation looks to be heated, even though they are talking quietly. Cal is holding onto a briefcase, and Matt has his arms crossed over his chest. The two men are glaring daggers at each other.

I start up my walk toward the lobby doors when I hear Cal say in surprise, "McKayla!"

Turning, I briefly take in his happy smile, and notice Matt's frown turning deeper. Because I'm pissed at Matt, I give my most radiant smile to Cal as he walks over to me, and I don't spare Matt another glance. "Hey, Cal. What are you doing here?"

Cal and I had actually had a great time over coffee. He read my Memorandum, gave me a few pointers, but overall pronounced it worthy of Lorraine's scrutiny. Then we spent another thirty minutes just chatting about our lives. We got along extremely well, and I almost thought he was going to ask me out on a date. But he didn't. Instead, he suggested we swap business cards, promising to call me for lunch one day. I wasn't sure if that would be considered a date, or we were just doing a business type of meal.

Regardless, I really hadn't given much thought to Cal since then because I had been so mired in my dark thoughts over Matt.

"I just finished a mediation with Matt. As usual, he kicked my ass today."

"Well, you can't win them all," I tell him in commiseration. I don't dare look over at Matt, but I can see in my peripheral vision that he is standing there watching us.

"So... I was going to send you an email tonight to see if you wanted to get lunch one day this week. Are you free?"

It's time to make Matt pay the price of using me as his sex toy and taking Lorraine out to a nice dinner.

I know Matt heard Cal ask me to lunch because I could tell his posture became more defensive. I make sure I'm just loud enough when I tell Cal, "I'd love to. After all, we had such a good time on Saturday."

Cal's smile becomes even bigger but, before he can even respond, Matt stalks over to both of us and says, "If you'll excuse us, Carson, I need to talk to McKayla about an urgent matter on a case."

Matt doesn't even wait for Cal to respond, but takes my elbow and starts ushering me back to his office.

CHAPTER Ten

When Matt opens his office door and pushes me inside, I finally tear my elbow away, spinning around to confront him. "What is your problem? Pulling me out of the lobby and manhandling me to your office like you own me?"

Glaring at me, Matt says, "What the fuck are you doing with Carson? You were with him Saturday?"

Part of me wants to give him enough innuendo about Cal that he'll think I screwed him, but I really don't have that in me. I hope a bit of honesty on my part may get Matt to open up to me. "Not that it's any of your business, but I met him in the law library and we had coffee. He helped me out with a Memorandum of Law."

I can see Matt visibly relax, and I know without a doubt that he thought I had slept with him. Pressing the advantage, I ask, "Where were you this weekend since we're... you know... all sharing and shit?"

His eyes cloud over, and his face becomes a mask of steel. "None of your business."

"What? You demand to know what I was doing, but you don't share what you were up to?"

"That's right. I'm twisted that way," he sneers, taking two steps to bring himself flush with me. "Stay away from Carson. He's bad news."

I start to step back from Matt but his hand snakes out and slides around my waist, pulling me up against him. My hands come up and slap flat against his chest, trying to push him away. I'm tired of his caveman routine, and I'm furious he won't tell me where he went this weekend. I know it won't do any good to press the issue, but I'm not going to let him try to seduce me with hot touches. My body is a complete traitor when it comes to Matt.

Pushing hard, I finally break free from his grip, only because he chooses to let me go. The fight, though, is far from over. "You can't tell me what I can and can't do. It's a two-way street. I have no say so in your plans, then you have no say so in mine."

"I do when it comes to Cal Carson. He's off limits."

"Off limits?" I start to screech, and then lower my voice so we aren't heard outside of his office. "You want to talk about off limits, how about you taking Lorraine out to dinner tonight? She's in her office right now getting all dolled up for your date with her. Let me make the same proclamation you're making about Cal. She's off limits. Stay away from her."

Matt's eyebrows rise up, and a devious grin slides across his face. "Are you jealous?"

"Doesn't matter if I am or not. You say I can't see Cal, well, I say you can't see Lorraine. Cancel with her."

The grin fades from Matt's face, and he's deadly calm when he says, "Not going to happen."

"What? You won't even consider my feelings?"

"Not where this is concerned. It's none of your business."

"Then Cal is none of your business. We're even." I want to punctuate my statement with my patented 'neener' move, but I know that would be too childish.

Matt lunges at me, and I'm caught off guard. I try to take a step back to avoid his clutches, but he seizes me nonetheless, grabbing onto my shoulders and pulling me close. "You're trying my patience, Mac. Words don't seem to work on you. Let me try something else."

I know it's coming, and I'm powerless to stop it. Matt's mouth is hot and wet as it covers mine and I open willingly to him, my body going pliant and melting into his. I can feel his erection burning through both layers of our clothes as he grinds it into me. He commandeers my mouth, makes it his slave. I fall deeper and deeper until my fingers are curled tightly into his clothes to keep from falling.

Matt has complete and utter control over me in this way, and there's something niggling at the back of my head, trying to surface. I try to forget the sensations of his tongue swiping against mine, and the feel of his hardness against me. What is it?

Oh yeah, it comes ringing through loud and clear.

You are a doormat, and he's walking all over you!

With all the mental and physical strength I can muster, I tear myself away from his kiss. He's so surprised that he releases me. He's breathing hard, his eyes dark and fevered. I know I look the same, and it takes every bit of strength I possess not to leap back into his arms.

"Enough," I pant. "Stop doing that to me. I'm not your puppet."

"You are if I tell you to be," he taunts with silky smoothness.

Taking a deep breath, I let his last comment pass, trying to reason with him one more time. "Listen... I won't see Cal if that is what you want, but I want the same thing with Lorraine. I don't want you taking her to dinner tonight. Are we agreed?"

Matt is shaking his head in the negative, and he confirms his position with words. "I'm taking Lorraine out to dinner tonight. I can't cancel. But then I'll be over to your apartment after."

My heart sinks. I'm not asking for much—I know I'm not. I'm even willing to let go the fact he won't tell me what he did this weekend. I'm just asking he cancel one measly dinner date, and he can't do that for me. The only thing he cares about is getting in my pants tonight after God only knows what he's going to do with Lorraine.

With a clarity that is as crystal as it gets, I know that my time with Matt is at an end. My feelings are too involved, and it can't just be sex for me. Squaring my shoulders, I give him a sad smile... but my resolve is firm. "Then I'm sorry, Matt. This freak of a fuck show is over."

"What?" he asks in disbelief, his brow furrowing.

"You heard me. I can't do this anymore. If you want my resignation, you have it. Just let me know. If not, I'll show up and do my job well. But as far as you and I are concerned... we're done."

I walk past him, half expecting him to reach out and stop me.

He doesn't though. He just stays quiet as I walk out of his office.

VIOLATION

Volume 3

Sawyer Bennett

Legal Affairs
Vol. 3 - Violation
By Sawyer Bennett

All Rights Reserved.
Copyright © 2014 by Sawyer Bennett
Published by Big Dog Books

This book is a work of fiction. Names, characters, places and incidents either are products of the author's imagination or are used fictitiously. Any resemblance to actual events, locales or persons, living or dead, is entirely coincidental.

No part of this book can be reproduced in any form or by electronic or mechanical means including information storage and retrieval systems, without the express written permission of the author. The only exception is by a reviewer who may quote short excerpts in a review.

CHAPTER One

The rest of this week has gone remarkably well considering on Monday I cut ties with Matt. Well, personal ties anyway. I still had to face him every day as my employer and, while slightly awkward, I was weathering the storm.

My first true test was the very next day... Tuesday, when I had to listen to Lorraine gush about her date with Matt. I got a full-blown novel on their evening together, even down to what the china pattern looked like at the fancy five-star restaurant he'd taken her to, and the fact he ordered a two-hundred dollar bottle of champagne for both of them to drink.

Asshole hadn't even bought me a Big Mac, and I'd made him howl with pleasure. Where's the gratitude?

Yes, I was still a little bitter, but I didn't let it affect the way I was around Matt. There was no way I was ever going to let him know that my feelings were still hurt and that, annoyingly enough, I missed him a little.

So, whenever we had to interact at the office, I gave him my most pleasant smile, and I even made sure I answered every question he posed my way with a "Yes, sir," or a "No, sir." And yes, I danced an internal dance of glee when his teeth would clench together and that jaw muscle would pop every time I did that.

Sometimes, life was all about the little pleasures.

Past those few interactions, I kept my head down and concentrated on my work. It was driving me a little batty because I had run into a few roadblocks on the Jackson case, but I was nowhere near ready to go ask Matt for help, so I dug my heels in and tried to solve my problems on my own.

The brightest part of my week was hearing from Cal. True to his word, he sent me an email Monday night and invited me to lunch on Thursday. Still smarting from Matt's refusal to treat me even remotely like a human being with feelings, I gladly accepted and even made sure I wore a pretty dress that clung nicely to my curves. I even curled my hair.

When I walked into the office kitchen Thursday morning to get a cup of coffee, Matt was in there sitting at one of the tables and reading the paper. He glanced up when he heard me walk in, and did a double take over my appearance. For a brief moment, his lips started to curve up in an appreciative smile and I thought he might compliment me, but then one of the staff pool secretaries walked in and we started talking.

Yes, it was evil of me, but when she complimented me on how great my dress was, I couldn't help myself when I said, "Thanks… I have a lunch date today and wanted to look nice."

My back was to Matt so I have no clue what his reaction was, but he immediately stood up and walked out of the kitchen.

So, back to my lunch date.

Cal is pretty awesome. We meet at a great little Cuban restaurant and spend an hour and a half just talking and laughing. He's down to earth and completely charming. I find out he's been practicing law for ten years but is completely dissatisfied with doing insurance defense work.

When I ask what he really wants to do, he tells me with a sheepish look, "Honestly… I'd love to do the type of work Matt does."

He says it with admiration, and I understand exactly how he feels. As a lawyer, Matt is someone you would want to aspire to be like.

As a lover… not so much.

"So what's with you and Matt? He seems a little antagonistic toward you," I ask. I don't tell him that Matt had warned me off, because that would imply Matt had a personal reason to do so, and that is still very much a secret.

Cal's face tightens just a bit, although he tries to give me an apologetic smile. "Actually, that's kind of personal if you don't mind. Matt and I have a history together, and it's not good."

I reach across the table and grab his hand, because I can tell that I provoked some dark feelings. "Not a problem. Forget I even asked. In fact, let's just agree that Matt Connover has no place being involved in our conversation."

Cal rewards me with smile filled with gratitude that I didn't push the subject, and we lapse into a truly scintillating discussion about tort reform. Well, it's actually more of a debate than a discussion, seeing as how technically Cal's practice of law and my practice of law are on two opposite ends of the spectrum. Still, I can't tell you how refreshing it is to be with someone that may disagree about my opinion, but still respects me enough to listen to it.

Bitterly, I remind myself that Cal is proving to be

everything that Matt isn't. Cal seems totally interested in me and wants to spend time with me outside of the bedroom. Well, I have no clue if he wants to spend time with me in the bedroom, but I'm just going to assume he does because... well, he's a guy.

After Cal finishes paying for the bill, he looks at me with his warm brown eyes even as he tugs on the tie at his neck. A sign of pure nervousness, so I gave him an encouraging smile.

"McKayla... I was wondering if you'd go with me to the Patron's Gala for the New York State Trial Lawyers Association next week? It's a black tie affair... I thought it would be fun."

I stare at Cal and blink a few times, not quite sure what to say.

Gah, what is wrong with me?

My immediate reaction should be to say yes. Any girl would be happy to go out with someone as handsome and successful as Cal.

But my first thought is, What if Matt changes his mind and comes begging for my forgiveness?

The mere thought that I would forestall moving forward with someone that could be very good for me, all for the barest possibility that someone that was probably very bad for me might come running, causes bile to back up in my throat.

I am a pathetic mess, and I'm actually a bit ashamed of myself.

Before I can talk myself out of it or think one minute further on it, I give Cal a radiant smile and say, "I'd love to go with you."

CHAPTER Two

By the time Friday rolls around, there is no denying it. I am going to have to break down and seek Matt's help with the Jackson case. I've finished all of my research on biomechanical engineering and even interviewed three potential expert witnesses to hire.

The only problem now, is I have no clue who to hire and whether or not what they are charging is fair. Only Matt can answer that, and I need his guidance and help with this type of thing. Before I can change my mind, I send him a quick email asking for ten minutes of his time. He responds back to me immediately and tells me that he's in the office all day, and to just come down to his office when I'm ready.

That throws me for a loop because Matt is always meticulous about planning his day out. No one can get into his office and take a minute of his time unless it's pre-approved and scheduled ahead of time.

The mere fact that I have unfettered access to him all day puts my nerves into overdrive, and I keep putting the meeting off for one reason or another. When it gets close to six PM, I finally hitch up my britches and decide I need to get it over with. I know Matt is still here because he rarely leaves before seven. I make sure I'm armed with a bunch of "Yes, sir's," and "No, sir's," just in case I get in danger of being sucked into his hypnotic gaze or something.

I'm just about to stand from my desk when the door flies open and there stands five-foot-three of snarling, spitting, bleached blonde attorney.

Lorraine Cummings.

She walks into my office, carrying a file, and slams the door shut behind her so hard that my undergraduate degree, which is hanging on my wall, falls, causing the glass to crack down the middle.

I stare openmouthed at it for a second, and then the anger starts to rise. I turn to her to demand she pay to have it fixed, when she tears into me.

I've never seen Lorraine so mad before. Her face

is mottled an angry red, and her eyes practically bug out of her head.

Holding the file up in her hand so I can see it, she yells, "Do you know what this is?"

"A client's file," I say, my voice as calm as can be in the hopes that she will lower hers. I'm not too worried about any of the staff hearing us, because they all clear out right at 5:30 PM on the dot.

"Not just any fucking client's file," she screeches, and I resist the urge to put my fingers in my ears because damn... she sounds like a cat in heat. "This is the file for my hearing today in front of Judge Hudson that you were to prepare for me. And do you know what? The fucking Order you were supposed to draft wasn't in there."

She punctuates the last words of her statement with so much anger that spittle flies out of her mouth and hits me on my arm. Geez! What is it about people spitting on me?

"Don't you have anything to fucking say for yourself?" When I just stare at her blankly, because I know damn well the Order was there when I handed it to her this morning, her rage reaches a crescendo and she cocks her arm back, letting the file fly at me. I see it hurling toward me almost as if in slow motion, turning end over end. All the loose papers inside take flight into the air, and then it's just an empty folder flying toward my head. I duck quickly to the left, and the folder splats harmlessly on the wall behind me.

It's my personal belief that Lorraine's greatest rage comes not because the Order was missing, but because she failed to peg me with the file. The minute I ducked, her anger turned to molten lava, and she lets out an almost inhuman screech.

"You're such a fucking screw up, McKayla!"

Okay, enough is enough. Now I'm getting really pissed but before I can even open my mouth, my office door flies open so hard, that now my law degree falls off the wall and succumbs to the same fate as my undergrad degree.

I stare at it sadly, and say, "That's just great."

Looking back toward the door, I see Matt Connover standing there, his face furious. He glances briefly down at my two degrees broken on the floor, and then turns back to me. He doesn't yell, but then he doesn't need to. He's Matt Fucking Connover.

"What the hell is going on here?" he asks, his tone measured and calm, even though I can tell he's bristling with anger.

"You broke my frame," I say lamely, because I'm really not sure what else to say. I told Matt on my first day of employment that I would never bring my problems with Lorraine to him. I'm a big girl, and I can handle this.

Matt gives me an exasperated glare and turns to Lorraine. "I repeat… what is going on here? I heard yelling clear down in my office."

Lorraine stands there nervously, wringing her hands together. She gives me a sidelong glance to see if I'm going to spill the beans on her. I avert her gaze and start organizing the papers that flew out of the file.

Hey… look at that. I pick up a piece of paper that had fallen out of the folder and hold it up to Lorraine. "Here's your Order."

Lorraine's face blanches, and not because she just yelled at me for nothing. She's terrified that I will tell Matt exactly what she did, even though she had no cause to yell at me like that.

The power I hold over her right now almost has a ticklish feeling.

She and I engage in a staring war, and I slowly open my mouth like I'm going to rat her out. Lorraine's eyes plead with me and I make her wait out her sentence for just a few more seconds, then I let her off the hook.

Turning to Matt with a smile I say, "Nothing's wrong. Just a little disagreement, but we cleared it up. Right, Lorraine?"

Lorraine lets out a huge, pent-up breath and smiles at me, although the light doesn't quite reach her eyes. "Right. No problems here."

Matt stares back and forth between us, and I can tell he doesn't buy a word of what we're saying. Finally, he sighs and says, "McKayla... let's meet on the Jackson case so I can get out of here. I've got plans tonight."

Great.

Another pointed reminder that Matt's plans do not revolve around me.

CHAPTER Three

When we reach Matt's office, he motions me in and then shuts the door behind us. I take a seat and wait for him to take his normal chair behind his desk. Instead, he takes the chair beside me, sitting in it with casual care and turning to look at me. The proximity is a little disconcerting and, I swear, I can actually feel a vibration between us.

Glancing at his watch, he says, "I've got twenty minutes before I have to leave for dinner."

He hesitates, and then he adds on, "Bill and I are meeting our accountant tonight."

I shrug my shoulders, as if I could care less that he is making a concerted effort to let me know exactly what his plans are. Sorry, bub... it's a little too late. "Not any of my business."

Matt just stares at me, and I don't get the nice little jaw pop that I've come to gain sustenance from, so I add on, "Sir."

There we go... the jaw is popping away, and I feel a peaceful calm enter into my heart. It's easier than fucking Yoga to find my Zen place by antagonizing Matt.

He continues to stare at me as if I grew a second head, and I just placidly look back at him. Finally, he says, "I want to know what was going on between you and Lorraine."

I shrug my shoulders again. "Nothing. Just a little misunderstanding, but it's solved now."

"Misunderstanding?"

"Misunderstanding," I reiterate.

"Lorraine was screaming at you. Just before I walked in, she called you a fucking screw up. I don't care what the reason was, but we don't talk to each other like that at this firm."

"I'm sorry. It won't happen again," I tell him with genuine remorse.

"Fuck, McKayla," he says in exasperation. "Why are you apologizing? She was the one screaming at you."

"And like I said... it was just a misunderstanding. No harm, no foul."

Now he's in full jaw-popping mode, and his teeth are clenched. I cannot believe how much I'm reveling in the fact that I'm getting under his skin. Finally, he manages to grit out, "I'll just have to talk to Lorraine myself, I guess. Give your degrees to Miss Anders and she'll get them fixed for you, at my expense."

"No, thanks," I say politely. "I can handle it."

Now I can practically hear his teeth scraping against each other, and I get almost giddy over the thought. I give him a lovely smile, so he knows that my non-cooperation, which is in turn causing him discomfort, is giving me quite a bit of pleasure.

I'm so fucking childish, but I just can't help it.

Matt stares at me a long moment until I see a bit of a hard glint reflecting back at me. His jaw stops popping, and his mouth parts slightly. Finally, his lips curve upward in a smile that says, You're not going to win this one, Mac, and a slight feeling of dread starts to creep up my spine.

Standing from his chair, he leans over his desk and presses the speaker button on his phone. After a small chime, I can hear Lorraine pick up her extension.

"Yes, Matt?"

"Lorraine... can you come into my office for a minute?"

I can almost hear Lorraine take a nervous gulp on her end before she says in a voice filled with a tinge of fear. "Sure. Be right down."

Matt presses the button to disconnect and turns toward me. He leans back against his desk, crosses his arms over his chest, and just stares at me with a triumphant look.

I get a nervous feeling in the pit of my stomach that magnifies once his office door opens, and Lorraine steps in. Matt's gaze lingers on me for just a second, then he steps away from his desk and motions for Lorraine to sit down beside me. King Connover takes his throne on the other side.

I watch as Matt leans back in his chair, confident and casual. My nervousness increases because this was the pose he assumed just before deposing the witnesses in Chicago.

Just before he shredded them.

Oh, shit… he is going to expose our lies. He stares a moment at Lorraine, and I can almost feel her shudder in fear. His gaze then lazily moves over to me, and the glow in his eyes almost takes on the look of a lion hunting its prey. I suppress the urge to run, and stick my chin up a little higher. I can tell this amuses him by the way his eyes crinkle.

He leans forward slightly, like he's getting ready to pounce. I recognize this move. He's getting ready to go in for the kill.

"Lorraine... I'd like to know exactly what just happened in McKayla's office."

I can see Lorraine's hands shaking just a bit when she says, "It was just a disagreement. No biggie."

"So I've heard," Matt says drily. "But any time you scream at someone and call them... what were the words you used? 'A fucking screw up'... well, I need to delve a little deeper, you see?"

Lorraine nods her head but doesn't say anything. Matt leans forward a bit more and places his elbows on his desk, steepling his fingers as he stares at her. "Let me see if I can put this together... you had a hearing this morning?"

Lorraine dutifully answers, "Yes."

"And you couldn't find the Order the judge was supposed to sign?"

"Yes."

"And you assumed that McKayla had failed to draft the Order and put it in the file?"

"I couldn't find it while I was in court—"

Matt holds his hand up to cut her off, and her mouth snaps shut.

"Yet the Order was, in fact, in there?"

"It appears so," Lorraine grits out.

"So, you went into McKayla's office and slammed the door shut, causing one of her degrees to fall and break?"

"Yes."

"And then you screamed at her for failing to draft the Order?"

"Yes." she says, her voice now a whisper.

"And then yelled that she was a 'fucking screw up'?"

"Perhaps I was a bit hasty—"

Matt holds his hand up again, and Lorraine snaps her mouth shut for the second time.

I feel like I'm in the Twilight Zone. I had dutifully kept my mouth shut about what had happened between Lorraine and me because I'm not a rat and I can handle my own battles, yet within just a few minutes, Matt has Lorraine spilling her guts.

He's amazing.

Matt stands up from his chair and looks down at Lorraine with determination. "I'm going to honor the deal we made with each other Monday night, but I'd like you to go ahead and pack up your stuff and leave now. I don't condone that type of behavior in my business."

Lorraine looks sick to her stomach, and I can't help but blurt out, "What? You're firing her?"

Matt walks to his door and opens it, motioning for Lorraine to leave. "That's right. Effective immediately."

CHAPTER Four

Lorraine stands from her chair and smoothes her skirt down. Then she turns on me, and her eyes are blazing in fury. "You fucking bitch, you just had to rat me out."

What? I did no such thing. "Lorraine… I never said a word."

"Save it," she spits out, and yes, by spit I mean I get hit again with her saliva. I reach up to wipe it off my cheek, even as she leans toward me to sneer. "You're fucking him, and you have him wrapped around your finger. All he talked about Monday night was 'McKayla this and McKayla that'. And now you have him doing your dirty work for you."

I'm so stunned by what Lorraine is saying that I can't even think to defend myself. But apparently, I don't need to because Matt's voice is deadly dangerous when he says from the doorway. "You need to leave right now, Lorraine, before I change my mind about sticking to our deal."

Lorraine spins on him, and her voice is icy. "Try to go back on your word, and I'll sue you."

"I'd like to see you try that, but I'm giving you to the count of three to get out of this office... or I'll have security escort you out."

I just watch this interplay with my jaw hanging open. I have no clue what's going on. But that's a good way to describe my overall feeling since I met Matt Connover.

I'm freakin' clueless.

Lorraine looks at me once more and growls, causing me to shrink back just a little in my chair. Then she stomps out of the office. As soon as she's gone, Matt closes the door and walks back over to his phone. He dials an extension and says, "Please go to Miss Cummings' office and watch her pack up. Do not let her on her computer and escort her out of the building. Get her key before she leaves."

He hangs up and sits down in his chair with a sigh. "I'm sorry you had to go through that."

"Sorry I had to go through that?" I blurt. "You just fired someone because we had a little fight. You're an asshole."

I can't help myself. I'm not just angry he fired someone so quickly. I'm angry at everything Matt has put me through the last two weeks. I'm pissed he seduced my body and mind, I'm pissed he doesn't want anything but sex, and I'm pissed that he has secrets that keep me in the dark.

An idea strikes me though.

"Wait... you didn't fire her out of some misplaced sense of obligation to me because we were having sex, did you?"

Matt's eyes narrow at me. "Absolutely not. While I enjoyed your charms immensely, I don't make business decisions based on how good my last fuck was. And watch who you call an 'asshole'. I just fired someone for practically the same thing."

I reel as if he slapped me in the face, and I can see the regret already forming on his face. His words are softer... gentler, when he says. "Look Mac... I didn't fire her because of you. Lorraine had been exhibiting some very bad behavior the last two weeks. She's been yelling and screaming at the staff left and right, and she's pissed off a few of my clients to the point they're threatening to fire our firm. She's not a good fit here."

"And what was the deal that you mentioned to her? Or is that none of my business?"

"It's none of your business," he confirms, but then he adds on, "but... for the sake of making sure you understand that Lorraine being fired wasn't your fault, I'll tell you. Bill and I decided this weekend to let her go. But we were generous... we offered to buy out her caseload and give her a severance package to help get her on her feet if she wanted to start her firm back up again."

Bells go off in my head. "That's why you took her out to dinner... why you bought her champagne."

"I took her out to dinner because I didn't want to do it at the office in case she made a scene, which I'm betting she would have. And yes, I bought champagne so she would understand what a sweet deal I was offering her. We weren't going to have the deal go into effect until the end of the month, so she could make some plans to re-open her firm. But I'm not going to leave poison in this firm to cause discontent. And she is poison."

I nod my head and gaze at the floor, thoughtful. Yes, she is poison, and yes... it seems Matt did a kind thing rather than a vicious thing. It appears he had a lot of reason to fire her other than her screaming at me.

"It's also why I couldn't cancel my dinner with

her Monday, and because it was firm business, I couldn't tell you what it was about."

My head snaps up. "Wrong, Matt. You could have just said I'm taking her out for a business matter. You could have said that, and it would have been fine. I would have been fine."

We would have been fine.

"You should have trusted me it was about business. I shouldn't have had to explain myself."

"Trust?" I ask with a laugh that sounds semi-hysterical. "What trust? You pointedly told me over and over again, it was just sex. We've never even had a real discussion other than over the five minutes it took to wolf your pancakes down. You don't do relationships, Matt... remember? So tell me... why should there have been trust?"

Matt has no answer. For all of his wit and razor-sharp intellect, he has no response. He just stares at me, his eyes almost filled with resignation that perhaps he had screwed up. But I also see determination that he's not going to apologize or admit he was wrong.

So I stand up and say, "You're late for dinner. Better get going."

Matt nods his head and I turn around to walk out of his office, more confused now than ever over my feelings. Yes, Matt handled the whole 'dinner with

Lorraine' thing badly, but I also learned that he has no romantic interest in her as I thought.

And I keep dwelling on the fact that Lorraine said Matt did nothing but talk about me during said dinner. In fact, it led Lorraine to believe that Matt and I were in a relationship.

Maybe it was possible that Matt did have feelings for me, but he just didn't know how to act on them?

Chapter Five

"I know I've told you once already, but you really are stunning tonight," Cal says.

I smile and thank him because, yes, I remember the appreciative look in his eyes when he picked me up at my apartment a bit ago. He raked his eyes down the form-fitting red ball gown I was wearing—yes, red is apparently my color and the gown was compliments of Macy again—and told me how beautiful I looked.

I felt like a princess tonight, but the only problem was... I wasn't with my prince. As the days ticked down toward the Gala and my date with Cal, my mind kept filling more and more with thoughts of Matt.

Should I have trusted him when he went to dinner with Lorraine? Is it really that big of a deal that he wouldn't divulge what was actually private firm business? And most importantly... did he have feelings for me? Something more than just the passion we shared between the sheets?

"So what do you think?" Cal asks as he sweeps his arm out toward the ballroom. I look around, taking in the setting. Heavy crystal chandeliers hang over the room, dimmed down to just a soft glow. Large tables seating eight are parceled around the room, ladened with bouquets of lilies. An orchestra is playing music, and the dance floor is filled.

"It's amazing," I tell him.

And it is.

It's just... I wish I weren't here. Cal seems like a really great guy, and I can't find a single fault with him, other than the fact that he isn't Matt. Which is fucked up, because Matt is just not cut out for what I ultimately need to be satisfied long term.

Sometimes, when you obsess about a desire long enough, it can magically appear before you. As if I had been secretly wishing for it to happen, and maybe I had been, I hear Matt's voice say, "Mind if we join you?"

Looking up from my seat, Matt is standing there, resplendent in a tailored tuxedo. His gaze flickers back and forth between Cal and me, not paying too much attention to me. Then I notice he's not alone. A lovely, statuesque blonde is beside him, her arm tucked into his elbow. She's wearing a black concoction that showcases a tiny waist and huge boobs. She's utter perfection. How can I ever compare to that?

Cal doesn't look pleased to see Matt, but he stands for introductions. "Sure... it's open seating so help yourself. I'm Cal Carson," he says to the blonde as she shakes his hand.

"Melody," she says in a sexy purr, and I hate her and her cursed sexiness.

She doesn't turn to me or even acknowledge me in any way, so Matt takes it upon himself. "Mel... this is McKayla. She's an associate in our firm. McKayla, this is Melody. She's a partner over at Weinstein Fannerty."

Melody turns her baby blue eyes my way and gives me a nod of her head. I do the same and envision poking her eyes out, but my nails aren't long enough, nor are they perfectly manicured the way hers are.

Matt chooses to take the seat next to me, and Melody sits beside him.

"You look nice tonight," Matt says as almost an afterthought to me.

Nice? Cal said I looked stunning and beautiful. What in the world is wrong with me that I long for a man that says I look nice?

"Thanks, Matt," I tell him pleasantly. "You clean up well yourself."

He gives me a wide smile and then turns his back on me to talk to Melody. I reciprocate and turn to Cal, making it my mission that I'm going to give him a chance, and I'm going to find something within me to let Matt go.

The most obvious thing at this point is to get away from Matt and the dangerous pull he seems to have over me. I suggest to Cal that we dance, and he is all over that. He leads me out onto the dance floor, and we sway to a slow song. We chat about work and politics, and he even tells me a funny story about his dog. He's great.

Really, really great.

So why are my eyes intentionally seeking out Matt's every time Cal spins me around?

They're seeking him out because Matt's eyes are glued on me. I noticed it like a slap in the face the first time Cal twirled me that way.

He's talking to Melody and her back is to the dance floor, but he's watching me dance with Cal.

And I can tell he doesn't like it. Even when he stands up from the table and steps a few feet away from Melody to make a phone call, his eyes stay glued on me.

But I'm not sure if he doesn't like it because he has feelings for me or because he just seems to hate Cal, but yes... he is definitely not happy at this moment.

When the song ends, Cal walks me back to the table, as dinner will be starting soon. Matt is sitting there alone, and he guardedly watches us as we walk toward him. As soon as Cal holds my chair out for me, his phone rings and he gives me a sheepish look as he takes it out of his pocket. Looking at the number, he frowns and says, "I'm sorry... this is an urgent call. Excuse me."

As Cal walks away, Matt stands and takes my elbow. "Let's dance."

I have no choice but to walk with him, but I wouldn't want any other choice. I'm a freakin' moron for pining for his touch, but I'll take it any way I can get it.

"Where's Melody?" I ask.

"Off powdering her nose or whatever it is that you women do when you have to go to the restroom."

"I believe it's called peeing. I'm sure she's just

peeing," I tell him, and Matt rewards me with a bright laugh as one arm goes around my waist and the other cups my hand.

"Ah... Mac," he says wistfully. "I've missed your crazy humor."

My heart flops over, because I don't get many glimpses of light-hearted Matt Connover. I feel immensely happy that I made him laugh, and I can't help but snuggle in closer to him.

Matt leans his cheek against my temple, and we dance silently for a few minutes. He breaks into my thoughts by murmuring, "You look amazingly and fantastically gorgeous tonight. Every woman in this room pales next to you."

"Even Melody?"

"Even Melody," he confirms. "By the way, she's just a friend. We went to law school together."

My night just keeps getting better and better. "So, you're saying I look better than just... 'nice'?"

Chuckling, Matt says, "That's all I could say to you in mixed company. I don't think anyone would understand an employer calling his employee 'amazingly and fantastically gorgeous', wouldn't you agree?"

"Totally agree," I whisper, and I let the music and Matt's arms carry me away.

"Mac?" Matt says near my ear.

"Hmmm?"

"Leave with me right now. I need you, and it's killing me not to be with you." His words are harsh and urgent. He sounds like a man in pain, and I pull my head back in surprise to look at him.

His eyes are molten, his look serious. He wants me... desperately, and, unfortunately, I want him, too. How can I say no? There's no way I'm saying no, because I'm an idiot, but I'll be a well-fucked idiot come sunrise.

Then it crashes in on me. "I can't... I'm here with Cal."

Matt spares a glance over at the table and confirms that neither Cal nor Melody are back.

"Make up an excuse," he urges me.

My mind is blank. "Like what?"

A devious grin forms on Matt's beautiful face. "How about fake a bout of diarrhea? I heard that worked well with Lorraine."

My mouth hangs open for just a second, stunned that he knew about that. "What? How did you know?"

Matt gives me a particularly quick spin on the dance floor while he laughs at me. "Everyone in the office knew about it, and people think you are incredibly clever."

A smile breaks out on my face, and I laugh. "It did work nicely."

Matt suddenly releases me and pushes me in the back toward the edge of the dance floor. He leans down and whispers. "Now go. Make an excuse. I'll ditch Melody and meet you at your apartment."

I turn to look at him, trying to gauge if he's really serious.

Yes... yes, he is. I see it in his eyes.

I try to take internal stock of my feelings. I'm going to give myself one last chance to make the right decision for my sanity and for the health of my heart. Am I going to give in to this... my desire for Matt and what he's offering me right this very minute?

Yes... yes, I am.

I nod at him and say, "I'll meet you at my apartment."

I start to walk away but Matt grabs my hand, pulling me back to him so I'm close enough to hear him murmur. "Don't plan on getting any sleep tonight, Mac. We have a lot to make up for."

My tummy feels like butterflies are flying around inside, so it won't be a complete untruth when I find Cal and tell him I need to leave because I'm having stomach problems.

CHAPTER Six

It's been ten days since Matt and I have been together in an intimate sense, and I feel like an addict in desperate need of her next fix. I hit my apartment, thankful that Macy is out on a One Night Only date, and start pacing around.

What should I do? Light candles? Put on a teddy? Strip naked?

The doorbell rings, and I yelp in surprise because I didn't expect Matt so soon. I was able to cut away from Cal pretty quickly with the old stomach bug excuse, but I figured he might need a few more minutes to make a polite excuse to Melody.

I open the door and there he stands, looking exquisitely handsome with a hungry look on his face. He steps toward me, and I back up.

He keeps walking and I keep backing up, in pace with his stalking. His eyes roam over me as he shuts the door. He keeps sauntering toward me as he takes off his jacket and lets it hit the floor. Next comes his tie and then he's loosening his cuff links, all while hunting his prey.

Except this prey wants to get caught, so I stop walking backward and wait for him to push all up into my personal space.

He doesn't disappoint, coming to stand flush up against me. His gaze is searing... electric, and I can feel it down into my toes, in my breasts, and yup... right between my legs.

"First time's going to be quick," Matt warns me, his breath coming out in a harsh pant.

"Works for me," I tell him, taking pleasure in the flash of lust that overtakes his face.

His hands reach down, grabbing the tight material at my thighs. I can feel him grip the dress and pull it slowly up until it settles around my waist. He glances down, and I follow his gaze. I watch with anticipation as he fingers the lacy material of my panties at my hipbone, and then he rips it away. The force of his move is sudden and causes me to jerk, then gasp, and then his hand is between my legs as I moan in sweet surrender.

It's all Matt needs to hear before he's lifting me up and pulling my legs around his waist. He takes three steps over to the wall that separates the living room from the kitchen and pins me against it. While keeping me held up with one strong arm, his other goes down to his pants, and he makes short work of the button and zipper.

And then he's shoving into me and my body melts around him, because just seeing him in my doorway made me ready

"God… you feel so good," he says through clenched teeth, and he just holds still for a second… savoring the intensity of this moment, his face pushed into my neck. I can feel his breath, rapidly blowing out and sucking in, almost as if he's fighting for control.

His fingers dig into my skin, and then relax.

Dig. Relax.

Matt makes a small circle with his pelvis, causing him to bump up against something delicious inside of me, and then he goes still again.

"I'm not going to last long," he says, almost sadly. "This feels too good."

"I'm not worried," I whisper in his ear. "I know you're good for it. Now… just let go."

He pulls his face from my neck and stares at me a moment. Yes, I still see lust and desire filling his eyes, but I see something more. I see amazement, and then happiness. He gives me a full-out, dimpled smile, and then pulls his hips back, only to slam back into me.

The sensation causes my breath to explode from my lungs, and I gasp, "That's what I'm talking about."

Matt snickers, and then crashes his mouth into mine.

Then it's a full-out, hot, make-out session, while he pumps into me with long, hard strokes.

He is magnificent, beyond mere descriptive words. Every nerve is firing in my body, and he keeps going on and on. Contrary to his original opinion, he lasts quite long, slowing down when he gets close, and then speeding up again to start the climb higher.

I hold on, my hands clenched into his hair. I periodically break away from his lips to layer hot kisses along his jaw or neck, all the while groaning in supreme satisfaction. It's only after I start to climax that Matt says, "That's what I've been waiting for," and he starts to really let my body have it, rattling the pictures on the wall as he slams repeatedly into me.

When his long groan of satisfaction starts to pour out of those sexy lips, I lean back against the wall and watch as pleasure takes over his face. His eyes close, his mouth hangs open, and wait for it... wait for it... there it is.

The sweetest words I ever heard come from Matt as he shoots into me.

"Mac... Mac... Mac..."

CHAPTER Seven

The sun is hitting me in the face, causing a blaring sort of light that hurts my head. I open my eyes and blink... once... twice... and find Matt hovering over me. He's on his side, head propped on his hand, and staring at me with a smirk on his face. I'm surprised he stayed all night.

I watch as he takes his finger and hooks the edge of the sheet that is draped across my chest.

"It's about time you woke up," he says, dragging the cotton material past my breasts and down to my stomach.

"Have you just been watching me while I sleep?"

I ask as he stops his descent around my belly button.

Matt leans over, flicks a tongue over one of my nipples, and says, "Mmmmm. Hmmmm."

My hands come up and grasp his head to my breast, and I'm smiling when I say, "That's kind of creepy, you know?"

"You love it," he murmurs against my skin before biting the swell of my breast.

"I love that," I tell him and pull him tighter against me.

After a few more kisses and licks that have me sighing, Matt lifts his body and rolls on top of me. My legs spread and he settles in between them, giving a slight shift of his hips that brings him right in line. He just gazes at me while he maneuvers himself in place, and with tiny pushes that cause me to gasp each time, he works his way in.

When he's fully seated, he leans down and kisses me. "Good morning."

"Definitely a good morning," I agree, and then I give over to the sensations of him rocking against me.

He goes so slowly, so tenderly. It's a world of difference from the crazy and rough coupling we normally do. It's like we're always in a race to the finish, knowing what glory lies at the end.

But this morning, Matt is in a mood to take his time. His moves are soft and deliberate. He roams his hands all over my skin with just a whisper of sensation, murmuring quiet words to me rather than the normal dirty talk that gets my motor revving.

He's touching more than my body right at this moment. He's now touching my heart, and it causes a painful thrill to rush through me.

"Do you have feelings for me?" I ask, not even subconsciously forming those words before they pop out of my mouth.

Matt goes still inside of me—even his mouth stops moving against my lips. Slowly, he raises his head and I'm almost afraid to meet his gaze, but I do it because I need to know how he feels, and the eyes are the windows to the soul or some shit like that.

"You really want to have this conversation now?" he asks, but he doesn't seem perturbed by the question. As if to make sure I am aware of all my options, he flexes his hips so I've no doubt that he's still deep inside of me. The move feels so good and causes me to bite down on my bottom lip, my eyes to flutter closed.

He must take that as acquiescence because he starts a gentle rhythm again, which sweeps me away in pleasure.

But no... I want to know the answer. I don't want to get sidetracked by his magical penis. "Wait... I do want to talk about this now."

Matt groans like I just told him I was sentencing him to death and slowly pulls out, rolling off me and onto his back. What I'm sure is just for dramatic flair, he rests the back of arm across his forehead and sighs. "I can't believe I just got cock blocked by you... while I was inside of you."

I turn over on my side to face him, now mimicking his earlier pose by resting my head on my hand. Ignoring the 'cock block' comment, I ask, "Well... do you?"

He's silent for a moment, but he turns to look at me straight in the eye. "Honestly... I don't know."

I'm not really sure what I expected him to say, but I actually did sort of expect the little pang of hurt from whatever was going to come out of his mouth. I had been bracing for it because I really didn't have high hopes that he was going to profess his mad and undying love.

Not that we were anywhere near close to that, but it's more than probable that Matt is just in this for the convenient and steamy sex. There doesn't appear to be much more between us.

But Matt then surprises me when he says, "I know I hated seeing you with Carson last night."

"Nothing is going on between us," I assure him.

"I know," he says without surety, but then his voice gets hard. "But you don't know how bad I just wanted to punch him when he was dancing with you."

The possessive tone in his voice mollifies me a bit. "What is it between you and Cal?"

"You mean you didn't ask him?"

"I did... but he said it was private."

Matt gives a sardonic smile. "And I suppose you'd get in a snit again if I told you to mind your own business, right?"

"Right," I say emphatically.

Rolling over to face me, he smoothes his fingertips along my jaw. His voice is soft. "I'll tell you, but I'm only going to say this once and no questions, okay?"

I nod at him, about ready to burst that he's actually going to share a confidence with me. Matt's gaze holds mine, his eyes flicking back and forth, until he's sure that he has my full attention. "Cal used to be my best friend, but he slept with my wife. So I'm sure you can understand why I hate him."

Of all the things that Matt could have told me, I was not prepared for that. I'm in information overload, and the only thing I can think of to say is, "You're married?"

"Sorry. I mean ex-wife."

"But, when did this hap—?"

My words are cut off as Matt puts his fingertips

over my mouth. "No questions. That's all you need to know."

His hand falls away from my mouth and he stares at me, making sure I'm going to keep quiet. When I keep my promise and leave all the questions rattling around inside of my brain, Matt reaches over and pulls me on top of him.

"Now that I answered your question, how about you make it up to me?"

"Oh, yeah... what did you have in mind?" I ask, settling my hips over him and placing my hands on his taut chest.

He gives me a salacious grin. "Well, for starters... how about you fuck me silly while you're on top, and then after, let's stay in your bed all weekend and only get out to eat. Deal?"

I still have a million unanswered questions, but I'm not going to push my luck. Not when he's offering me an entire weekend. Reaching down between us, I find Matt is hard and ready to go.

"Deal," I affirm as I maneuver myself and saddle up, settling my warmth over him.

CHAPTER *Eight*

True to the game plan, Matt and I spent practically all weekend in my bed, unless it was to crawl out and answer the food delivery person on the other side of the door. Luckily, Macy had been in and out at all the appropriate times, and never once caught Matt streaking to the refrigerator for a bottle of water.

Now I'm off to spend my Sunday afternoon with Macy.

"Penny for your thoughts," Macy asks me as we stroll through the racks of clothes at Saks. I can't afford to shop here, but I never mind watching Macy try to burn through her fortune.

Our routine is usually thus. Macy makes me try on clothes I'll never buy. Then she surreptitiously tries to slip them in with the clothes she's buying. I catch her in the act, pull the clothes out, and then we get into a big fight. Macy acts like a drama queen, and the saleslady gets very uncomfortable. Finally, she relents and I hand the clothes over to the attendant to re-stock.

Right now, we haven't even made it past the initial perusing of items to start our normal shopping practice.

"I was just thinking about what a fuss you're going to make later when you try to buy me clothes, and I stop you from doing so."

Macy snickers and pulls a Nanette Lepore dress from the rack to hold up in front of my body. "Here, try this on."

I take the dress from her and roll my eyes, but I'll try it on because it will make her happy and will give me something to do while she relentlessly tries on clothes.

"So what's going on with you and Matt? I could hear you two going at it all weekend in your bedroom. I was getting damn horny just listening to you two."

"Eww, Macy. Don't listen to us. That's just intrusive and gross."

Her jaw drops, and Macy just stares at me.

"Seriously? Do you have any idea how loud you two got? I mean... I'm a screamer but you damn take the cake, Mac. I was kind of proud of you and jealous at the same time."

Flipping through a rack of blouses, I say, "Sorry. We'll be quieter next time."

"You think there will be a next time?"

Shrugging my shoulders, I say, "I suppose so. I mean... we can't seem to get enough of each other."

"Then why are you so down in the dumps about it?"

Sighing, I grab Macy by the elbow and lead her over to a sitting area outside of the dressing rooms. "Okay... here's the deal and tell me what you think. Matt has been clear from the get-go that this is just sex, and he doesn't do relationships."

"Sounds like a man after my own heart," Macy muses.

"I know, right? You two would be perfect for each other."

"Which doesn't make him perfect for you," she concludes, because she knows where I'm going with this.

She and I are polar opposites when it comes to the male persuasion. Macy sees them as nothing but a good time and only wants them around if she can get an orgasm out of the deal. I'm the type that really doesn't do one-night stands, and I love being in a relationship.

So, if Matt is the perfect type of guy for her, that means he's really not the type of guy for me.

"Yet, I still keep looking for him to want something else with me. I keep hoping he'll change."

Macy grasps my hand and holds it up to her heart. She does that when she's getting ready to lay a truth that will hurt on me. "Babe… you know men don't change unless they want to. Doesn't matter how much you want them to change… they have to want it."

Standing up from the bench, I pull my hand from Macy's. "I know. So how much longer do I let this go on?"

"You're having phenomenal sex with a gorgeous man. I don't see where the downside is to this."

"The longer I stay involved, the more I want from him. I can feel myself getting sucked in deeper and deeper," I grumble, kicking my foot out in frustration. The tip of my shoe catches a stand that has a mannequin decked out in Prada, and the whole thing wobbles precariously. Just when I think disaster is averted, the head of the mannequin pitches off the side and cracks hard against the floor, causing her nose to chip off and go scuttling across the marble.

I just stare at it dumbly as a sales associate comes

over to us with a disapproving look on her face.

"Can I help you ladies with something?" she asks.

"Yeah, my friend just beheaded your mannequin," Macy says with a smirk. "I think it needs CPR or something."

I bring my hand up to my mouth to hide my giggle, but the saleslady just shoots us an annoyed look, and then reattaches the head sans nose. When she leaves, bending over to scoop up the nose, Macy turns to me. "Look, Mac. You know I love you, right? I only want the best for you, and most friends would probably tell you to run as fast as you can from this guy. But not me. I'm going to tell you to stick with it, because even if you will eventually be miserable, you are at least happy right now. Even if it is only just sex… at least you are doing something that is out of your comfort zone."

"Just like when you first signed me up with One Night Only," I add.

"Just like that. So I say take the bull by the horns… Or, in your case, by his incredibly talented dick, and enjoy the ride."

"So your advice is just keep doing what I'm doing?"

"Stay the course."

"Enjoy the ride?"

"Yes, Mac… enjoy the ride."

CHAPTER Nine

After a few texts and an email from Cal checking up on my 'stomach' problem, I finally break down and meet him for lunch. He chose a little Italian place about halfway between our two offices, and I see him as soon as I walk in.

He looks superbly handsome, and I'm not blind to the fact that a few women are checking him out. I sigh. I wish I wanted to check him out that way. But my feelings are so conflicted. First, there's the fact that I'm completely in lust with my boss, and we spent all weekend doing the nastiest of things to each other. I mean, things that could get us locked up in certain states.

But more importantly, and something I have only recently discovered, is that Cal had allegedly slept with Matt's wife. I say 'allegedly' because I don't know the truth of the matter. I only know the very brief bit of information that Matt told me and since he refused to talk about it any further, I just didn't know what to believe.

I intend to find out more today.

Cal stands when I reach the table and gives me a hug. He looks me over and says, "You look much better. I take it you're feeling fine now?"

God, if only he knew how fine I felt. After the amount of orgasms I had this weekend, I was feeling loose and relaxed in a way that no professional masseuse could ever make me feel.

"I'm fine," I assure him. "I'm really sorry for bailing on you last week."

Cal shoots me a winsome smile. "No worries. Shit happens... no pun intended."

I laugh and pick up the menu to peruse it. As I'm weighing my options, Cal says, "So, I was hoping I could talk you into dinner one night this week."

Glancing up, I see the earnestness in Cal's face. He likes me... he wants to get to know me. He's asking me out on a freaking date because he wants to build something with me. It's written all over his face.

I should be whooping with joy, crawling on his

lap, and smothering him with kisses just before I say 'yes'. He is everything that I lost when Pete dumped me, and everything I thought I was looking for.

But he's not Matt.

Placing the menu down, I hope to hell I have the right words. "Cal... um... I don't know how to really say this, but... I don't think I can go out with you. Not on a date."

Cal's lips turn downward from the rejection. "Because you're interested in someone else."

He says it as a statement, not as question. I hesitantly nod at him.

"And that someone is Matt Fucking Connover, right?" His voice isn't mocking or even angry. He says Matt's voice with a sort of reverence.

My mouth hangs slightly open in disbelief. "What? What makes you say that?"

Leaning back in his chair, Cal gives me an indulgent smile. "For lots of reasons. First, it was the way you looked at him when he arrived at the ball... like someone that was starving and he was the buffet. Second, the way you glared at Melody. I thought there might be a catfight. Third, the way Matt watched you while you were dancing with me. He hated it."

"I can't believe it's that obvious," I whisper, my eyes cast downward.

The waiter comes up to the table, and Cal shoos

him away. "It's not really. What really brought it all together was the phone call I received as I was walking you back to the table. It was my co-counsel on a case we have against Matt, which we've been desperately trying to settle with him. He told me Matt had just called him and made an offer. Said we had fifteen minutes to accept it or not."

I stare at him dumbfounded, and my mind flashes back to the memory of Matt stepping away from the table to make a phone call while I danced with Cal. "Why didn't Matt just tell you that while we were all sitting there?"

"Why indeed?" Cal says with a chuckle. "But isn't it obvious? He knew my co-counsel would call me, and he knew he'd call me right that very moment, which happened to coincide with the time I was leading you back from the dance floor. He knew I'd then have to scramble to get up with my clients and get their permission to pay the money. He also knew my clients are in London, five hours ahead of us, and it would be extremely difficult to do so. He knew that would give him time to get you alone, and I'm assuming enough time to convince you to leave with him."

"Son of a bitch," I say, although not in a way that I'm mad about. It's more of an 'I'm totally fucking in awe of Matt Connover and his wicked ways right at this very moment' sort of saying.

"That he can be," Cal agrees.

"Did you settle the case?"

Cal's eyes flash with anger. "Of course not. It took me longer than fifteen minutes to get the permission to settle. Took me about an hour in fact. I texted Matt that we accepted, but he texted me back the next day and said too late… wasn't within the fifteen minutes."

"Holy shit, he's like scary smart," I say.

"More like scary devious," he adds.

I look Cal in the eyes. "I'm really sorry. I tried to deny the feelings I have for him. I wish I could."

Cal gazes at me in sympathy but gives me a reassuring smile. "I get it, Mac. The heart wants what the heart wants. But… please be careful. Matt is just… hard to get close to. He has the ability to really hurt you."

"Matt told me that you two used to be best friends."

Cal nods, and I don't fail to notice that his face goes slightly red. "Did he tell you the rest of the story?"

"Not much. He only said that you slept with his wife. But he refused to say anything more. Is it true?"

It's a pair of very sad eyes that meet mine. "It's true. I betrayed him in a moment of drunken weakness, and it cost me my best friend."

The air comes out of me in a rush, because I guess, deep down, I couldn't believe Cal would do something like that. He seems broken up by it though... completely remorseful.

"And you've regretted it ever since," I say, because I can hear it in his voice.

"Every fucking day," Cal says.

CHAPTER Ten

Lunch with Cal turned out to be quite informative. He unburdened the entire story to me, but there really wasn't much to it. Apparently, Matt's ex-wife came on to him after a party she held while Matt was out of state on a case. Cal was really drunk, but he also takes responsibility. He insists he should have known better, no matter how drunk he was. It's sort of my belief that when a man is faced with a beautiful woman that has disrobed in front of him, he's probably going to fuck her, no matter how wrong it is.

I left lunch feeling weird. Oh, it was all good

between Cal and me, and I believe we have started what may be a really good friendship. I don't judge him for what he did. Plus, he's paid the price. He lost Matt, and that tears him up.

But I felt weird because Cal gave me some insight to Matt. He told me that Matt changed after he found out they'd slept together. He said the divorce was really bitter, and there was a huge and ugly fight over custody of their son.

Yes... Matt had a son, and I didn't even know about it.

So, yeah... I have some weird feelings right now.

As far as Matt and I are concerned, we settle into a weird sort of routine.

At work, we hardly see each other but when we do, there always seems to be some sort of secret smile that we manage to pass on to each other. The two times we actually had to meet in his office to go over cases, he was extremely professional, although once he slid his pinky finger over the back of my hand. When I glanced at him, he gave me a look filled with heat and desire, and I felt lit up from within over just that slight touch.

At the end of the day, Matt will stroll into my office and ask what I want to eat. I'll hem and haw, and finally decide on something. He'll then leave, and I'll pack up to head home. About an hour later, Matt shows up at my apartment with food and then well… you can guess what happens after that.

As if on cue, my doorbell rings and I open it up. There stands Matt, holding a bag of Chinese food and a bouquet of flowers.

I'm stunned, my jaw dropping open.

I mean, I was expecting Matt and the Chinese food, and I had been sitting here for the last ten minutes hoping he'd get me an extra egg roll, but never in a million years did I think he'd bring me flowers. This was way better than an extra egg roll.

Before I can say anything, I hear from behind Matt, "Yum! Chinese! And I'm starving. Oh hey, nice flowers."

Macy steps around Matt, who is still standing in the doorway, and walks into the apartment. I move back so Matt can come in. "Matt… this is my roommate, Macy. Macy… this is Matt."

"Hey," Macy says, as she looks him up and down like he's a slab of meat. "Dayum, Mac. He is H-O-T. If you ever get tired of hitting that, let me know. I'll take him for a test drive."

I roll my eyes as Matt just stares at Macy as if she were a circus attraction, which sometimes… she might as well be.

She saunters up to him and takes the food out of his hands. "Nice to meet you, and thanks for the food. I'm starving."

Matt raises his eyebrows and shoots me a bewildered look. I call out into the kitchen, "That's Matt's and my dinner."

She yells back. "I'm willing to share. Come on in and let's eat."

"I'm sorry," I lean over and whisper to Matt, taking the flowers from him. "We can make up some plates and go eat in my bedroom if you want."

I get a wide-eyed stare, and then he starts walking toward the kitchen as if in a trance... strangely hypnotized by Macy's own brand of weirdness. "No way," he says in wonder. "I want to get to know this roommate of yours a little bit better."

Giggling, I follow him in and make myself busy putting the flowers in water. I didn't even get a chance to thank him properly, but I can do that later. I know just the thing that will make him very, very happy.

We all three settle in to eat, and actually have a pretty good time. The thing with Macy is that she always likes to shock you when she first meets you. Then, after that, she settles right down into a charming conversationalist. She has no problem keeping Matt amused, and I use the time to watch him interact on a personal level and away from the office.

He laughs so easy, his eyes crinkling at the

corners and his dimples making periodic appearances. He reaches over to me every once and a while, rubbing my leg softly just so he can have contact with me. The secret smile we share doesn't have to be so secret here, and it graces both of our faces when we look at each other.

I wish it could always be this way between us.

"So, Matt… where do you live?" Macy asks.

"I live over in Chelsea," he says as he takes a bite of egg roll.

"That's closer to your office—how come you two just don't go there after work? I mean, it's not like you do anything but eat and screw like bunnies."

That's a good question, so I turn to Matt with a smile and playfully punch him on the shoulder. "Yeah, how come you never take me to your place?"

Matt doesn't miss a beat. "Because I never invite the women I'm just fu—"

He stops abruptly, sudden realization of what he was about to say hitting him. He looks quickly to me, guilt lying heavy on his face.

I'm not going to lie… it hurt to hear him say that.

"You mean, you don't invite the women you're just fucking over to your place," I clarify, trying to keep my voice light and unaffected.

Macy cautiously rises from her chair. "I think I'm

going to head to bed now and give you two a little space."

I don't bother looking at her as she leaves, and Matt's eyes never waver from mine. When she's gone, he says, "I'm sorry… that was crude. But it's the truth. I told you I don't do relationships, Mac. I always—"

Holding my hand up, I stop him. "No, what you said was honest and you're right… you've been very clear about things with me. If there's one thing I appreciate about you, is that you always give me honesty."

I try to give him a warm smile, to let him know my feelings aren't hurt, but deep down… they are. But in fairness to Matt, he's never led me to believe this would ever be anything more.

"Do you want me to go?" Matt asks softly.

"No," I assure him with a half smile. "Stay. Finish eating and let's go shake the apartment's foundation."

"Okay," he says, giving me a tentative smile of his own.

We finish dinner and hit the bed… hard.

Nothing has changed in that respect. He touches me, and I melt for him. I grasp onto him, and he shudders. We still have that sizzling hot chemistry between us, and for the first time, I am beginning to truly accept… that is truly all there is.

Chapter Eleven

For the last eighteen hours, I haven't thought of Matt.

There are too many other things on my mind. Far more important than Matt.

I glance around the hospital room, taking in the gray paint on the walls, the gray floor, the gray tone to my mother's skin.

Nope. Haven't thought of Matt once in that time. All I can think about is my mother's broken body... her broken brain that has swollen so much they had to cut a hole in her skull to relieve the pressure.

Matt had left my apartment around nine PM the night before and I immediately fell into an exhausted sleep, so deep I apparently didn't even hear my cell phone when the hospital called.

Macy shook me awake, the look on her face so terrible that I almost vomited knowing something horrific had happened. She pulled me into a warm hug and told me she had bad news.

Then she proceeded to destroy my world when she told me my mom had been in a terrible car accident and was in critical condition in my hometown of Nashville. She watched me apprehensively, waiting for me to melt down, but that never even crossed my mind.

Instead, I sprang into action, booting up my laptop and looking for a late evening flight out. There was none until the next morning, and I knew I could make the thirteen-hour drive faster. I hastily packed a suitcase, having no clue what I really put in there, all the while Macy paced nervously, wringing her hands.

She begged me not to drive, and I shut her down with a glare.

She begged to come with me, but I told her I didn't need her. My gut didn't even clench up when I saw the look of hurt and worry pass over her face. I'm not sure why I told her that, other than to say I probably wasn't thinking straight, because I would never intentionally hurt her.

Within twenty minutes, I was heading to the parking garage that housed my car, which I hardly ever drove because it just wasn't needed in the city, and prayed that the fact I hadn't had the oil changed in over a year wouldn't hurt my chances of making it to Nashville. I had merely told Macy before I left to please call my office in the morning and tell them I wouldn't be in and had no clue when I'd be back.

She tried to give me a hug before I left, but I was icy cold with the knowledge that my mom could be dead before I made it home, and I didn't spare her another glance as I left the apartment.

I fueled myself up on coffee the entire trip and never got stopped once for speeding. I drove straight to the hospital, praying for the best and expecting the worse. Mom's doctor had called me with an update just as I was hitting the Virginia border.

He made me feel hopeless.

It was hopeless... pretty much.

My mom... my champion... the one that has been there for me through thick and thin, was essentially brain dead. The doctor droned on and on about what all the tests had shown, and while they wanted to get one more neurosurgeon to evaluate her, they wanted to prepare me for the worst. They told me she was on life support and was not in any pain, but that I would have some decisions to make.

Decisions.

I know what they mean by that. I look at the respirator attached to my mom, watch the way it's breathing for her, and I follow the electrical cord from the base of the unit to the wall plug. They want me to make the decision to unplug her.

But how can I just unplug my mom from this life? I'm not sure I can, and I don't have anyone else to help me with this decision. My dad, God rest his soul, died four years ago from a heart attack at the tender age of forty-six. I'm an only child. It's just been my mom and me since then, and I've always been the one leaning on her.

Now she's leaning on me... needing me to do what's right by her.

Tears well up in my eyes and start leaking out. I let them slip slowly down my face, making no move to wipe them away. It does no good because they'll just start up again.

It's all I've been doing since I got to the hospital five hours ago... staring at my mom from across the room, and weeping.

I'm a fucking rock in the storm, my sarcastic voice says, and more tears slip down my cheeks. I check my cell phone and see missed calls from both Macy and Matt, both of whom left voice mails that I have no desire to listen to. I assume Matt probably wants to know when I'm coming back or something. I shoot off a quick text to Macy to let her know I'll call her tonight.

A nurse comes in, giving me a sad smile. She checks my mom's vitals and switches out a saline bag on her IV. All the while, the ventilator rasps and the monitor issues a soft beep every few seconds.

When the nurse leaves, I stand from the chair and stretch, grimacing over the popping bones in my vertebrae. Glancing at my watch, I note it's almost four PM, and I know the doctor will be in some time this evening to discuss options.

As if I really have an option.

My stomach growls, and I realize it's been more than twenty-four hours since I've eaten… unless you count the gallons of coffee that I drank on the way here.

I walk up to the edge of my mom's bed and look down at her. Taking her hand gently in mine, I bring it up to rub against my wet cheek.

"Oh, Mom," I whisper. "What am I supposed to do?"

She doesn't answer, but I don't expect her to. I watch her heart monitor, and there's no change. Nothing about my touch or my voice will rouse her from her coma. No amount of love for me is going to pull her from those dark depths.

The tears start pouring now in earnest, because the clock is ticking and the doctor will want my decision in a few hours. I call upon God, but he gives me no answer. I wrack my brain for every conversation I may have ever had with my mom about dying with dignity. For the life of me, I have no clue what her wishes were when it came to this sort of thing, although I can't imagine she'd want to live life this way.

I am so lost and I don't see a clear path anywhere, so I do nothing but hunch over my mom and quietly cry.

"Mac?"

My body goes still, and my breath freezes in my lungs.

It's not possible.

Turning away from my mom, I let my gaze follow the voice. Standing in the doorway is a man, but my eyes are so tear-filled that he's just a hazy apparition. I blink once, pushing the liquid away, and my vision clears.

And there Matt Connover stands, looking at me with sympathy. He opens his arms up, and there is no other choice in my mind but to walk into them.

MITIGATION

Volume 4

Sawyer Bennett

Legal Affairs
Vol. 4 - Mitigation
By Sawyer Bennett

All Rights Reserved.
Copyright © 2014 by Sawyer Bennett
Published by Big Dog Books

This book is a work of fiction. Names, characters, places and incidents either are products of the author's imagination or are used fictitiously. Any resemblance to actual events, locales or persons, living or dead, is entirely coincidental.

No part of this book can be reproduced in any form or by electronic or mechanical means including information storage and retrieval systems, without the express written permission of the author. The only exception is by a reviewer who may quote short excerpts in a review.

Chapter One

I vaguely note that Matt is wearing jeans, a t-shirt, and tennis shoes... an outfit that I've never seen him in before. It's a far cry from the tailored business suits and silk ties he always wears.

No matter what he's wearing, when I release my mom's hand and turn to walk into his outstretched arms, I finally feel a small measure of comfort.

Matt wraps himself around me, and I lay my head on his chest. He smells like fresh soap, and I could care less how obvious I am when I turn my nose into his shirt and inhale him deeply. Unfortunately, it makes me painfully aware that I probably smell like a garbage dump since I haven't showered in over a day and a half.

Pressing his lips to the top of my head, Matt just holds me until I'm ready to break free. But I'm not sure I'll ever be ready. This is the first time in our tortured game that he has held me just to comfort me, with no expectation of getting anything in return. It's a side of Matt I've never seen, and I probably won't see again after he leaves.

Which now makes me realize... why is he here? This is very anti-Matt. We eat dinner together... we have sex. That's all there is.

But I can't let that be one of my worries because I have enough on my plate. For now... I'll just enjoy Matt's strong embrace and worry about everything else later.

Unfortunately, my peaceful moment is disturbed when my stomach gives an incredibly loud and embarrassingly long rumble of hunger. It sounds like Chewbacca and a T-Rex having a mixed martial arts contest inside my stomach.

Matt pulls slightly back and looks down at me. "When's the last time you've eaten?"

"When I had dinner with you, I guess," I answer, because I think that's the last time I'd eaten. Wracking my brain, I couldn't remember putting anything else in my stomach other than coffee, which is probably why it felt full of burning acid right now.

Grabbing my hand, Matt says, "Let's rectify that."

I pull back, glancing in worry at my mom laying in the bed... the respirator slowly whooshing in and out. "I can't leave her."

Matt's eyes turn warm, but they are stern. "Mac... she'll be fine if you leave for just a few minutes. The nurses' station is right outside her door. We'll come right back, but you need to eat to keep up your strength. Okay?"

He waits for me to decide, which again is very anti-Matt. The Matt I've come to know and 'love to hate sometimes' would have dragged me kicking and screaming down to the cafeteria and shoved food down my throat. Now, he's presenting me with an option and leaving the choice up to me.

"If you don't want to leave her," he continues, "I'll go down, get you something, and bring it back. But I think you should come with me... stretch those legs a bit."

I glance back at my mom and feel tremendous guilt for leaving her side for even a minute. But then rationality comes back and I realize... she won't even know I'm gone. She won't know anything, ever again.

I nod at Matt and he takes me by the hand, linking his fingers with mine as we walk through the hospital. Following the signs pointing to the cafeteria, we walk in silence for a bit because I'm still stunned that he's here. I can't figure out why. It's not something he should be doing as my employer. But he doesn't seem to have any feelings for me outside of the bedroom, so that doesn't make sense either.

Deciding to go ahead and put this worry to rest so I can concentrate on the more important things, I stop and turn to look at Matt. "Why are you here?"

"Because no one should go through something like this alone," he says simply.

"Yeah... but I'm not your responsibility or concern."

Matt shrugs his shoulders and resumes walking. "Truth be told, Mac... I'm not really sure why I'm here. When I got into the office this morning, Miss Anders told me what happened. I guess Macy called her."

"Yeah, I vaguely recall telling Macy to call the office for me."

"Well, I called Macy back to get more details. She was beside herself fretting about you. Said you hadn't called her, and you weren't returning her calls. She wasn't sure whether to get on a plane to fly to be by your side or not, but then she said you sort of told her you didn't want her there, so she didn't want to intrude. I'm telling you... she was a mess."

Guilt courses through me for doing that to Macy,

and honestly… I don't even remember doing that. I think I was operating in a state of shock. I make a note to call her as soon as I finish eating something.

Matt continues. "Anyway, I decided to take the worrying away from Macy and told her I would fly down here to help you out. I made a quick stop at home to pack a small bag, and here I am."

"Thank you for coming," I say in a small voice. "You really didn't have to."

"I know," is all he says, and then the subject is closed.

Matt walks me through the line but nothing looks good to me, so he proceeds to fill my tray up with a variety of items. After he pays, we find a seat and he points at the food. "Eat."

"You always have to be in control, don't you?" I grumble, even as I pick my fork up and take a small bite of mac and cheese.

Damn, that's good.

Matt just gives me a knowing smile and watches me while I eat. If I look like I'm ready to slow down, he points at the food and that's all he has to do to urge me to eat. When I'm done to Matt's satisfaction, I push the tray off to the side and lean back in my chair. I'm exhausted, and I scrub my hands over my face in an attempt to revive myself.

Finally, I focus on Matt, who is patiently waiting for me to talk… if I want to.

Chapter Two

"I don't know what to do," is the first thing I say to him.

He gazes at me in understanding and sympathy. "Tell me what's going on, and we'll talk it out."

I inhale deeply, sucking all the oxygen in that I can hold. After slowly letting it out, I tell him, "The doctor is going to come by tonight and talk to me in more detail about her condition, but from what they've told me so far, she isn't going to recover. She has minimal brain activity... The machines are keeping her alive right now. I think tonight... I think he wants to talk to me about taking her off life support."

"Did your mom have a Living Will or any other health care directive?"

I knew this question would be coming from Matt—he's a lawyer after all—but it's like a sharp slap in the face when it comes. Tears well up in my eyes, and I shake my head in the negative.

"I'm so stupid," I say vehemently. "I'm a fucking lawyer, and I never thought to have my mom do one."

Reaching across the table, Matt takes my hands and attempts to soothe me by rubbing them gently with his own. "Don't do that to yourself. It has no purpose here to dwell on those things."

Pulling my lower lip between my teeth, I bite down hard to feel some type of physical pain that will force the emotional tears back. It works and, with a few blinks, the wetness dissipates.

"Did you and your mom ever talk about this?" Matt asks.

"No," I say miserably, staring at the Formica table in front of me. "Not even when my dad died. He had a heart attack. It was so quick... We never thought about something like this happening. I never thought I'd have to make these decisions."

Matt's quiet for a moment, and then he says,

"Okay… let's figure out what your mom would want then. Tell me about her?"

A slow smile creeps onto my face, and I raise my eyes to Matt's. I know what he's doing, and it's brilliant. He wants to make me focus on the type of person my mom is… I mean really focus, so that I could determine what her inherent wishes may be.

"She's energetic… always on the go. She works full time, but in her spare time, I don't think she sleeps. She's always been so active with her church, and she does volunteer work. Oh, and she loves to garden. She always said she was happiest when her hands were about three inches deep in soil."

"Tell me about her church," Matt says. "What sorts of things does she do there?"

And it goes on and on. Matt sits there, using all of his skills he's acquired as an attorney, and he questions me like I'm a witness with a juicy piece of information that he's trying to discover. He's trying to help me discover what my mom would want. Except he's amazingly gentle with his questions, like he's leading a small child on the witness stand.

Matt gets me to talk for almost an hour straight, and things start to get clearer. My mother loved life too much to ever want to live life in a bed, stuck to a respirator.

"What about you, Matt? What would you want if this happened to you?"

"If I was just like your mom? I'd want to be let go."

I nod, because that's exactly what I would want, too.

Matt and I head back to the room and wait for the doctor. I marvel at how Matt seems to be at ease in this situation, and I can only guess that has come from years of dealing with people, such as lawyers, judges, and doctors. I think it's probably very hard to get Matt Connover flustered about anything. He's a rock, and it's something I sorely needed today.

While we wait for the doctor, Matt and I work a crossword puzzle together. Every once in a while, I'll take a break and walk over to my mom. I'll stroke her cheek or hold her hand for a bit.

I start my goodbyes.

The doctor finally comes, and I introduce Matt as a "friend". Dr. Fritz is a neurosurgeon and was called in last night to evaluate my mom. He's a warm and outgoing guy, maybe in his mid-fifties, and I don't think I've ever met a doctor more personable. But he's very grave when talking to me about my mom's condition. He uses a lot of large words that I don't understand, but at the end of the conversation, he pats my knee gently and says, "Bottom line... there is almost absolutely no hope of your mother regaining brain function."

Matt reaches out to take my hand, and I'm grateful for the contact. He turns to the doctor and says, "Put it in a percentage for us to understand, Dr. Fritz."

The kind doctor looks at Matt seriously. "Less than a one-percent chance. I mean... far less than one percent. It would be a medical miracle."

Less than one percent. A medical miracle. The thing that sucks about that phraseology is that it still implies there is some hope, no matter how infinitesimal it is.

"If it was your mother... what would you do?" I ask.

Dr. Fritz gives me a knowing smile, and I can tell this is not the first time he's been asked that question. "Miss Dawson, if my mother was in the same exact circumstances as your mother... there's no question. I'd discontinue extraordinary measures and let her go."

Taking a deep breath, I nod. I know what has to be done.

CHAPTER Three

Matt checked us into the The Hermitage in downtown Nashville and immediately sent me to take a hot shower while he ordered room service. It took a whole lot of fighting on his part, but he finally got me to agree to sleep in a hotel rather than in a chair in mom's room. My time with her is running short, and I want to be with her every minute. I feel guilty now... at this very moment, as I stand under the hot water and let it cleanse my body. I feel guilty because I only have precious hours left with my mom, but here I am in the comforts of a swank hotel.

The only reason I'm here is because Matt gently reminded me that my mother is essentially gone already. That she has no comprehension, and she wouldn't know if I was sitting by her side or sitting in a hotel. But the real kicker—the way Matt got me—was he told me that based on what he'd learned about my mom that day, she wouldn't want her daughter suffering and would want her to get some rest.

I caved, and now here I am.

I had made my decision to discontinue extraordinary measures for my mom. Dr. Fritz asked how much time I would need for friends and family to say goodbye, and I honestly wasn't sure. My mom and dad's families were all out in California. Mom and Dad had settled in Nashville when I was three years old.

After a brief call with Aunt Kay, my mom's sister, she felt we should let her go now rather than wait for them to all fly in. No one really wanted Mom suffering on the respirator for very long, and Aunt Kay promised she'd be in the following day to help with the funeral. That left her friends locally, and I merely called her pastor and advised him that if anyone wanted to visit, they could come by in the evening.

I told Dr. Fritz I wanted to do it first thing in the morning, and so we scheduled it for eight AM. I even put an appointment entry on my iPhone calendar, and then realized that was a fucking moronic move. There was no way I was going to forget this particular appointment, so I erased it.

Finishing my shower, I brush my teeth. I take a few minutes to dry my hair before I throw on the hotel robe that Matt had apparently stuck on the back of the door because it hadn't been there when I stepped into the bathroom.

When I come out into the room, I see that Matt has some food laid out.

"I know you ate just a few hours ago," Matt says as he uncovers everything, "so I just got something light... some soup and sandwiches. And after you eat, you're heading straight to bed to get some rest."

He pulls the chair out for me to sit down, so I do. He even takes my napkin, snaps it out, and lays it on my lap with flourish. I really and truly cannot help the giggle that comes out. That seems to egg Matt on so he opens the bottled water and holds it out for me to inspect, stating, "Our finest vintage, madam."

"It looks spectacular," I tell him, and we both chuckle while he pours me some water.

Matt keeps my mind occupied as we eat. He tells me that Lorraine seems to have calmed down, and they are rationally discussing Bill taking over her caseload. I also make a quick phone call to Macy just to tell her how sorry I am for my behavior and assure her I wasn't thinking clearly. She told me she was catching a flight to Nashville in the morning and that she would stay here until I was ready to come back.

When we finish eating, Matt takes the tray and sticks it outside our room door for housekeeping to pick up. I root through my bag, trying to find something to wear but, apparently, I didn't throw in a single pair of pajamas. Grabbing a pair of underwear, I slip them on under the robe, and then stand up. I place my hands on my hips, looking around in confusion.

"What's wrong?" Matt asks.

"I forgot my pajamas."

"No worries," Matt says, and he lifts the t-shirt he's wearing over his head. He tosses it at me. "Put this on... it will be more comfortable than wearing that robe to bed."

I open the robe and shrug it off my shoulders, dropping it to the ground. I have no modesty where Matt's concerned... he's seen it all.

Hell, he's licked it all.

Just before I put his t-shirt over my head, I lock eyes with him, and he's watching me with an odd mixture of what I think is lust, but also compassion. It's the weirdest thing I've ever seen, and it unsettles me. I have a rush of desire for him in that moment, but I also have no want or need to act upon it.

Instead, I inhale his scent from the t-shirt and look longingly at the fluffy pillows on the bed, which are calling my name.

Matt pulls back the covers and motions me under. When he has me tucked in, he walks to the other side and takes off his jeans. Even though I'm exhausted and heartsick, I lie on my side and watch him with appreciation. His body is utterly beautiful, and I sigh knowing that tonight it's only for me to look at. Matt catches me checking him out, and I'm not even embarrassed. But I am so tired that I can do nothing but give him a tiny smile.

Matt then pulls out his laptop from his briefcase.

"Do you mind if I do some work?" he asks me.

Still smiling at him, I give a tiny shake of my head.

Setting the laptop on the bedside table, Matt gets under the covers and turns to his side so we're staring at each other.

"Do you want me to hold you until you fall asleep?" he whispers.

His words are like a soothing balm over my shredded heart, and I nod. He pulls me into his embrace, tucking my head under his chin. His hands slowly stroke my back, up and down. Long, measured strokes... not too light and not too firm. Just enough to relax me and, before I know it, my eyes start to close.

I think my last thought before I went to bed was that if Matt treated me like this all the time, I'd probably fall head over heels in love with him.

CHAPTER Four

Macy had begged me not to return to work so soon. I just buried my mom two days ago, having flown back to New York the day after the funeral. I just couldn't stand being there... in my mom's house... without her there.

Even worse, I longed to see Matt again, and I'm ashamed to say that also prompted my quick return. He stayed in Nashville with me the morning after I had fallen asleep in his arms. He stood by my side when they disconnected my mom from the machines. He kept his arm around me while we waited for her to die, and then he let me sob in his arms when they pronounced her gone.

But he didn't stay too much longer after that. Not that I expected him to. He told me the day he arrived that he had to get back to the firm soon, so I never, ever expected him to stay for the funeral. I was just so very happy and so very touched that he chose to come be by my side for the hardest thing I've ever done in my life.

I'm sure Matt saw what he did as nothing more than a kind gesture, but I saw it for so much more. Matt can gripe, moan, bitch, and complain until he's blue in the face that he's only in this for the sex with me, but he'd be a damn liar. There are feelings there on his part, and I intend to flush them out.

So while I'm still grieving for my mother, I intend to get back into the swing of my life in an effort to help ease the pain. I'm also going to push at Matt until I can break him out of his rigid rule of 'sex only' encounters.

When I arrive at the office, I'm met with tons of my new colleagues giving me hugs and kind words of compassion. It touches me deeply and, when I get into my office, there's a huge bouquet of flowers and a card signed by everyone in the firm. I let my fingers drag slowly over all the names while tears fill my eyes.

"Welcome back," I hear from the doorway. I look over to see Matt standing there. He's holding onto the doorframe with both hands and just sort of leans into my office. I quickly blink away the tears, but I know he saw them. He doesn't look ill at ease though and just smiles at me.

"Hey," I say in soft welcome. Seeing him is even better than I could have imagined, and I envision him walking in and wrapping his arms around me.

He doesn't do that though. He just stays where he is, appraising me. "So... everything okay? Sure you're ready to be back to work already?"

"I'm sure," I tell him with a confident smile.

"Good," he says. "There's a new case I just assigned to you... You'll see an email about it. Review it, and you'll be handling the depositions next month."

"Oh-kay," I drawl out.

I wait for him to say more... to ask how I'm feeling, to ask about the funeral, to ask to make sure I'm really, really okay. I kind of sort of wait for a hug. Cocking my head to the side, I wait for it.

And wait for it.

Finally, Matt looks left and right down the hall and, confident no one is nearby, he leans in a little further and lowers his voice. "Can I see you tonight?"

"Yes," I say quickly, relieved that he does indeed want to be with me. I was starting to think his cool demeanor might have meant our time was at an end... yet again, and I just wasn't ready for that.

"What do you want me to bring to eat?" he asks with a smile.

"Surprise me," I tell him.

He gives me a nod, and then he's gone. I stare at the empty doorway for a few moments, trying to determine if I should be worried or not by his behavior. I mean… it's typical Matt behavior. Slightly cool, a little aloof, but still interested in hot orgasms with me. Nothing odd there.

Except, I think maybe I expected him to be a little warmer to me. He had, after all, stood by my side while my mother died, letting me cry in his arms. He held me in his arms all night. Yes, all night. I woke up with him holding me, his laptop in the same exact position he had left it before pulling me into his embrace.

Regardless, I shake the thoughts, content for now in knowing that I would be with him tonight, and I could gauge things then.

Booting up my computer, I start wading through what seems like a gazillion messages. I see the email from Matt telling me about the new case he assigned to me… a slip and fall at a grocery store. I have to smile at it. He said, "This is a crap case and you're going to lose it, but it's perfect to cut your teeth on."

There's an email from Cal wanting to know how I was doing and asking to get together for lunch soon.

I smile because I was in turmoil about Cal before, knowing that he was interested in me, but I wasn't interested in him. Now that he knows I have feelings for Matt, he truly seems to want to be friends and that is something you can never have enough of. I shoot him a reply stating that I was free any time this week. He responded back immediately, and we made plans for Friday.

The rest of the day goes by quickly, because I have a ton of stuff to do but not enough hours in the day. It's almost seven PM, and I need to get home.

No, I want to get home… so I can see Matt.

CHAPTER Five

Nothing has changed between Matt and me since I returned from Nashville.

Every night this week, he's shown up like clockwork and proceeded to wring the most exquisite pleasure out of my body. I returned the favor to him, time and again.

No, nothing has changed in that regard. We are still combustible. We are still insatiable. There is a driving need for him to be inside of me, and there is a raging desire for me to let him get there.

I tried to get him to open up to me. That first night after I returned, I waited until we had collapsed on my bed. Both of us rolled onto our backs and gasped for air as we stared at the ceiling. When our pulses started to decline, I rolled on my side to face him and said, "I wanted to thank you again for coming to Nashville. That really meant a lot to me."

Matt slowly turned his head to look at me, his face impassive. He gave me a dim smile and said, "It was no biggie."

No biggie? The man dropped everything and flew to be by my side while my mom died. How can that be nothing?

So I tried again, "It was a big deal, Matt. It changes things... don't you think?"

I couldn't believe it... it was panic that I saw flare bright in his eyes. He looked like he was ready to bolt from the bed while I stared at him in interest. Then, the panic receded and was replaced by desire. He dragged his gaze down my body and said, "I have a better idea—less talk and more action."

He then proceeded to render me speechless with just his lips alone. By the time he was done with me, I had no desire for more conversation. I was well and truly spent, and I fell asleep almost right away.

Of course, he was gone when I woke up the next morning.

Now my doorbell rings, and I want to kick myself in the ass for the way my blood fires up, knowing Matt is on the other side. Tonight will be the same—wonderfully hot sex with an emotionally closed-off man. As you can see, there are pros and cons to this scenario.

The pros? That's easy... I'll get a minimum of three orgasms, and if I only get the minimum, that means Matt's having an off night. I'll get to have hours of pure heaven, having a man that is focused usually on just my pleasure, only taking his when he's confident he's given me all he has.

The cons? Every day that I allow this pattern to occur, I'm only reiterating to Matt that this relationship—or lack thereof—is acceptable. I am giving him no reason to want more with me, because frankly... he's getting everything he desires.

I have to ask myself, What do you really want, Mac?

Figure it out and go get it. And if you can't get it, cut ties and run.

So with a burst of renewed spirit to take the bull—which is Matt—by the horns, I open the door and say, "We need to talk."

There's no panic this time, just a self-assured confidence as he steps through my doorway. He sticks the tips of his fingers into the waistband of my shorts, giving me a small jerk to make my body press up against his. He inclines his head and whispers against my neck, just after he flicks his tongue out. "Talk later... I want you too much right now."

My knees turn to jelly just from that small touch, but he doesn't have me completely under his thrall just yet. I give myself a mental shake of the head and push back from him.

"No. Talk now. Sex later." I give him my most-determined look.

He appraises me, and then his lips curl upward in a challenging way. "I tell you what. If you can carry on a rational conversation with me for just thirty seconds while I try to seduce you, I'll give you my undivided attention for the next two hours. You can talk until you're blue in the face. Deal?"

Hmmmm. Could I keep my head on straight for thirty seconds? For the opportunity to get two hours of talk time with Matt? I'm practically drooling over the prospect of having his attention for that long.

"Deal," I say emphatically, confident I have this in the bag. How hard could thirty seconds be?

Matt lunges at me, and I don't even have time to prepare. In fact, his sudden move shocks me so greatly that all of my thoughts scatter to the wind. Within the first five seconds, he picks me up, tosses me on the couch, and pulls my shorts and underwear off. His hands are quick and assured when he drops to his knees in front of me and spreads my legs.

He gives me one look... filled with challenge. "Come on, Mac... you have about twenty seconds left to carry on a conversation. Let's make it easy. Tell me about your favorite movie."

Then Matt dives his mouth between my legs. He goes straight for the main attraction, clamping his lips on me tight and sucking hard. My hips buck up so violently that I almost throw him off, but his hands grip me tighter and he doesn't let go. This is an all-out attack by Matt, and he is utterly merciless.

I'm experiencing the most intensely erotic thing he's ever done to me so far. I know I'm supposed to be talking about something, but for the life of me, I can't remember what it is. I can only think of his tongue, his fingers, his lips... and the way the stubble on his cheeks rubs the insides of my thighs because my legs are practically clamped onto his head.

I can't think... I can only feel, and I start to think... maybe this is best. Maybe I should only feel with Matt and quit trying to out think our relationship.

I fail miserably at my task. I am doomed. I can't even say one intelligent word while Matt feasts, causing electric pleasure to explode within me.

Still floating among the stars from my orgasm, I'm vaguely aware of Matt pulling me up, walking me around the other side of the couch, and bending me over it. I can hear the pop of his button and the zip of his pants coming undone, and then he's plunging into me while I hang practically upside down.

It's wildly intense what he's doing to me, and he manages to bring me to another quick orgasm before he's shooting into me while he groans, "Mac... Mac... Mac..."

When my heart rate returns to normal, when Matt lets me up off the couch... when I manage to get my legs underneath of me to stop shaking, I practically cry with frustration. "I can't do this anymore, Matt."

He grins at me.

Yes, the son of a bitch grins at me and says, "Yes, you can. Want me to prove it to you right now?"

"No," I say firmly. "I'm tired of being controlled by you sexually. I'm tired of this... this... I don't even know what this is, but I'm tired of it."

Matt doesn't believe me, and he still wears that cocky smile as he steps forward and reaches out to me. His fingers are just inches away, when fury rolls up inside of me.

"No!" I yell, but then I take a deep breath and let it out slowly. I look him dead in the eyes and say more calmly, "No. I need you to leave."

Matt stares at me for a few minutes, and the

smile never leaves his face. He still doesn't believe me. I can see an almost-indulgent look in his eyes as he zips himself up and heads toward my door. He doesn't even look back at me as he walks out, saying, "You'll never be able to give this up, Mac. Not for long anyway."

CHAPTER Six

"That has to be the most pitiful display of happiness that I've ever seen," Cal says as he glances at the menu. We decided to meet up at a Greek restaurant today. I had high hopes I could lamb kabob my way out of despair, because yes... they are that damn delicious.

My gloom-and-doom attitude has apparently taken over every facet of my personality. I thought I had on a bright smile when I responded to Cal's question of, "How have you been doing?"

I told him I was fine, even though I knew my smile wasn't really all that convincing.

"Spill it," was all he says as he puts the menu aside.

Taking a deep breath, I bare my soul to him. I tell him that I still go to bed every night with a deep hole in my heart now that my mom is gone. I lament that I'm in a job where I feel completely in over my head. And most importantly, I tell him about Matt.

I don't get into the nitty-gritty details of our sexually depraved lifestyle, but I do tell him that I'm just not cut out for a sex-only relationship.

Cal actually winces when I say that, and I flush with embarrassment.

"I'm sorry," I say quickly. "I probably shouldn't talk about sex with you. Especially not sex with Matt."

Cal's eyes smile at me... truly smile at me. "It's okay, Mac. You need someone to vent to, and remember... I know Matt way better than you do."

Our waiter chooses that moment to interrupt my whining, and we place our orders. I double up on the lamb kabobs, telling myself it doesn't matter if I get a fat ass. It's not like Matt will be looking at it anymore.

Once the waiter leaves, I let out a heavy sigh. "Why am I such a girl? I mean... why can't I just accept great sex? My roommate Macy lives her life that way, and she's one of the happiest people I know."

It's with great wisdom that Cal says, "McKayla... I'm betting Macy isn't as happy as you think she is. As humans, we are wired to need social interaction and intimacy. Most people are happiest in a relationship. I know I am, and I can't wait to be in one again."

Now I wince, because I'm not sure if that's a pointed reminder that Cal had perhaps looked at me in that light. "I'm sorry," I say again. "I didn't mean to hurt you."

Chuckling, Cal reaches across the table and pats my hand. "You didn't hurt me, Mac. Honestly... we didn't know each other all that well when I realized you had it bad for someone else. I'm just making a general comment that I'm a man, and I want a relationship. I'm ready to settle down. Some men do want that type of thing."

"So, you think what I did... breaking things off with Matt, was the right thing?"

"I think if you were unhappy with the way things were, then yes, it was the right thing. You can't wait for him to change because frankly... I don't think Matt wants to change."

This is what I don't get. I saw a glimmer of true caring and openness in Matt when he came to Nashville. He has the ability... hell, he's a fucking natural at taking care of people. Why doesn't he open himself fully to it?

"It's because he was hurt so badly." Cal's voice cuts into my thoughts.

I look at him in surprise. "What are you? A freaking mind reader?"

"I just know that look. It looks like you're trying to solve a great mystery, and the greatest mystery in your life right now is Matt."

"How badly was he hurt?" I ask softly, not really wanting to know the answer, because I'm afraid it will soften my resolve to stay away from him.

Cal is so very sad when he says, "I damaged him badly. It's my greatest shame. But Marissa, his ex-wife, what she did to him... I think that was the destroying factor. I was not the first person she cheated on him with. In fact, I was the last. Matt had a private investigator following her for weeks before I ever slept with her. He protects himself now. I guarantee you Matt thinks it's better to be alone than to open himself up to hurt again."

We chat a little bit more about Matt, but then our food arrives and we move on to other, more amiable things to discuss. We finish with a promise of getting together the following week, and I find myself looking forward to it. Cal has become a very good friend to me.

Back at the office, I struggle with the Jackson case. The other side has served me with

Interrogatories… a long list of questions about the case that I have thirty days to answer. My palms get moist as I look them over, and I seriously start to question my sanity in taking this case. Hell, I seriously question my sanity in wanting to be a lawyer sometimes.

At the end of the day, I start getting more melancholy. It's getting to be that time that Matt normally stops by my office and asks me what I want to eat. It fuels the anticipation that, within a few hours, I'll be wrapped up in his strong arms.

I won't be getting that today. After asking Matt to leave last night, I am in no way surprised when seven PM rolls around, and there is no sign of him.

But this is for the best, I remind myself.

This is what I wanted.

CHAPTER Seven

I don't fucking believe it.

I go a solid week without seeing or hearing a peep from Matt. The first few days, I would sometimes stare longingly at my office door, hoping he'd come through it and tell me that he saw the error of his ways. But then I started to settle in to my new life without Matt Fucking Connover in it.

Even when I had some questions on the Jackson case, I was able to pick a few of my colleague's brains and save myself from having to deal with Matt at all.

But this morning, he walks into my office at eight AM and hands me a folder. He tells me that I'm going to argue a Motion to Compel for him in court and that I have thirty minutes to get ready for it. He tells me this is in a calm voice… no menace and no anger, so I don't think he is doing it to punish me. In fact, he assures me that this is a slam-dunk motion. He points me to the actual rule on civil procedure that will, in fact, win the motion for me, as long as I argue it properly, and tells me that he will be by my side if I run into any trouble.

Then he walks out of my office after telling me to be ready to go in half an hour.

I then commence to have a full-blown freak out. I think I even start hyperventilating. Handing in my resignation is the only way out of this, and that scenario is looking pretty damn good.

But then… after about five minutes of spazzing out, I remember that Matt said this was a slam-dunk motion, and he wouldn't have given me something I couldn't handle. So I log on to our legal library, pull the rule up, and read it. I print it and read it a second time. It looks pretty straightforward, but I still manage to memorize it in my allotted time frame.

Now, here we sit in front of the Honorable Jericho H. Stanback, a kindly looking judge with snowy white hair and wire-framed glasses, and my armpits are pouring sweat. I feel a little light-headed actually, and try to take a deep, calming breath.

It doesn't work.

Matt leans over and whispers, "You got this, Mac. Piece of cake."

I turn to look at him. He's looking at me with such confidence that I feel a bit of it infuse inside of me. He continues to stare at me, conveying the same message.

You got this, Mac.

When the judge asks for my arguments, I stand on shaky legs. I will admit there is a moment where I think all my brain function has died. I go blank.

Then it comes flooding back to me, and I start talking. I give the judge a short background of the case and explain why we are before him today. I quote the Rules of Civil Procedure, even perfectly laying out the portion that applies to our case. I assure him that there is no law to the contrary, that the facts of the case fall squarely within this rule, and that I respectfully ask His Honor to grant our Motion to Compel.

When I'm done, I sit back down and listen carefully to the other attorney make his argument.

It's kind of lame to be honest.

Then the judge is granting my motion... in essence, claiming me the victor. I want to stand up and do a football-touchdown dance, or do my "neener" move to the other attorney, both of which would assuredly land me in jail on contempt of court charges. So I just walk over to my opponent and shake his hand.

Matt gives me a short smile and congratulates me. He then tells me to head back to the office on my own as he has a few other matters to attend to at the courthouse.

I'm riding so high on my first real court appearance... and a victory to boot, that all my other worries just sort of melt away. This is what I'm supposed to be doing. McKayla Dawson is going to make a hell of a litigator.

When I get back to the office, I can't help but relate the entire scenario to our receptionist, Bea, but I can tell when her eyes glaze over that she could care less. She listens to me with a painted smile and nods like she understands, but I'm betting inside she's probably wondering what to eat for dinner that night.

With no other victory parade to attend to, I head back to my office and get back to work reviewing the slip and fall case Matt had given me. He's right... the case is pretty craptastic. It was some bonehead walking through a grocery store that didn't notice the dark red cranberry juice that had spilled in a huge puddle on the white flooring.

Hello, open and obvious danger.

Yeah, I was going to lose this case, but Matt said

it would be good to cut my teeth on. That also meant no pressure.

A knock on my door causes me to look up, and it's Matt. I'd like to tell you that I could look at him without my blood racing through my veins or my heart tripping all over itself.

But I'd be lying.

"Can I come in?" he asks.

"Sure," I tell him and watch as he steps in and closes the door behind him.

I expect him to sit down across from me, but he walks right up to where I'm sitting. His hand reaches out and cups me behind the neck, pulling me up from the chair.

I'm powerless to stop, my body betraying me quickly.

Matt leans in and nuzzles my neck. "I'm coming home with you tonight, Mac."

His voice is low, husky… filled with promise. It makes my toes curl inside my pumps.

Yes, home with me. That is what every part of my body is telling my brain.

Well… not every part. My heart rears its ugly head up and practically roars at me. "Don't be a fool, McKayla."

My hands come up to Matt's chest, and I push him back. I keep pushing until he releases me, and there's a foot of space between us.

"No," I tell him firmly. "You're not."

Anger flashes across his face. "I don't get it. You want me, and I want you. Why are you being this way?"

"I do want you," I admit. "I want you a lot. But I want more than just sex. I need more than just sex."

He stares at me, confusion written all over his beautiful face. His words are slow and cautious when he asks, "What more do you need?"

"I want a relationship. Dating, conversation, shared secrets. I want it all, Matt. I deserve it all."

He soaks in what I'm saying, but then his shoulders sag slightly. "I don't have that to give."

"Yeah, you do," I tell him. "You showed me you do in Nashville. You have a lot to give."

I reach my hand out, intending to take his in mine. To give him soft and reassuring contact, so my skittish beast of a man doesn't flee.

Too late. He steps back out of my reach and his face hardens. "Are you seeing someone?" he asks with suspicion. Then it's like a look of horror that crosses his face. "Fuck... please don't tell me you're dating Cal."

"No, I'm not dating Cal. We're just friends."

Mocking condescension. Yup... that's all over Matt's face right now. "Please... that man just wants in your pants, and he'll get there, too."

"He doesn't want in my pants," I snap. "You're just going to have to trust me on that."

One side of Matt's upper lip curls skyward, and he practically snarls at me. "See, that's just it. I don't trust you."

That feels like an arrow shooting straight through my heart. I try to remember what Matt has been through, and I try to reason to myself that he's this way because of past betrayal. But damn... it still hurts.

"I'll ask one more time... Let me come home with you tonight. I won't ask again, McKayla." His voice is soft... with an almost underlying hint of pleading in it. I want to give in. I want to take him home and show him how good I can be to him... for him. But I'm deluding myself that it would ever lead to something that is good for me.

Shaking my head sadly, I say, "I'm sorry. I can't."

Matt doesn't like that. Doesn't like it at all. His eyes go frigid, and his chin comes up. He's mad, but he's also being rejected, and I know that hurts. I hope to God it is just anger speaking when he says, "No skin off my back. You're not the only game in town."

He turns away before I can even respond and saunters out of my office.

CHAPTER Eight

I'm struggling when I get off the elevator, trying to hold my coffee, hitching up my briefcase over my shoulder, and tottering in four-inch heels and a skirt that doesn't do more than let me shimmy around. Add on to that the fact I haven't gotten any sleep this week, and I'm in a poor to piss-poor mood.

If you're counting, that means I haven't had a good night's sleep in exactly six days. Not since I told Matt that this was over, and he implied that he was heading back to One Night Only.

Bea watches me walk in, her face grim and full of doom. My stomach drops. "What is he?"

"I'd say about a fifteen?"

"A fifteen?" I ask in shock.

"Yup. It's bad."

Turning to look back longingly at the elevator, I briefly consider just heading home and having a sick day. I can't take another day like this. I wonder if Matt's bad mood is because he's not getting his regular sex fix from me, but then I shake that thought away. He's getting it... just not from me, so that can't be the reason.

You see, each day Bea and I have taken to a ranking system to judge Matt's mood. It's becoming increasingly fouler every day. It's a simple one-to-ten scale, and he had topped out at a ten yesterday when he yelled at a secretary, causing her to run from the office in tears with Miss Anders hot on her heels, trying to comfort her.

But today... Bea says he's a fifteen, and that is probably bordering on a nuclear explosion.

My plan? Keep my head down and stay buried in my office, only surfacing to make a mad dash to the bathroom to pee. But if I don't drink any coffee or water, I can probably go all day without having to leave the sanctity of my office and risking a run in with Matt.

I'd like to tell you every day away from Matt is easier, but it's not. I miss him, plain and simple. Yes, of course I miss the sex. Hello… have you read what we've done so far? But it is more than that. I miss his wit, his intellect, and his charm. When he's operating at a fifteen though, it's guaranteed I won't be seeing that any time in the near future.

When I get to my office, I log on to my computer and check my email. My eyes go immediately to the one that is flagged in red from Matt. It says, "Jackson Case - Urgent - see me when you get in."

That's it… nothing else, no indication of what's wrong. And now I have to go into the bear's den when he's at a fifteen. This is shaping up to be a spectacular day.

Matt grunts out a terse, "Come in," when I knock on his door. For once, he's not on the phone but sitting behind his desk, reading a file. When I sit down, he pushes the file aside, reaches across his desk to grab a thick document, and then hands it across to me.

At a glance, I can see it is the rough draft of the Answers to Interrogatories I prepared in the Jackson case for him to review. Seeing as how it was the first set I had ever done, I needed him to review them for legal accuracy. What stands out the most to me, is the red ink that spreads across the top sheet. Flipping briefly through the pages, I see more red ink…

slashes and slashes of it, marking up my words, and mauling my legalese. It looks like Lizzie Borden got ahold of it... a freakin' blood bath.

When I look up at Matt, his face is hard and his eyes icy. "I'm disappointed in you, McKayla. The draft you handed in to me was sub-standard at best. A first-year law student could have done better."

My face flushes red, embarrassment practically seeping out of my pores. I am a perfectionist and to be told my work is bad tears me up inside. I don't understand it because I had done meticulous research and studied several examples of other Interrogatory answers to use as a go-by. When I handed it in to Matt, I thought I'd get it back with an A+++ and a smiley face... maybe a gold star glued to the front.

Flipping through the pages, I focus on his mark-ups to see exactly where I failed. As my eyes move from red mark to red mark, my face goes crimson again, but this time, it's heating up with fury. Matt's corrections have nothing to do with the quality of my legal work. They're all picky issues over the semantics on how to word something. For example, he crossed out the word "instantaneously" and wrote above it "instantly". And that was just one example. Page after page I flip through, and I only spot one area where he has a legitimate gripe... where I placed an objection improperly.

When I glance back up at him, he's watching me with interest, his eyebrows raised slightly to see what my reaction will be. He's ready for me to erupt, and I think he'll be disappointed if I don't. He's expecting a fight, and he wants to uncork the tempest that must be brewing inside of him.

He's a fifteen, I remind myself. So I say with measured calm, "Matt... some of these corrections are just semantics. I think it's a little unfair to call my work sub-standard when you are basically disagreeing with word choices."

His voice is sharp and laced with disdain when he says, "Word choices in a legal document can make or break a case. You could sink an entire claim with just one poorly chosen word. It's a lesson you desperately need, and I'm going to make sure you learn it. Furthermore, you are not to ever question my opinions on your work again."

Okay, that does it... Fifteen or not, I'm not going to let him walk all over me. Matt Fucking Connover is going to get a piece of my mind.

CHAPTER Nine

Standing up from my chair, I put my palms on his desk and lean in. "You are being completely unfair. You're taking your anger out on me when it's not deserved."

Matt stands up, placing his palms opposite mine, and leans in as well. His voice is controlled, but laced with menace. "I'm not taking my anger out on you. I'm telling you that your work product is poor. Learn the difference."

My control sort of snaps at this point, and I shove the bloodied document under his nose. My voice raises an octave. "This is not poor work product. This is you desperately trying to find some fault with my work so you can punish me."

"Punish you?" he sneers as he grabs the document out of my hand. "Why would I possibly do that?"

"Because I cut you off, and you can't handle the rejection," I snarl.

Matt laughs at me... a full-blown, mocking laugh. His eyes glint with danger. "Get over yourself, Mac. You were replaced and forgotten just like that." He snaps his fingers to punctuate the point.

Pain lances at my heart and fury courses through me such as I have never felt before. I have to dig my nails into the palms of my hands to stop from smacking his face.

My voice is venomous, and I'm just one decibel short of an all-out yell. "I can't take this shit anymore. I did nothing to deserve this."

I grab the document out of his hand, hoping I leave him with a paper cut or two, push off from his desk, and spin toward the door, intent on leaving. But Matt is quick. I have no clue if he vaulted his desk or ran around it, but within a nanosecond, he has my elbow clutched and he spins me around.

If I thought Matt was angry before, I didn't know what true anger was. His face is practically contorted in rage when he roars, "You did nothing to deserve this? You fucking denied me."

You would think that this would be a somewhat selfish and bratty statement on his part. But the anguish with which he says those words cuts me deep. He's hurt. Truly, deeply hurt, and a pang of sympathy goes through me.

However, I hold my ground but soften my voice. "I denied you nothing, Matt. I simply asked for more."

Matt's face undergoes an amazing transformation. The terrible lines of rage disappear. The darkness of his eyes lightens to amber, and his hand falls from my elbow. In an instant, he's no longer furious but appears stricken by my words.

His eyes lower from my face, and he reaches up to brush his fingers through his hair in bewilderment, turning slightly away from me. Shoulders sagging, he walks back around his desk and sits heavily in the chair. He stares at his computer, but I can tell he sees nothing. He's only staring at it to avoid looking at me.

"Get out," he says quietly. "I want another draft of those Answers by the end of the day."

It's eerie... the level of uncertainty in his voice right now. Gone is the furious animosity, and all that's left behind is confusion.

And pain.

My heart tumbles over itself in empathy, and I have a brief moment of hope that maybe... just maybe, that Matt will be receptive to discussing our relationship. I take a step toward his desk. His gaze rises up, and he stares at me blankly.

"Matt... I'm sorry you're hurting. I am, too. Maybe if we talked this out, we could figure—"

He cuts me off, his face starting to harden again. "There's nothing to talk about. Now leave."

I'm losing him, and it makes me desperate. "Please... I want to make this better—"

I'm cut off again by Matt's mocking laughter. His eyes are once again dark, and my stomach flips over in wariness. "You want to make this better?" he sneers as he stands up from his desk, his hands going to his belt buckle. "The only way you can make this better, Miss Dawson, is if you get over here on your knees."

Agony courses through my bones over the hurtfulness of those words. This is not the Matt Connover who held me while my mom died. I have no clue where he is, but he's gone, and I can't stop the tears that well up in my eyes.

We stare at each other for a moment. His eyes piercing... mine wet.

I suck in a shaky breath, just so I can have the oxygen necessary to say quietly, "You're despicable."

Turning around, I start walking toward the door, glad he has only my back so he can't see the tears that now slide down my cheeks.

"Mac," he says in a desperate sort of way, but I don't stop.

When I open the door, he tries again... this time a little more desperate. "Mac."

I ignore him, stepping out of his office and closing the door behind me. I jump slightly when something crashes from inside his office, and I hear him yell, "FUCK!"

I'm on autopilot. I walk to my office and log off my computer. Packing a few files in my briefcase, as well as shoving Matt's slaughter of my document in there, I turn my office light out and close the door.

Walking past Bea's desk on the way through the lobby, I say, "Send all my calls to voice mail. I'm taking two sick days. I'll be back in on Monday."

I get just a flash of a surprised look from Bea as I walk by her, and she hesitantly asks, "Are you all right?"

"I will be by Monday," I tell her confidently.

And I am confident. I'm purging Matt Connover from my mind.

Correction... I'm replacing Matt Connover.

It's time for another trip to One Night Only.

CHAPTER Ten

It's Friday night. Macy and I have decided to have a "junk" night. That's where we buy or prepare our favorite "junk" food, and we slug out on the couch to watch movies. It was actually Macy's idea, which surprises me because this is really not how my girl likes to spend her weekend nights. She'd much rather be knocking boots with some hot stud.

But this is perfect for me. I have my bestie hanging out with me, food to help console me, and my yoga pants on so when I gorge on my "junk" food, I can still feel comfy.

Besides, it's not like I had anything better to do. I

mean... who was I kidding? When I walked out of the office yesterday morning, telling myself the only way to get rid of Matt Connover from my existence was to screw someone else, I was living in a dream world. I just didn't have it in me to use rebound sex as a means of forgetting. I was stuck depending on the only true cure... time.

Yesterday, I worked from home making the changes that Matt demanded on my document. I emailed them to him with a short note saying, "Here are the changes requested."

He immediately fired back an email, clearly not even having bothered to read the attached document. It said, "Are you okay? Miss Anders said you were taking a few sick days."

I actually laughed out loud at that. I mean, how dare he act concerned? He told me just a few hours before to get on my knees—a thought that actually had me slightly horny and greatly embarrassed that it made me horny.

Bastard.

I didn't even bother replying, and he never sent me another email.

Macy walks out of the kitchen with her hand stuffed down a bag of Cheetos. She plops on the couch next to me, daintily nibbling on the end of one. "So, what movie do you want to watch first?"

LEGAL *Affairs*

Leaning over, I pick up the DVDs I rented. "Let's see... we have Thor, Captain America, Iron Man, or The Avengers."

"Hmmmm. I'm sensing a theme here," she muses. "Why the need for super-hero action?"

Shrugging my shoulders, I grumble, "I just need to see some hot men in tight clothing to distract me."

Macy leans over and pats me on the knee. She knows exactly what happened with Matt on Thursday and has been babying me a bit since then. I suspect that's why she's with me now on "junk" night rather than hooking up with some random.

Grabbing Thor, because let's face it... he's the yummiest of the choices, I put it in the DVD player and head back to the couch. Just as I'm sitting down, my phone buzzes, indicating I have a text. Picking it up, I feel a zap of electricity course through me when I see Matt's name.

The text merely says, I'm sorry.

"It's from Matt," I say to Macy, and she leans over my shoulder to look at it.

I immediately write back, For what?

Because if he's going to apologize sincerely, I want to make him work for it.

A few minutes pass and nothing comes through. Macy and I exchange looks, and then I set my phone down so I can start the movie. Just before I can hit the "Play" button, I get another text.

Fot ebwryrhing

"He's a terrible texter," Macy comments.

"And he clearly has his auto-correct turned off," I add.

I text him back. ?????

For evwtthimf

I start to text back another, "?????" when another message comes through.

Fuck

Macy snickers and I start to text something, but then the phone starts ringing. It's Matt.

I answer it and press speakerphone so Macy can hear. "You're a terrible texter."

Matt doesn't say anything, but I can hear a lot of background noise. Loud music and people talking, some yelling, some laughing.

"Matt?"

"H-e-e-e-e-y Mac," Matt practically sings into the phone, his voice happy and carefree. "Didja get my text?"

"Are you drunk?"

"Abso-fucking-lutely," he says, and then he yells at someone, "You missed... drink, motherfucker."

There's a lot of laughter and then some cheering. I'm glad he's having such a great time while I'm eating junk food and letting my belly hang out in my yoga pants.

"I don't have time for this shit. Call me when you're sober."

I start to hang up, but Matt says, "Wait! I need to tell you something."

"What?" I ask in exasperation.

"I just... it's just... Aw, fuck. I just miss you, McKayla."

I suck in a quick breath, my heartbeat tripling with his proclamation. Glancing over at Macy, she just sadly shakes her head. She's thinking the same thing I am... drunks have no inhibitions, and he probably won't remember a damn word of this tomorrow.

Which pisses me off. I'm getting sentimental and sappy by his claim that he misses me, and come tomorrow, when he's sober, he probably won't remember it, and if he does, he'll probably push it deep down and become the cold-hearted bastard I've recently come to know.

"I'm hanging up, Matt. Don't call back."

Again, I start to disconnect when Matt says quietly, "I lied, McKayla."

Macy tries to grab the phone, startling me. I grab it out of her reach and mouth the word, "What?" to her.

She whispers, "Hang up... you don't need to listen to his bullshit."

But I can't… because he might say words that I have been longing to hear, and although they may be drunk words, I will take whatever I can at this point.

"What did you lie about?" I ask him.

"I didn't use One Night Only again. I just couldn't go through with it."

"Why not?" I whisper.

He's silent for a moment, and all I can hear are the noises of the bar that he's in. Then he says, "Because I can't stop thinking about you. You're all I want."

I'm all he wants? My heart flutters in response and my hopes that Matt and I could truly be something start to rise.

But then Matt causes me to come crashing back down again, because he says, "It's why I left work at two o'clock today and hit a bar to get shitfaced. So I could drown you out of my mind… even if only briefly. You're a blessing, Mac… but you're also my curse."

I'm stunned speechless and, before I can even say anything back to him, he disconnects and the line goes dead.

CHAPTER Eleven

I wish there was a magic pill I could take that would ease my heartache. And another pill that would magically ease the way my body still aches for Matt.

This fucking sucks.

All weekend I stewed over his call on Friday night. I vacillated amongst a variety of emotions, trying to decide how to handle the situation.

When I was pissed, I would work myself up and decide to put in my resignation. I even sat at my computer on Saturday and typed it up. It was simple.

Dear Matt,

I hereby tender my resignation effective immediately.

You suck, and I hate you.

Sincerely,
McKayla P. Dawson

But there were moments when I would get overwhelmed with sadness for Matt. He's a man that is clearly struggling, and I don't know how to help him. During those moments, I wanted to do nothing more than go into work tomorrow, crawl onto his lap, and hug the hurt out of him.

And finally, there were my moments of weakness. When I thought about what he told me on the phone, that I was all he wanted, it would cause pleasure to fire hotly through my veins. My memory would pulse and flash with images of Matt and me together... naked, writhing on the bed, and moaning in pleasure.

It was at those times that I wanted to be in Matt's office bright and early tomorrow, lying naked across his desk when he walked in. His eyes would darken heavy with lust, and he would take me fast and hard. Just the mere thought of it caused me to shiver.

Then I'd get pissed all over again, because Matt

has such a hold over my sensuality that I want to give in to him just because my body demands it.

My heart doesn't stay quiet though, and it reminds me that it doesn't want to get shredded in the process.

The buzzer in the kitchen goes off, and I walk in to take the cookies out of the oven. It's a compulsion of mine... baking when I'm sad, confused, angry, or whatever. Bottom line—every emotion that Matt is making me feel right now calls for massive amounts of chocolate chip cookies.

Setting the hot pan on top of the stove, I scoop a cookie up with my spatula and then grab it with my hand. It's hot as hell so I toss it from hand to hand, little bits of boiling chocolate sticking to my skin. I take a tiny bite—burning the hell out of my tongue and top of my mouth—and drop my cookie on the floor, but not before I am rewarded by a big dribble of chocolate down my chin and onto my t-shirt.

Of course, that is when the doorbell decides to ring.

Licking my fingertips, I walk into the living room and look through the peephole. Matt stands there gazing at the floor, looking so very perfect with his hair windblown and his sun-kissed skin. He's casual in a navy blue t-shirt, faded jeans, and black Chuck-Ts. He looks young and edible.

I open the door, and he glances up. I amend my

earlier statement. He actually looks like shit. His eyes are bloodshot, and he hasn't shaved in several days. Dark circles hover just under his eyes.

"You have chocolate on your chin," he says as he steps up to me and wipes it off with his thumb. He then sticks said thumb in his mouth and sucks the chocolate off.

No matter how mad I am at Matt, that simple act practically causes me to moan.

"Can I come in?" he asks.

Nodding, I turn to walk into the kitchen and he follows. As I stoop to the floor to pick up my dropped cookie, he says, "Is Macy here?"

"No. She's at the gym," I respond, tossing the cookie carnage in the garbage. I make myself busy by taking the remaining cookies off the sheet with a spatula and placing them on a plate.

When I'm done, I turn to him and cross my arms over my chest. "You look like hell, Matt. Did you go on a bender or something?"

A guilty look flashes across his face. "Actually… I did. I never drink like that, but I pretty much stayed drunk Friday and Saturday."

"Did it help?"

"No," he says quietly. "It didn't help at all. I can't get you out of my mind."

Matt sounds so forlorn that I can't help but be

moved. "I'm sorry."

His eyebrows shoot up. "Sorry? You have nothing to be sorry for. I'm the asshole. I have so much to apologize for that I don't even know where to begin."

My hope starts building again. Here is Matt... standing in my apartment and telling me he's sorry. This is a man that rarely apologizes... for anything. I feel the burning need to let him off the hook quickly, my evil plans to make him grovel completely abandoned.

"Matt," I say gently. "It's okay. I understand what was driving you."

I actually get a little dizzy when Matt walks up to me, standing toe to toe. He smells so good, and his eyes are glowing golden. Both of his hands come up to frame my face, his long fingers circling to the back of my head to hold me in place... to make sure my eyes stay on him.

"No, it's not okay, Mac. I have to make up for this, and I'm hoping that I haven't messed things up so badly that you won't let me start over by taking you out on a date. I want to give you what you want. At least, I want to try to give it to you... if you'll let me."

I can literally feel the burden of sadness and frustration lift from my shoulders, while a thrill of hope and excitement fills my body. My skin is even a little tingly.

"A date?" I ask in wonder, my wildest fantasies—not involving Matt naked—are coming true. "What made you change your mind?"

Matt's eyes are deep pools of regret and sadness. His voice is quietly calm, but resolved. "I finally started realizing that the pain of loneliness is much worse than the pain of betrayal and heartbreak that I was trying to avoid."

The power of his words and what they mean slam into me so hard, I have to close my eyes to savor them. He is saying he's lonely without me, and for someone that has shunned relationships and emotional bonds, that is saying a lot. He's also saying that he's ready to take a risk.

He's ready to step out onto the ledge and risk it all.

When I open my eyes, he's smiling at me. It's a tentative smile, because I still haven't given him an answer. I smile back and nod. "I'd love to go on a date with you."

Relief floods Matt's face, and the haggard look he's been sporting suddenly lifts. Leaning in, he whispers his lips over mine gently... just a ghost of a kiss. When he pulls back, he says with a low voice, "I'm probably going to be really bad at this dating thing... I hope you have patience with me."

Grinning at him, I say, "I'm sure you'll do just fine."

Chuckling, he leans in and kisses me on the forehead. Giving me one last look of longing, he turns toward the door to leave.

"Wait! Where are you going?" I ask, confused as to why he's leaving so soon. I had maybe sort of hoped he'd continue to kiss me, and then we could just jump right into the make-up sex.

He doesn't even look back at me as he opens my door, but he does call out over his shoulder. "I'm going home so I can call you and ask you out all nice and proper."

"But… but…" My words trail off, but it doesn't matter.

Matt has already walked out and closed my door behind him.

Turning back toward my cookies, I give out a squeal of excitement and pump my fist into the air. Glancing at my watch, I see that I can get one more batch of cookies done before Matt calls me.

REPARATION

Sawyer Bennett

Legal Affairs
Vol. 5 - Reparation
By Sawyer Bennett

All Rights Reserved.
Copyright © 2014 by Sawyer Bennett
Published by Big Dog Books

This book is a work of fiction. Names, characters, places and incidents either are products of the author's imagination or are used fictitiously. Any resemblance to actual events, locales or persons, living or dead, is entirely coincidental.

No part of this book can be reproduced in any form or by electronic or mechanical means including information storage and retrieval systems, without the express written permission of the author. The only exception is by a reviewer who may quote short excerpts in a review.

Chapter One

Monday's usually suck, but not today. I step off the elevator, and I have a bit of a spring in my step. I'm looking awesome in my black pencil skirt with a white, silk, wraparound blouse. I'm wearing the Louboutins that Matt first fucked me in, and I'm on top of the world.

Bea does a double take when she sees me. "Damn, Mac... you look fantastic."

Yes, I curled my hair today, put on a little extra makeup, and fine... I actually put on a darker shade of lipstick to accentuate my mouth so that when Matt looked at it, he would think of a wet blow job.

But I can't help it… I want to be pretty for Matt today. I want him not to have a doubt in the world that I'm the best damn risk he'll ever take.

"Thanks, Bea," I chirp at her and sashay by.

"He's a negative five by the way," she calls out.

I stop and turn around to look at her, my eyes wide in wonder. "A negative five?"

"Yeah, it kind of freaked me out. He came in with boxes of donuts for everyone. He smiled at me, and I swear a freakin' rainbow shot out of his butt. He even complimented the scarf that I'm wearing."

I giggle because Bea sounds totally shell shocked by Matt's behavior. It was only last week he was cursing at the staff, causing them to run from the office in tears. But just this weekend… he and I made our amends, and Matt asked me out on a date.

I squeal inside like a high school drama queen. Yay, me!

Matt had called me Sunday as soon as he got home. We talked for almost two hours and he did, indeed, ask me out for a date on Friday night. I'm not sure what exactly changed for Matt, but he seemed to let go of all of his fear and anger, and he actually seems to be embracing this attempt to have a real relationship with me.

I'm on fucking Cloud Nine.

When I get in my office, the first thing I spy is

the white daisy laying on my desk on top of a cream-colored envelope. Picking up the flower, I hold it to my nose and smell its wildness. I set it back down and open the envelope. There's a cream, linen card on the inside that says:

> *I don't think I can wait for Friday to take you on a date.*
>
> *How about tonight?*
> *Matt*

The swelling of elation inside me is overwhelming. I hum with unbridled energy, and I feel like I could conquer the world. Because Matt Fucking Connover... the man that is relationship averse and emotionally closed off... cannot wait until Friday to go on a date with me.

It's like I'm in high school and just got asked to the prom by the star quarterback. I want to jump around my office and do a little dance.

In fact, I think I will. Hopping back a few feet from my desk, I bend my knees, stick my ass out, and shake it all around, while waving my arms in the air.

I'm pumped up... high on Matt.

"That's some pretty funky dancing."

Yelping, I spin to the doorway and see Matt causally leaning against it, his hands in his pockets and the cutest grin on his face, making his dimples extra deep.

My face flushes hot, but then I decide to own it. Sticking my chin up, I say, "I was just excited. It appears I might have a hot date tonight."

Matt does his quick look left and right down the hall, and satisfied that no one is around, steps into my office. He shuts the door and walks up to me with purpose, a cocky grin on his face.

He is spectacular today, wearing a dark gray suit with a blue power tie. It's tailored so well, I can practically see the muscles in his shoulders straining against it.

Matt takes his right hand and skims his fingers along the side of my neck, all the way around to the base of my skull. I feel his hand open wide and then he grabs a handful of my hair, twisting it several times around his wrist. When he has me well and truly captured, he pulls slightly, causing my head to tilt back and expose my throat. Bending over, he places light kisses along my jaw, all the way to my ear, where he murmurs, "I take that is a yes to my invitation to go out tonight?"

I nod my head, even though he has my hair tightly fisted.

"Good," he says roughly against my ear and then pulls away, releasing his hold on me. My knees are shaking slightly, and I guarantee you I have an utterly stupid look on my face. Yes, with just a few whispered words and light kisses, Matt has rendered me the village idiot.

"I'll pick you up at eight. The restaurant I'm taking you to is dressy," he says as he opens my office door to leave. "Oh, and Mac?"

"Huh?"

Yup... still the village idiot.

"Do me a favor... wear those white, lace boy shorts tonight under your dress. You know... the ones that drive me crazy?"

I just nod at him, the power of speech gone... obliterated... destroyed.

I almost collapse when he shoots me a radiant smile, which causes his dimples to pucker deep. He gives me a quick wink, and then he's gone.

He told me Sunday to have patience with him... that he wasn't sure that he was very good at this dating thing.

Who is he kidding?

He's fucking fantastic at it so far!

Chapter Two

Our first date could not have gone off any better if a Hollywood screenwriter had choreographed it. When Matt picked me up at my apartment, he didn't bring me flowers. Instead, he had a full carton of Ben & Jerry's Chocolate Peppermint Crunch, because I had made some obscure reference to it one night after we had sex. He walked into my kitchen and put it in my freezer, telling me that it was for dessert later.

He then took me to a lovely restaurant that was quietly intimate. I'm not sure if he arranged it ahead of time, but we got seated in the back in a tiny corner that sort of cut us off from the rest of the patrons. The wine was spectacular, the waiter unobtrusive, and the conversation flowed with such ease that I felt like I'd known Matt for years.

I was worried about it honestly. Whether or not we could have normal conversation that didn't revolve around phrases such as, "That feels so good" and, "Harder, please."

Turns out, we converse quite well. We laughed, we joked, and most special of all, Matt told me about his son, Gabe. He spoke with such pride, such love… such unconditional emotion, that I almost had tears in my eyes. Matt the Cold-Hearted—which would have been his Viking name if, well if he were a Viking— had the squishiest, warmest soft spot for a little seven-year-old boy.

He didn't say much about his ex-wife, Marissa, other than she had primary custody of Gabe, but he had liberal visitation. In fact, he reminds me of the day I had asked him if he had plans one weekend, after we had returned from Chicago. He reminds me with a soft laugh that I looked green with jealousy when he had told me that he did, in fact, have plans all weekend. He assured me tonight that said plans were with a little, brown-haired boy, and that was the only thing that would have kept him away from me.

My skin went all warm when he told me that, and

my heartbeat hummed out in appreciation.

Now dinner is done, and we are back at my apartment. I unlock the door and open it, stepping into the foyer. Matt grabs ahold of my wrist and stops me.

"This is where I give you a kiss and say goodnight," he says as he pulls me close to his body, wrapping his arms around my waist.

My hands dig into his chest muscles slightly with surprise. "What?"

"You heard me. Kiss me good night, and then I'm heading home."

"Oh, hell no," I say with sass and gumption. "You had me specifically wear lace panties for you, and I've been thinking about you peeling them off me all night. There's no way you're going home, buddy."

Matt leans in to give me a quick kiss, smiling with amusement when he pulls back. "You are adorable, but I'm being a gentleman tonight. I'm showing you that you are more than just sex to me."

"You've shown me that already," I whine like a big baby. "I want sex… tonight!"

Chuckling, Matt says, "Are you pouting?"

I stick my lower lip way, way out.

"No," I grumble and stomp my foot down.

"Did you just stomp your foot?" he asks with a smirk.

"I'm a grown woman," I snap as I stomp my other foot. "I would never do something as childish as that."

Matt releases my waist and brings his hands up to clasp my head. He presses his lips to mine, and I can still taste the smoky peat of the Scotch he drank tonight. My mouth opens, and his tongue slips in. I sigh, and my body melts into his.

Then he kisses me deeply... with quiet hunger.

I feel starved for him, and I whimper when he pulls away.

"Tell you what," he says, tucking a lock of hair behind my ear and looking me straight in the eye. "How about I tuck you into bed?"

My eyes alight with victory, but he squashes it instantaneously.

"I will not be fucking you though," he says firmly.

My lower lip goes back out, and he reaches down to nip at it.

"However," he says with a lecherous smile. "I could be persuaded to peel those panties off you. I mean... if it's really that big of a deal to you."

I jump up and down like a schoolgirl, clapping my hands in excitement. "Yes, please. Panties and bra. Tuck me in, tuck me in!"

Matt busts out laughing and scoops me up in his

arms. Kicking the door shut, he walks through the living room. Macy is on the couch, watching CNN. She glances up at us, her mouth hanging open, as Matt carries me by. I shoot her a quick wave and a broad grin as he takes me to my bedroom.

I bounce on the mattress slightly when Matt drops me there. He's efficient... wasting no effort and, within seconds, I'm lying there in only my white, lace bra and boy shorts. His eyes feast on me, roving over every part of my body.

Looking up at him with my most seductive stare, I stick my foot out and run it up the inside of his leg, causing his gaze to move from my breasts down to where I'm getting perilously close to his cock. "Matt... please don't leave me like this. I'm dying here."

I can see his erection pushing hard against his pants, and I move my foot to gently rub over it. He hisses out in pleasure, but then grabs my foot and lowers it to the bed.

"I'd never leave you wanting, McKayla," he tells me with lust flooding his words.

Crawling onto the bed in between my legs, Matt does indeed peel my panties off me. He lays his fingertips in the center of my chest, and then lightly drags them down my body, straight down in between my thighs. I arch off the bed like a cat stretching after its morning milk when he slips a finger inside of me.

I stare at him in fascination, because he's staring at me in fascination... where his hand is wedged firmly against me. His gaze slowly moves up and locks with my own.

"Watch, Mac," he whispers, and then nods his head back down to my hips. Both of our eyes travel south, and mine stayed glued to his hand working me.

But then the feelings get to be too much. My blood is pumping faster, and Matt's fingers are hitting deeper. My eyes have no choice but to flutter closed as my head falls back in utter surrender. I hear Matt give a soft laugh at my ability to do nothing more than focus on my feelings, and he adds his thumb to the mixture of pleasure.

Then I'm flying high and a long moan flows up from my throat and filters into the air, just as my body earthquakes itself into an orgasm. It shreds me from the inside out and seems to go on for an eternity. I'm completely wrecked when it finally stops spasming.

I'm vaguely aware of Matt removing his fingers from me. It sort of penetrates my brain that he's covering me up with my comforter. I'm almost asleep by the time he presses his lips to my forehead and says, "Good night."

"Good night," I murmur back, and then I'm out.

CHAPTER Three

Being in a new relationship is fun, particularly if you have someone that has a good sense of humor. For example, check out this text exchange between Matt and me this morning.

Me: Are you like my boyfriend now?

Matt: I'm not sure. Don't I have to ask you to go steady or something?

Me: Good question. Grade school was too long ago.

Matt: Let me see if I can figure this out. Do boyfriends get blow jobs from their girlfriends?

Me: Definitely!

Matt: Do boyfriends get to go down on their girlfriends as often as they like?

Me: Most assuredly!

Matt: Do boyfriends get to fuck their girlfriends senseless?

Me: I'm horny.

Matt: Focus and answer the question.

Me: Yes! Yes, they do!

Matt: Unfortunately, I don't think we are technically boyfriend/girlfriend yet. We're not doing any of those things.

Me: :(

Matt: Did you just sad face me?

Me: Yup.

Matt: Tragic.

Me: I know. You know, you could fix this and just have sex with me.

Matt: All in good time.

This is the Matt Connover that I've been pleasurably dealing with all week. He's like a different man. I mean, when he decides to take a risk, he goes all in. He's not the type to dip his toe in the water and test out the currents first. Nope. He dives in headfirst, never even checking to see if he's at the shallow or deep end.

I admire that. I admire the bravery with which he is giving me a shot. He's gone from being completely bitter and closed off, to being adventurous and open-minded.

And best of all... he seems to be enjoying the new way in which we are discovering each other.

Glancing at my watch, I note it's only three PM. Only five hours left until my date with Matt. That is... the original date he had asked me on last weekend. It's kind of sort of a big deal, even though we've done something together almost every night this week. We've caught either a quick dinner after work, or maybe even just a drink. One night, we just sat in his office because we were both working late and talked.

But tonight... tonight is where I'm going to demand he fuck me so we can get back on the track of having a full-blown relationship. I'm done having him try to woo me.

I'm wooed enough already.

Thinking of all the ways that Matt is trying... I mean, really trying, to give me what I've asked for, suffuses me with warmth and appreciation for him. It's a feeling of tenderness I had not yet really possessed.

It makes me want to tell him that right now.

Standing up from my desk, I walk down to his office, nodding at various colleagues I pass in the hallway. Matt's door is closed as always, but after a light knock, he grants me entrance. When I step in, the brow that was furrowed as he looked at a file smoothes out and an appreciative smile comes across his face.

"To what do I owe this pleasure?" he practically croons softly at me, and it makes me want to crawl on his lap and rub up against him.

"Get up," I tell him. "Let's go for a walk."

His eyebrows rise. "What? In the middle of a workday?"

I roll my eyes at him. "Shocker, yes, but people are allowed to take breaks in their work day. You and I have been at it for seven hours straight already, and neither one of us took lunch. Let's go take a short walk to stretch our legs, and I'll buy you a cup of coffee."

Stroking a finger across his chin, he stares at me with contemplation. "I can see merit to this idea."

"It's a fantastic idea. Come on, law boy. Let's beat feat."

Slapping his palms on his desk, Matt stands from his chair, looking almost like a child that's been told he can go out and play.

"You've never done this before, have you?"

"What?"

"Go for a short walk midday. Taken a moment just for yourself."

Matt gives me a sheepish grin and shrugs his

shoulders. "I guess not. It feels kind of wicked."

Laughing, I start for the door. "I haven't even begun to show you the ways you can be wicked during a workday."

I'm brought to an abrupt halt as Matt reaches out and wraps his hand around my wrist. I turn toward him, looking at him in question. He gets this sexy little grin on his face and pulls me slowly back his way, until I'm mashed up against his body. Inhaling, I appreciate the woodsy-citrus smell of his body wash. He never wears cologne, and I love that fresh smell he always seems to have.

Pushing his fingers through my hair to the back of my head, he grips me and pulls me closer. His lips are so soft when his mouth touches against mine. It's a kiss of gratitude, hope, and happiness.

But Matt still has sexy down to a science because as he pulls back, he says, "Are you ready to get fucked tonight?"

Oh God, the man can cause my body to shudder violently with just a few words, and he looks triumphant as he feels the tremors rumble through me.

He smiles at me like he just won an Olympic gold medal. "I'll take that as a yes."

I open my mouth to tell him yes when his office door flies open. We both hear it at the same time and jump apart like we've been zapped with an electrical current.

Spinning around, Bill Crown stands there, looking between Matt and me with a look of shock on his face. He closes the door and steps back against it, giving us a grave look. My heart is racing a million miles an hour because I got my proverbial hand caught in the Connover Cookie Jar.

Sneaking a glance at Matt, he has a light smile on his face as he faces off against Bill.

Turning back to Bill, I steel myself, getting ready to absorb the tongue lashing I know will be coming.

Instead, the serious look vanishes and a wide grin spreads across his face. "I knew it," he says triumphantly. "I knew there was something going on between you two."

Matt starts laughing and slips an arm around my waist. "I was going to tell you, but truth be told, it really wasn't until this week that I was sure it was going to work."

I look wildly between the two men, not really understanding half of what's going on. Matt is my boss… he should not be within five feet of me in an intimate nature. Bill, as his business partner, should be pissed about this.

Yet, he looks almost giddy.

"I don't get it," I say dumbly, pulling slightly

away from Matt because I still feel like he's forbidden fruit. "Aren't you mad?"

Bill chuckles. I note that when he smiles, he looks about ten years younger. I always thought Bill looked haggard and worn out, and I'm wondering if it's because he's generally unhappy. But now... he's looking at Matt like he wants to shake his hand and slap his back.

"I'm thrilled for Matt, actually," Bill says. "He's been single far too long, and he's a great guy. He deserves happiness. But... obviously, this should stay secret. I'd suggest keeping your make-out sessions to a minimum."

"Point taken," Matt agrees. "I assume whatever you came in for can wait? I have a short walk I need to take with my girl. I'll be back in ten minutes."

Bill is still grinning when we leave Matt's office.

Chapter Four

This is huge. I mean, really big—and I'm not talking about Matt's package. Although, that is really big, too.

No, I'm referring to the fact that I'm standing on the threshold to Matt's apartment, knocking on his door.

No, I'm not stalking him. Before he left work for today, he stopped by my office and asked me if I would I like to come to his apartment for dinner, for our date.

His. Apartment.

The man that doesn't take women that he's fucking home.

See... huge!

Because that means he definitely sees me as more than just a great lay. He is truly seeing that maybe we are relationship material. He's progressing far faster than I ever thought possible, and it makes me admire him even more for the efforts he's making.

The door opens, and a moment of pure giddiness possesses me when I see Matt. He's beyond gorgeous as he stands there in dark-washed blue jeans and a tight, white t-shirt. His feet are bare, and he has a corkscrew in one hand. He is relaxed and happy to see me, and I melt a little more for him.

"That's not a new sexual toy you bought to use on me, is it?" I ask, looking at the corkscrew. "It looks like it may hurt."

Matt steps back to let me in, giving me a grin. "I don't need toys to use on you, baby."

"No, you don't," I whole-heartedly agree.

Looking around, I take in Matt's apartment. It's totally a man's home. It has light beige walls, dark leather furniture, and a TV in the living room that practically takes up an entire wall. It's comfortable looking though, and I immediately kick off the heels I wore with my jeans and peasant top, placing them near the door.

"Come in the kitchen," Matt says. "I'm finishing up dinner."

"Smells delish... What are we having?"

"Nothing fancy. Just a quick, chicken casserole. I'm not that great of a cook."

"Then I'm very impressed that you are trying to cook for me. I think you might get lucky tonight."

Matt pulls a bottle of wine from a rack beside his refrigerator and opens it up. "We're both getting lucky tonight," he says softly.

The tone of his voice... it's seductively promising, and warmth rushes through me. He stares at me as he pours two glasses of wine, his eyes burning bright.

"You're very good at this," I say as I take the wine that he offers me. I take a sip and sigh with pleasure.

"What's that?" he murmurs as he takes his own sip. His eyes blaze into me over the rim of his glass.

"Dating me... trying to give me a relationship. It's more than I expected, so thank you."

Matt sets his wineglass on the counter and walks up to me. He takes my hand and lifts it up to his mouth, pressing a warm kiss on the inside of my wrist. He stares at me as his lips move across my skin, and my pulse flutters madly in response.

"You know," he says as he takes my glass from my other hand and sets it on the counter, "I told myself I wasn't going to touch you when got here, but when I opened my door and saw you, I knew that was a lie."

Taking my other wrist, he pulls it up to his mouth to give it a warm lick, followed by a soft kiss, all the while pinning me with his gaze. "Then I told myself I would wait until after dinner to have you, but now... touching you... tasting you like this..."

Another warm kiss to my wrist, and then he continues, "Well, I knew that was lie, too."

Still holding my wrist, Matt walks up to the oven and turns it off. I have no choice but to follow. Turning, he leads me through the living room and down a hallway. His walk is casual, but I'm feeling anything but.

He's leading me to bed, where I know he'll do terribly wicked things to me. The thought causes my most intimate muscles to clench almost painfully, and my panties to become damp.

Matt wastes no time. He clasps my face in his large hands and pulls me in for a bone-melting kiss. It's deep and luxurious... with deep swipes of his tongue and his breath hot against my lips. His hands seem to be everywhere on me... grasping my hip to pull me in close, cupping the underside of my breast, and trailing fingertips over my collarbone.

Our clothes seem to melt away, and we stumble to the bed. Then it's skin on skin. His palm cruises along my outer thigh while he sucks at my nipples. My fingers dig into his shoulders as my hips flex up into his because I need the contact.

He murmurs things to me.

As his hand goes between my legs, he says, "You're perfect, Mac. Just fucking perfect."

His other hand squeezes my breast, and then he pinches a nipple, all the while whispering, "Beyond beautiful."

When he finally sinks into me, I watch his eyes close as he gives into the pleasure. He moves in and out of me in long, measured strokes that are neither too fast nor too slow. They are perfect, deep, and invading.

Matt curls an arm under one of my legs, resting it in the crook of his elbow, and he hikes it up high. Angling his hips down, his next push in goes deeper than ever and he says, "Heaven... this is what Heaven must feel like."

All Matt's words are just as seductive as the way he moves inside of me. His cock seduces my body, but his words seduce my heart.

"Are you close?" he whispers in my ear, all the while with deliberate pumps between my legs.

I nod, pressing my face into the skin at the base of his shoulder. I give a tiny lick that causes him to shudder. "So close."

"Me too," Matt says as he picks up the pace. "I want us to come together."

"Yes," I breathe out. "Together."

It only takes Matt's hand slipping between our bodies to rub up against me, in just the right spot, and my orgasm tears free... racing up my spine, then back down again.

I call his name out... loudly.

He gives one last, hard push and then he's jetting hot inside of me, murmuring, "Mac, Mac, Mac..."

CHAPTER Five

I wake up alone in Matt's bed, the sunshine streaming through the window. I don't need to wonder where he is though, because I'm immediately assaulted by the smell of bacon, which is... as you know... only like the best smell in the entire galaxy.

Crawling out of bed, I grab Matt's white t-shirt that got so carelessly discarded and head into the kitchen. I can't help the way my breath catches a little as I watch him standing at the stove, wearing only his jeans. His back is tanned golden, and his muscles are supremely beautiful. His hair is sticking up all over the place, and he looks like a man who spent all night fucking his girlfriend.

Just thinking of the things we did last night causes heat to flash between my legs. I mean, sex with Matt has always been beyond amazing, but there's something different about it now that we have moved into relationship territory. It's more intimate, and the craving goes much deeper.

"Something smells good," I say, and Matt turns to look at me. His eyes travel down the length of me, and my nipples harden nicely against his cotton t-shirt. He doesn't fail to notice and I know this because first, his gaze is stuck to my chest, and second, his golden eyes darken to a mocha color.

Matt reaches out and turns the stove off. His tongue peeks out and swipes at his lower lip as he walks up to me. My pulse speeds in response, and I hold my breath to see what he'll do.

Bending down, Matt picks me up to wrap my legs around his waist. The maneuver has his hands clutching my bare ass, and my legs dutifully lock around him.

"Christ," he mutters, flexing his fingers into my skin. "You're not wearing any underwear."

I smile at him and lace my fingers into his hair. "Nope."

"Good girl," he commends and spins around to

set me on the counter. He steps in close, and it's the perfect height as his pelvis is in direct alignment with mine. Our mouths meet in open surrender to one another, and our kiss is fueled with lust.

Hands roam roughly across hot skin. Matt whips off my t-shirt, moving his mouth across my breasts, while my hands stroke up his back.

When he sticks one hand between my legs, he murmurs, "So wet. Can't wait."

In a move so quick I'm not even sure I understand how it happened, Matt has his jeans unzipped and his dick pulled out, slamming it inside of me. I gasp at the intrusion, not because it's unwelcome, but because if feels so fucking good.

"I love the way you feel inside me," I moan in his ear, and that causes him to pump harder between my legs.

"Do you like the way I fuck you?" Matt rasps out just before he presses his teeth into my shoulder.

"Y-e-e-e-s," I manage to stammer while he sucks hard at my skin.

"Do you want it harder?"

"God, yes."

Matt pulls my hips off the edge of the counter and, with a palm to the center of my chest, pushes me to lay flat on my back. Then he starts to slam into me so hard it feels like my hipbones are going to pop out of joint.

Still I cry out, "Harder."

Matt groans over my words and gives it to me harder.

And about twenty seconds after that, we are both crying out each other's names as we experience the mother lode of all simultaneous orgasms.

There is a requisite period of rest, when Matt leans his head on my chest while our breathing gets back to normal.

"That was insane," I tell him, my fingers slipping through his hair to rub his scalp.

"We're completely depraved," he observes, pushing his head harder against my palm. "I thought I might break you there for a minute."

I laugh softly. "It felt so good. You have complete permission to hammer at me that way any time you want."

Matt looks up at me and smiles, holding my gaze in a way that says, You really are like the perfect woman.

He stands and zips himself up. Tearing off a paper towel, he gently cleans me up, placing soft kisses on my belly as he does. Then he pulls me up, places my t-shirt back over my head, and points me to a bar stool while he makes me a cup of coffee.

I watch as Matt cooks me breakfast. It's simple... just scrambled eggs and bacon, but there's something touching about watching your lover cook for you.

When he turns to place my plate before me, my cell phone, which is laying on the counter, starts to ring. I glance down at it at the same time Matt does, and I internally groan when the name "Cal Carson" displays across the screen. I reach out and slap at it to disconnect the ring, knowing that Cal will leave me a voice mail.

I look up at Matt, prepared for him to go ballistic. There is a tiny tick in his jaw muscle, but his voice is fairly calm when he says, "Why is Cal calling you?"

"We're friends, Matt. Just friends."

Matt stares at me, his brow furrowed. "I don't like it."

"You don't have to like my friends," I tell him.

"You can be friends with him, even knowing what he did to me? I mean... you do know the sordid details, right? You know his friendship has no loyalty, right? And that's the type of friend you want?"

He's angry, and I get it. He has every right to be, and I'm suddenly very confused. I want to be friends with Cal, but my loyalty has to be to Matt, right? I mean... he is my boyfriend.

A pleasurable rush goes through me at the thought of Matt being my boyfriend. It's something I want... very much.

Matt looks at me intently. "Mac... I don't know if I can do this with you if Cal is a part of your life."

CHAPTER Six

My heart actually hurts for Matt because I see him standing there, looking at me with fear. He's afraid I'll walk away, and that Cal will destroy another relationship. But I'm not going to let that happen.

I hop off the bar stool and walk up to him. Taking both of his hands in mine, I rub my thumbs over the backs in an attempt to soothe him.

"Matt... if you want me to choose, then I choose you. Always. But before you ask me to do that, will you at least hear me out?"

Relief washes over his face and his arms wrap

around me, pulling me in. He doesn't respond, so I pull back.

"Will you? Just listen to me... for five minutes... and then you can ask me to choose if you want."

Matt purses his lips in distaste at my request, but he knows it's not unreasonable, so he nods his head. Before he can change his mind, I lead him into the living room and push him down on the couch. Because I want to touch him, and because I want him to understand how much I love the intimacy we share, I crawl onto his lap and straddle him.

His hands immediately come up to my waist, skimming under the edge of the t-shirt. I rest my hands on his shoulders and take a deep breath. "Okay... here's the thing about Cal—"

My words are cut off by a moan as Matt's hand slides over the top of my thigh, and he sinks a finger into me. Closing my eyes, I submit to the feeling, but then I realize he is just distracting me from my mission.

Pushing back against him, I hop off his lap and glare at him. "You promised you'd listen to me."

He smirks at me and shrugs his shoulders. "Sorry. You can't sit your bare ass on my lap and not expect that to happen."

I glare at him harder, which causes his smirk to deepen. He's leaning back on the couch, his long legs stretched out in front of him so they rest just under the edge of the coffee table. Sighing, I step over his legs and sit my rump down on the edge of the table. Leaning forward, I place my elbows on my knees and clasp my hands. This is my "I'm getting ready to have a serious talk" pose.

Matt's gaze holds mine. Good, he knows I'm serious.

I start to open my mouth when I see Matt's eyes travel downward.

Down… down… down.

Until they are focused right between my legs.

"Sorry, babe… you can't expect me to pay attention when you're flashing that at me. You've got five seconds to get some underwear on, or I'm going to throw you on the floor and fuck the shit out of you."

My skin breaks out in tingles, and for a split second, I almost let him do it. But then I realize that I need to have this talk, and besides… I'm betting I can convince him to fuck the shit out of me when the conversation is over.

I run into the bedroom and slip my panties on, then I run back out before Matt gets up and changes his mind. But he's still there, waiting patiently, and I decide to sit on the opposite end of the couch from him. I even tuck my legs up demurely under me, and I ensure all my goods are covered.

With a sigh, he turns and angles his body toward me, throwing one arm casually over the back of the couch.

"Okay... spill it," he says with resignation.

I take a deep breath. "Okay... I have the floor. Just listen. Cal feels horrible about what happened."

"Good," Matt sneers. "He should."

"Hey! You said you'd listen, so shut it. Like I said... his guilt is crushing him. He's hurting right now."

Matt rolls his eyes. "Am I supposed to feel sorry for him?"

I don't answer his question, because the answer is obvious. Instead, I say, "He must have been a really great friend."

"Why do you say that?" Matt asks suspiciously.

"Because... I know you wouldn't be hurting this bad if he had not been so dear to you."

Shrugging his shoulders, Matt doesn't even hedge. "Save it, Freud. You think I don't know this already?"

"Matt, do you even know what happened between Cal and your ex-wife?" I don't think he does, because if he did... if what Cal told me happened was the truth, then I'm not so sure Matt would be this unyielding.

"I know all I need to. She was married to me...

he fucked her. What more is there?"

"You're not interested in the details?"

"Why would I be?" he asks, incredulous. "I don't get where you're going with all of this."

"I'm just curious if there is room in your heart to forgive him. I'm not saying you have to ever be friends again, but forgiveness goes a long way toward having a peaceful heart."

Matt considers my words. He stares at me deeply, chewing on his bottom lip. But then his gaze hardens. "I'm sorry, Mac. I just don't have it in me. I've worked really hard to put it behind me and move on. Please don't ask me to do more than that."

My heart sinks a tiny bit, but I also completely understand Matt's feelings on this.

I understand, and I respect them.

"What do you want me to do?" I ask.

"I want you to promise me you'll end your friendship with Cal and have no further contact with him."

I smile at him. I smile at him in sadness and understanding. Pushing up onto my knees, I crawl across the couch and climb onto his lap. I'm relieved when his arms come around me to hold me tight.

Laying my cheek on his chest, I whisper. "Okay... I'll do that for you."

His lips press into my hair, and he quietly says, "Thank you."

Chapter Seven

True to my word, I called Cal and explained what was going on with Matt and that he had asked me to cut ties. Cal was extremely understanding but was also sad to be losing a friend. I was very sad, too, because I genuinely liked Cal and understood his side of the story. I wasn't giving up though. I would continue to work on Matt.

Speaking of Matt... I was hoping to see him soon. He's been in a trial all week and working late, late hours, so we haven't had any time together other than a few stolen moments in the morning before he'd head off to court. He would always call me late at night when he was finally leaving the office, usually around midnight, just to say goodnight.

I missed him and couldn't wait for this damn trial to be over with, so I could have him back.

The phone on my desk buzzes, and I can see that it is Bea calling me. Picking it up, I drawl, "What's up?"

"He's a fifteen again," she whispers. "He just barreled through the doors, and he's pissed. I think he lost the trial."

Slamming my phone down, I take off for Matt's office, my heart sinking. He's going to be devastated as he was so invested in this case. Just as I round the corner and see Matt's office, I catch a glimpse of him stepping inside and slamming the door behind him.

I walk—okay, run—toward his office and don't even bother with a knock. I open the door, slip in, and shut it behind me. Except, the door pushes open, moving me out of the way. Bill walks inside and shuts the door again.

Matt is pacing back and forth, anger all over his face.

"What happened?" I ask quietly.

Snapping his head my way, Matt glares at me. "What do you think happened? I fucking lost the case."

"It's not a big deal," Bill urges. "We didn't even

have that much money invested in it."

Matt spins around, and I swear I see flames leaping from his irises. "It's not about the fucking money, you jackass. My clients' lives are screwed up. The judge totally fucked us on the jury instructions."

Stepping forward, I hesitantly lay my hand on Matt's arm. "Is there an appealable error?"

The fire seems to die out of his eyes, and he takes a deep breath, letting it out in one big rush. He picks up my hand, which is resting on him, and brings it to his lips, giving me a tentative smile. "Yes. There are several errors for appeal. I'll have you help me get the Notice filed."

Glancing over my shoulder at Bill, he says, "I'm sorry I yelled, Bill."

Chuckling, Bill heads back out of the office. "No worries. And I think Mac is better equipped to deal with your snarly ass than I am."

Matt takes his jacket off and tosses it on a chair. I watch as he undoes his cuff links and rolls his sleeves up, appearing to be lost in thought. He takes a seat behind his desk, and loosens his tie around his neck a bit. His original outburst is done, but I can still see the tension radiating off him as he stares down at his desk.

I glance back at his door. Bill had left it opened a crack, so I walk up to it and shut it. I turn the lock, and it makes a distinctive snick that reverberates through the room.

Matt's head snaps up at the sound, and he pins me with his eyes. "What are you doing?"

I start to walk toward him, making sure my hips sway provocatively. Unbuttoning the yellow, silk blouse I'm wearing, I let it fall to the floor so he can appreciate the lacy, white bra I'm wearing.

"I'm getting ready to make all your fantasies come true," I purr as I step around his desk and come up to his side.

Matt turns his chair slightly and looks up at me. He stares at my breasts in longing, and his voice is thick when he says. "What do you mean?"

Leaning over, I kiss his neck and whisper, "I'm getting ready to give you a five-star blow job."

Matt groans, leans his head back against his chair, and closes his eyes.

"I don't need that," he murmurs.

Laughing softly, I drop down on my knees in front of him. Quickly removing his belt, I slowly unzip his pants past the already huge erection that he's sporting. "Baby... I've never seen anyone in more need of a blow job than you right now."

"Fuck," he hisses through his teeth. "You're killing me here."

Pulling his pants and underwear down slightly, I take his length into my hand, marveling at the silky feel of his hot skin against my palm. I squeeze him gently, rubbing my thumb along the tip, and Matt gives a groan.

"Shhh," I whisper as I start stroking him. His hips press upward, urging me on.

"What if someone calls me?"

"Answer the phone," I say nonchalantly as I lean forward and lick him from base to tip. He actually grunts at the contact.

"What if someone knocks on the door?" he gasps when I lick him again.

"Tell them to go away." This time I take him all the way in, straight to the back of my throat, where I relax it so I don't gag him out. He tastes divine, and I can feel him trembling all over.

"What if—?" he starts to ask, but I cut him off.

Releasing him from my mouth, I say, "Baby... shut up and enjoy this."

He grins at me and leans his head back again, closing his eyes. I take him back in my mouth, and then I go to town on my man. I pull him in deep, relishing the way he slides between my tongue and the roof of my mouth. Bringing his hands to my hair, he grips me hard. His hips start moving on their own, and I can tell he's completely powerless to stop them.

I let my hand in on the action. As I pull up on his cock with my lips, I let my hand squeeze and stroke him around the base. Apparently, this feels good to the male persuasion because at this point, Matt starts babbling almost incoherently. I can make out a few words like "fuck," "blow," and "come," but he butchers most of the English language with words like "woirsht" and "ferulsa".

No clue what they mean.

The time comes when I feel him get even larger, even harder, in my mouth, and I take a peek up at him. I love when he looks like this... eyes squeezed shut, mouth hanging slightly open, and eyebrows angled in. He's getting ready to come, and I relish it.

He erupts hot into my mouth on a down stroke, and fortuitously straight down the back of my throat. He moans low and long, and I'm pretty sure anyone walking by right now would hear it.

And you guessed it... he whispers my name over and over as I continue to move up and down his length a few more times until every spasm has quieted down, and his grip relaxes from my hair.

I pull away and tuck him gently back into his pants, pulling the zipper up. Standing up, I lean over and grab his tie, pulling him forward so I can give him a soft kiss. He breathes a relaxed sigh over me.

"Feeling better?" I ask him.

His eyes open and they are light golden, looking at me with awe and reverence. He nods and says, "You're amazing."

I flash him a quick smile and straighten his tie out. "I know. Now, let's talk about this appeal and figure what we need to do so we can kick those motherfucker's asses."

Matt's laughter rings out loud, and yeah… my chest puffs out a little that I did that to him.

Chapter Eight

"Hey, baby. I'd like another Slippery Nipple." I punctuate my statement by wriggling my bottom against Matt's lap. I can feel the rumble of a groan tearing through him, but he grips my waist hard to stop my movements.

Party pooper. Who cares if we're out in public?

"No more Slippery Nipples for you," Matt says emphatically. "You're going to be hating life tomorrow as it is."

Dude! Cut off by my boyfriend and during my celebration. That's messed up.

I look at my watch and I admit... I must be a little drunk because I have to squint my eyes to bring it into focus. It's only nine PM, which makes it even more embarrassing that I've been cut off.

We're celebrating because I had my first solo hearing today and won. Now, granted... it wasn't much of a fight, and yeah, the other side didn't even show up, so technically the judge had no choice but to grant in my favor. But hey, a win is a win is a win, and I wasn't about to say no to Matt when he suggested we go out for drinks to celebrate.

He surprised me even more when he suggested I invite Macy, and so now here I sit with my boyfriend and my best friend. It's a plethora of 'friends'.

Whoa... I just used the word plethora, so I can't be that drunk.

"Hey Macy... I just used the word 'plethora' in my mind," I say, genuinely impressed with myself.

Taking a sip of her vodka tonic, Macy grins at me. She's completely enjoying my inebriated state because she doesn't get to see me this way often. I don't like giving up control.

"That's great, Mac. But so what?" she asks, shooting Matt a conspiratorial wink.

"W-e-e-e-ll," I drawl out. "I'm obviously not that drunk if I can use big words in my head. Thus, I deserve another Slippery Nipple."

Matt's arms wrap around my waist, and I can feel the rumble of his chuckle against my back. He leans in and kisses me on the neck. "It's arguments like that that will make you a legal star. I'm convinced. I'll go get you another Slippery Nipple."

Matt deposits me back in my chair and heads off to the bar. I watch him as he walks away, leaning my head on my hand, and giving a swooning sigh.

"Girl... you have it bad," Macy remarks. "I never saw you act this way around Pete."

"Pete who?" I ask. "There is no Pete... there is only Matt. Hey... that sounds like a really deep, philosophical statement. Kind of like, 'I think, therefore I am'. Except now it's, 'There is no Pete... therefore there's Matt'. Man, I have layers."

Macy bursts out laughing at me. "I love you, Mac. I really, really do."

A silly grin breaks across my face. "Awww. I love you, Macy-girl. I love Matt, too."

"You do?" Macy asks, her laughing abruptly gone and replaced by genuine curiosity.

I glance over at the bar and take Matt in. He's leaning against it casually, watching a basketball game that's on the TV while he waits for my drink. Do I love him? Or am I just drunk? Can it be both?

No immediate answer comes to mind, and I realize I'm not quite the philosopher I thought I was just a few minutes ago.

"I don't know," I tell Macy. "I know I'm ridiculously happy with him. He's given me everything I asked for."

"Well, you'll know when you know. For now—enjoy the ride. And I do mean that with every bit of sexual innuendo I can muster."

Looking back at Matt again, I tell her, "Oh, he's giving me the ride of a lifetime. I'm definitely enjoying it."

After that one last Slippery Nipple, Matt convinces me it's time to head home. When we walk into the apartment, Matt says goodnight to Macy and drags me back into my bedroom. I wave at Macy, and she shoots me a smile that says, I'm really happy for you, Mac.

At least I hope that's what the smile means. Or it could mean, I hope you don't puke on your shoes but if you do, it's Matt's problem.

As soon as my bedroom door is closed, I spin toward Matt and reach out for his belt buckle. My fingers fumble for a second but then his hands close over mine, quieting my movement. "No way, baby. You're too drunk."

I make a pffft sound, which, in hindsight, really makes me sound drunk. "But honey… I want it."

I'm going for seductive and sexy, but I think I may be coming off as drunkenly whorish. To my relief, Matt gives me a soft smile and pulls me into a hug. He kisses the top of my head, and I can't help but sigh in contentment to be wrapped up in him.

"You can have it," he assures me. "Tomorrow…when you're sober. So for now, go brush your teeth and takes some aspirin."

I huff and puff but, honestly, the room is sort of spinning, so I totter off to do what he says. After brushing my teeth and popping two Tylenol, I quickly remove all of my clothes, leaving them lying on my bathroom floor. I probably am too drunk to have sex, and seriously, I don't want to have sex with Matt and not remember it. That would be a freakin' travesty.

When I come out of the bathroom, Matt is lying in my bed. His chest is bare, and the covers are pulled up to his waist. I know him well enough to know that he's completely naked underneath. He loves to sleep in the buff.

Although I'm drunk, I still have enough of my wits to enjoy the hotness of Matt Fucking Connover in my bed. He looks like perfection lying there.

I crawl over him to reach my side, wrestling my way under the covers and collapse beside him in a fit of giggles. Scooting closer to him, I put my head on his chest while his arm comes around to hold me close. Reaching out to the lamp beside the bed, he turns it off and plunges us into total darkness.

And as always happens when you've had too much alcohol and the inhibitions are completely obliterated, I lay it all out on the line.

"Hey, Matt?" I whisper loudly. Really, really loudly.

"Yeah."

"I think I love you."

I'm met with silence, but he squeezes me in response. I wait for something else, but he remains quiet.

"I'll probably regret saying that tomorrow, but I just had to say it."

"You won't remember it tomorrow, Mac."

"Yes, I will," I assure him with confidence. "I may not remember telling you, but I will remember I love you. That's just not something I can forget."

He leans over and glides his lips over my forehead. "You're something else, Mac."

His words are soft and genuine. He is not displeased by my proclamation. I may not get the words back in return, but I know that our relationship just got a little deeper.

CHAPTER Nine

There have been many times over the last several weeks that I've been nervous in my relationship with Matt. The first time we met and I stripped in front of him, my first day of work when I realized he was my boss, and my drunken proclamation that I loved him.

Yes, those were all moments of extreme apprehension.

And yet, none of them compared to the way I feel right this moment before I knock on his apartment door.

Matt has Gabe this weekend. It wasn't his

regularly scheduled visitation, but his ex-wife called him late last night and asked if he could take him. She apparently wanted to take an impromptu weekend trip with her new boy toy.

Of course, Matt jumped all over it. If there is one thing I've come to know about Matt, he loves Gabe beyond all measure. His entire reason for living is that little boy.

I was in no way disappointed when he told me last night—Friday night—that he had to go pick up Gabe and wouldn't be able to see me. I had just been packing up my briefcase with some weekend work when he had come into my office to give me the bad news.

Except… it wasn't bad news. When he told me he needed to forsake me in favor of Gabe, I was genuinely happy for him and I made sure he knew that. He gave me a soft kiss goodbye and murmured, "I'm not sure I deserve you."

Those words alone made it all worthwhile.

But then Matt called me this morning—Saturday—and asked if I wanted to go with him and Gabe to Coney Island for the afternoon.

I had asked, "Are you sure, Matt? You want me to meet Gabe?"

He never even hesitated. "Absolutely."

But now the nervousness abounds because, holy

hell... what if Gabe hates me? If he hates me, there is no future for Matt and me... no matter how good the sex is.

With moist palms, I knock on the door and, when it opens, I'm staring at a little miniature Matt. Dark brown hair and soft amber eyes. He smiles at me and, woe to his future girlfriends, he even has Matt's dimples.

"Hi," Gabe says. "Dad says come on in. He's just finishing up some work."

"Thanks," I tell him as I walk into the apartment, and he shuts the door behind me. "I'm McKayla. But you can call me Mac. All my best friends do."

"Want to play Wii bowling with me?" he asks, not even acknowledging my name but instead, focusing on what's really important to little boys.

Before I can even answer, I'm completely enchanted when he takes my hand and leads me into the living room. "I'm really good. I beat Dad all the time, and I'll probably beat you."

Chattering away, Gabe sets up my avatar and hands me the Wii controller. After explaining the basics to me, we begin the game.

Gabe clearly plays the Wii a lot because he gets strike after strike. He's a little ham too, because every time he does, he does a little dance in front of the TV and yells, "In your face, Mac."

We've only been playing for about twenty minutes when Matt comes out of his back office. I'm just getting ready to bowl when he says, "Poor form, Mac. I think you need to bend over a little more."

I shoot a smirk over my shoulder at him and say, "Behave yourself."

Chuckling, Matt sits down on the couch and watches his son totally beat my ass again. Gabe shrieks in glee, mocking my defeat at the hands of a child.

Laughing, I hand the controller back over to him. "You are just too good, Gabe. I'll never be able to beat you."

Turning to his dad, he says, "Want to play?"

Matt reaches out and tousles Gabe's hair. The look on his face is one of overwhelming love for his child, and it shoots a ping of joy through my heart. "Maybe later, buddy. Let's get ready to head out to Coney Island. Go get your shoes on."

Gabe leaps up and yells, "Hooray," before he takes off running to his room.

Matt turns to me and crooks his finger. "Get over here and give me a proper hello."

There's no room for hesitation. I willingly walk up to Matt and let him pull me down onto his lap. His lips find mine in one fluid move, and he's giving me a kiss that is possessive and deep.

It's also brief because that type of kissing usually leads to hands wandering and clothes shedding, and we, of course, cannot do that with Gabe here. He pulls back with a sigh. "So, what do you think of Gabe?"

Matt's words are full of pride.

"He's wonderful," I assure him, and then I ponder a moment. "He's you."

The light in Matt's eyes over my words shines bright. He knows his son is wonderful, and the fact I just said his son is just like him means that he is wonderful, too.

Gabe comes tearing back into the room and I start to get off Matt's lap, but he holds me tight. There's apparently no personal space to a seven-year-old because he runs to the couch and jumps on both Matt and me. "I need you to tie my shoes, Dad."

"Nope," Matt says. "You know how to do it."

"I forget how," he pouts.

"Well... I heard that in order to get into Coney Island, you have to prove you can tie your shoes. If you can't do it, we can't go."

Gabe looks at his dad, trying to determine if what he is saying is true. He's a smart kid though and not willing to risk rejection at Coney Island. He pushes away from Matt and me and starts tying his shoes.

Little stinker.

I look at Matt and giggle, and he just shrugs his shoulders. "All the negotiations skills I learned as a lawyer have been invaluable raising a child."

When Gabe finishes with his laces, he reaches over and grabs Matt's hand. "Come on, Dad. Let's go."

Matt and I stand up from the couch and start walking toward the door. He grabs his wallet and car keys off a table in the foyer.

"What do you want to do at Coney Island today?" Matt asks Gabe.

Gabe starts rattling off his agenda at about a hundred miles an hour. "I want to ride the Cyclone, play skeeball, eat hot dogs and cotton candy, and then go to the beach, and then we can ride the Cyclone again. I'll ride it once with you, and then Mac can ride it with me." He continues chattering, and I'm staring at him in wonder because it's amazing to me that a child can talk for that length of time and not even pause to take a breath.

Matt opens the door while my eyes are helplessly pinned to Gabe as he continues his speech. We start to follow Matt out but he comes to an abrupt stop, and I run into his back.

Looking up and around Matt's shoulder, I see a woman standing in the hallway. She was apparently getting ready to knock.

She's stunning. Pale blonde hair, deep blue eyes, and huge boobs. She's every man's wet dream.

For a brief moment, I think this is some woman that Matt is seeing behind my back. But then I immediately take in the way that Matt's shoulders stiffen and his jaw muscle starts popping. A sure sign that he is not a happy camper.

Then it becomes clear who this is.

Matt grits out, "Marissa… what are you doing here?"

Chapter Ten

So this is Matt's ex-wife. The one that screwed around on him. The one that left him with a bitter heart and made my work all that much harder.

The look she gives Matt chills my bones. It's calculating and vindictive. She pushes past Matt into the apartment, and I have to step back so she doesn't run me over. "I've had a change in plans, so I'm here to get Gabe."

Turning to me, she says, "And you are?"

Well, this is awkward. Do I stick my hand out and introduce myself? Before I can even think what to say, Gabe grabs ahold of Marissa's hand and says, "This is Mac, Mommy. She's daddy's friend."

Marissa's eyes roam up and down me briefly, and then they are dismissive. Turning to Matt, she says, "I don't appreciate you bringing your flavor of the week around our son."

Matt's eyes flash in anger, but his voice is completely calm. "Marissa... I'm not doing this with you. Not in front of Gabe. We're on our way out to Coney Island. I can bring him by your place later this evening."

"Sorry. That just won't work for me. I'm taking him now."

Gabe pipes up. "I want to go to Coney Island with Daddy."

Marissa hardly gives him a glance. "Not today, baby. We have other things to do."

"Marissa... don't make Gabe suffer because you want to get back at me."

She doesn't even bother to respond, but I see triumph in her eyes. Unbelievable. The bitch is punishing Gabe just to punish Matt.

I hate her. I literally hate her.

I am immensely uncomfortable witnessing this exchange, and I would love nothing more than to slink out of Matt's apartment right now. I consider it, but then Matt says, "Mac... would you mind taking

Gabe back to his room for a moment so I can have a few words with Marissa."

"Sure," I say softly. "Come on, Gabe."

Gabe looks from me, to his mom, to his dad. Matt nods at Gabe and says, "Go on, buddy. I'll work this out with Mom."

"Okay," Gabe says, and he grabs my hand to lead me back to his room.

"Marissa," I hear Matt plead softly. "Please don't do this. He's so excited about going to Coney Island."

I can't see Marissa's expression, but I can almost envision it. She's happy to have power and happy to have Matt beg her. I hear her response just before Gabe and I turn the corner to his room.

"Sorry, Matt. It's not your weekend for visitation, and it's my right to take him."

I close the door behind us, and I content myself to look at his collection of toys that he parades before me. I can no longer hear their conversation clearly and for that, I'm glad. It's painful hearing Matt have to beg on his son's behalf, probably knowing he'll never get anywhere with her.

After a few moments, Gabe's door opens and Matt stands there. He looks resigned, sad, and pissed off all at the same time.

"Hey, little man," he says quietly. "Let's get your stuff together. Mom has important stuff she needs to do, and you'll have to go with her."

Gabe immediately starts whining, not that I blame him at all. If I had to go with that bitch versus going to Coney Island, I'd whine too. "No, Daddy… I want to stay here with you."

My heart breaks… literally cracks right down the middle, particularly when I see the pain in Matt's eyes. Kneeling down, he pulls Gabe into a hug. "I know. I want you to stay here, too. But go with Mommy, and I promise that we'll go to Coney Island next weekend. Okay?"

Gabe grumbles a little but eventually nods his head. I watch while Matt packs his stuff up and leads Gabe back into the living room. Just before he leaves, he turns to me and hugs onto my leg. "Bye, Mac. See you next weekend."

I tell him goodbye while I stroke the top of his head, and then Matt leads him back into the living room. I wait a few moments until I hear the apartment door open and close, indicating Marissa is gone.

Seeking out Matt, I find him in the kitchen. He has both palms on the kitchen counter, and his head is hanging low.

"Are you okay?" I ask him hesitantly.

He raises his head, and his eyes are dark and bleak. His generous lips are now flattened in anger.

"No, I'm not fucking okay," he snarls, and his voice is filled with so much hatred and bitterness, I actually flinch. "How can I be okay after that?"

Clasping my hands in nervousness, I can only say, "I'm sorry."

He stares at me a long moment. He's appraising me, looking deep to find something. I'm not sure what he's seeking, but the desolate look in his eyes never lessens. Pushing away from the counter, he stalks up to me.

Slipping his hand into my hair and palming the back of my head, his voice is harsh and guttural. "Do you see, Mac?"

"See what?" I whisper.

"Do you see why I am the way I am?"

"Because of Marissa?"

"Yes... it's all because of her."

Matt just stares at me, his eyes flicking between mine. His face is hard and unyielding. Gone is the humor and easy sensibility. My stomach drops when I realize that Matt hasn't let go of his bitterness. But how could he... if he has to deal with that constantly from his ex-wife?

He may have opened up to me a bit, but when it boils down to it, he has his heart firmly protected.

Do I have the fortitude to break through those barriers? I think I might.

Bringing my hands up, I stroke his cheeks. Standing on my tiptoes, I bring my lips to his and press in. At first he doesn't respond, so I slip my tongue out and lick at his lips. With a slight groan, he opens up and my tongue plunges in.

I feel desperate, because I see that Matt has the potential to slip away from me. I have a whole new appreciation for the efforts he has been taking to give me the relationship I wanted. He has been majorly damaged, and this is painful for him. His risk to open up and let me in is far greater than I had ever imagined or gave him credit for. It would be so easy for him to give up, and I'm going to do everything in my power to make sure he doesn't.

"I need you," I murmur as I pull slightly away from the kiss to caress my lips along his neck.

He groans again, my words fueling his desire. His hands pull and tear at my clothes, and mine do the same to him. The desperation with which we are clawing to get at each other is different for both of us. I don't want to lose Matt, and I'm trying to get closer to him. Matt wants to forget what just happened with Marissa and lose himself in the haze of sex.

In a matter of seconds, Matt has me on the living room floor and he's driving into me. His entry is painful and pleasurable all at once, but my body quickly accepts him because it knows him. It knows he belongs.

Matt takes me roughly, which is not unknown to me. We've had plenty of hot, rough, and fast sex before. It's like the rush of a drug... or at least how I imagine it would be. If this is what he needs to purge Marissa's actions from his mind, then I'll give it to him.

Over and over again.

He drives me towards a blistering orgasm, and I'm still shuddering when he follows me with a quiet moan. My arms come around his back and pull him even tighter to me.

I wait for it...

For him to whisper my name in reverence like he always does.

But I'm met with nothing but silence.

AFFIRMATION

Volume 6

Sawyer Bennett

Legal Affairs
Vol. 6 - Affirmation
By Sawyer Bennett

All Rights Reserved.
Copyright © 2014 by Sawyer Bennett
Published by Big Dog Books

This book is a work of fiction. Names, characters, places and incidents either are products of the author's imagination or are used fictitiously. Any resemblance to actual events, locales or persons, living or dead, is entirely coincidental.

No part of this book can be reproduced in any form or by electronic or mechanical means including information storage and retrieval systems, without the express written permission of the author. The only exception is by a reviewer who may quote short excerpts in a review.

Chapter One

Things are off, and I can't quite put my finger on it.

Ever since Marissa showed up this past weekend and took Gabe, Matt has been a little withdrawn. When I ask him what's wrong, he gives me a bright smile and says 'nothing'. When I try to talk about something personal, he deflects and gets me turned around in another direction.

Some things are the same. For example, the sex is still nuclear and consistent. We can't get enough of each other and for that, I'm thankful. Still… I feel like I'm grasping onto Matt, like he's on the verge of slipping away, and that is causing me a lot of anxiety.

"That smells fantastic," Matt says as he comes up behind me while I stir the spaghetti sauce. He puts his hands on my hips and leans his chin on my shoulder to watch me cook. It's a simple gesture, but one that gives me hope that maybe things will be okay.

"Why don't you set the table? This will be done soon."

"Sure. Will Macy be joining us?"

I shake my head. "She's got a date, and by date, I mean she has a one-night stand."

Chuckling, Matt grabs a few plates and silverware to take to the table. "I thought I used that service a lot, but Macy takes the cake."

Turning to look at him, I try to keep the jealousy out of my voice. "Exactly how often were you using it before you met me?"

Setting the last fork down, he turns to gaze at me, with a knowing smile on his face. He walks up to me and holds my chin between his thumb and forefinger. Leaning down, he gives me a light kiss. "I used it a lot, Mac. But none of those one-night stands ever compared to you, and I don't miss it in the slightest."

And just like that, Matt has erased some of the uneasiness I had been feeling about our relationship.

After dinner, we both get comfy in my living

room. I have to review a deposition transcript, and Matt is watching ESPN's Sports Center. We sit beside each other companionably until I finish, which is indicated by the fact I throw the transcript on my coffee table and give a huge yawn.

Matt practically pounces on me. "About damn time you got done. I've been dying to fuck you."

Giggling, I wrap my warms around his neck as he kisses me like his life depends on it. "You could have had me at any time," I tell him when we come up for air.

"I was trying to be a gentleman," he says as he lifts me from the couch and carries me back to my bedroom. "But I'm not feeling so gentlemanly now. Think you can take it a little rough?"

I slide down the front of him when we reach my bed, feeling how hard he is already, and a thrill of excitement goes through me. "I can take anything you've got."

Eyes firing hot with desire, he pulls me back to him and crushes my mouth with his. It's carnal, possessive, and I love it. Just as he's pulling my shirt over my head, his phone starts ringing. The ringtone is Heart's Barracuda, and Matt tenses up when he hears it.

"Fuck," he says, stepping away from me and taking his phone out of his pocket.

Connecting the call, he holds it to his ear and snarls, "What do you want?"

I watch as he listens to, who I'm guessing is Marissa, on the other end. The ringtone sort of gave it away, but Matt's demeanor pretty much solidifies it. He listens for several minutes, his face getting even tighter. He even clenches one hand in a fist until the skin on his knuckles pales to white.

"Absolutely not," Matt says. "I won't agree to it."

He listens for a bit more, and I can practically hear him gritting his teeth. Then his face changes, softens slightly. His voice is warm and open. "Hey buddy. So what do you want to do this weekend?"

Again, Matt listens and his eyes close as if he's in pain, causing my heart to lurch for him.

A wounded smile graces Matt's lips, and he says quietly, "Okay, Gabe. Sure... I'll see you soon."

Another two seconds and, apparently, Marissa is back on the phone because Matt says, "You fucking bitch. Don't ever pit him against me like that again, or I will sue you for full custody."

Then he disconnects the phone and just stares at it.

Taking a step forward, I lay my hand on his arm. "What happened?"

Matt seems caught off guard and looks at me in surprise. Then his features smooth out, and he says,

"Nothing. Marissa's taking Gabe to Hershey Park this weekend."

"But it's your weekend. You were going to take him to Coney Island."

Matt gives a harsh laugh, and his voice is bitter. "Yeah... doesn't work that way with Marissa. Not when she bribes Gabe and then puts him on the phone to tell me how much he wants to go. I can't say no to him, and she knows it."

His body is radiating tension, and I feel the driving need to take it away. I step into him, wrapping my arms around his waist. Laying my cheek on his chest, I rub his back. Up and down, side to side, round circles. His heartbeat is galloping under my ear.

"Can you take her to court or something to get her to stop doing this?"

Another harsh laugh from Matt, but he doesn't answer me. Instead, he pulls my face up and starts kissing me. It's instantly deep and sensual, his tongue knowing immediately how to pull me into the game. I think briefly about pulling away and making Matt talk to me, but it's like he senses my thoughts.

He murmurs against my mouth, "No more talking, Mac. Just fucking, okay?"

His voice sounds pleading and needful, and it's not so much that he needs my body... he just needs to not think about Marissa and her evil ways. He wants to purge thoughts of her and what she does to him out of his memory.

While I really want to have a conversation about this with Matt, because I think he needs someone to vent to, I know that it is much easier to give into his physical needs right now.

I relinquish myself into the lust and passion that always flows hot between us. Within minutes, we are naked and he is sunk deep into my body.

CHAPTER Two

I unlock my apartment door and push my way inside, immediately depositing my briefcase on the floor as I kick off my shoes. I'm exhausted.

"What are you doing here?" Macy asks as she walks out of the kitchen, holding a glass of wine.

"I live here. Or did you forget?"

Macy turns around to head back into the kitchen, and I follow. "I didn't forget. It's just you're usually over at Matt's, or Matt is here with you. This is like the third night in a row you've been here... by yourself."

My shoulders sag under the pitiful reminder that

it is indeed the third night in a row that Matt has begged off spending with me. I'm sick with confusion over this.

"So what's the deal?" Macy asks as she pours me a glass of wine and hands it to me. She has something cooking in the oven, and it smells heavenly.

Sighing, I shrug my shoulders and lean against the counter. "I don't know. Last three nights he's apologized, said he has a ton of work to do, and kisses me on the forehead with a promise we'll get together soon."

Macy looks surprised and gives me a devilish grin. "I'm surprised Matt can go that long without banging you."

I grimace in return. "Well, he didn't really go that long. Right after he told me he couldn't come over tonight, he locked my door, pushed me up against the wall, and screwed the hell out of me in my office."

"Nice," Macy says, genuinely impressed.

"No!" I insist. "It's not nice. He's pulling away from me, Macy, and it's tearing me up. This is how he was before. Just wanting the sex and no intimacy. I've been feeling it ever since that weekend Marissa took Gabe away."

Not to be deterred, Macy sort of nudges my shoulder with hers. "But you got to admit... pretty hot screwing you right there in your office, right?"

Rolling my eyes, I take a deeper sip of wine. "Yes, that's hot, and I'm the first to admit I like that stuff. But I'm afraid that we're heading back to where that is all there is between us."

I finally get a sympathetic look from Macy. "Have you talked to him about it?"

I snort hard and take a gulp of wine. Waving my glass, I say, "Talk to Matt? Are you kidding? Like an actual conversation? Any time I try, he sidetracks me with sex. He's deflecting me by preying on my ovaries."

"Maybe he just needs a little time. I mean, this stuff with his ex-bitch just happened. Don't get all upset now when he may snap out of it in a few days."

I empty my glass of wine and pour another. Perhaps she's right. Maybe Matt's just having a few rough days, and I need to have some patience with him. It's hard though, because although it was never brought up again between us, I certainly have not forgot the night I was drunk and confessed I loved him. Yes, I remembered that clearly the next day, just as I remembered he didn't say the words back.

So I want to have some patience with him, and I want to help him work through his woes, but the feeling is made even more desperate by the fact that I'm in love with him and the thought of losing him is crushing.

And worse yet, Matt is just a portion of my woes.

At the beginning of the week, Matt introduced Kylie Wynn to the firm, the newest attorney on our legal team. She wasn't an employee of Connover and Crown, but Matt was contracting with her to help work the appellate case on the Pearson trial that he had lost a few weeks ago.

While Matt is fully capable of handling the appeal on his own, his trial load over the next several months is insane, so he wants extra help to work the case.

After Matt introduced Kylie to the firm, he called her and me into his office to discuss the appeal.

Let me just say, I hated Kylie from the minute she opened her mouth, and for a variety of reasons.

First, she's one of those lawyers that thinks her shit don't stink. Yes, I know that is bad grammar, but it punctuates my feelings rather well. She is condescending, rude, and arrogant, except with Matt, of course. She talked to me like I was a third grader, and spent an inordinate amount of time blowing rainbows up Matt's ass.

Second, and this is not being said with any hint of partiality or bias, but she has the hots for Matt. I can tell, and worse yet, I know Matt can tell. Oh, some of her signs are subtle, such as licking her lips and bending forward to expose cleavage.

Other signs are not so subtle, like the way she

sits in a chair and crosses her legs just so her skirt slides up and exposes the bottom of her thigh-high stocking. To Matt's credit, his eyes didn't stray down, but then she made a big production of pulling her skirt down in the hopes of garnering his attention. It was at this precise moment that I had seen enough and clumsily happened to knock my glass of water over on the table.

Kylie wasn't so much interested then in Matt looking at her legs, but was more concerned with saving her Ferragamo briefcase that was close to getting waterlogged.

The thing that upsets me the most, and hence why I intend on chugging this second glass of wine, is that Matt doesn't seem overly put off by her behavior. Again, he hasn't engaged with her, but he doesn't shun her the way he did with Lorraine. For example, Kylie had laid her hand on Matt's arm when she was making a point, and rather than pull his arm back the way he used to do with Lorraine, he left it there… let her touch him and didn't even appear to want to stop it.

To cap it all off, Kylie made it clear that I was going to be her little bitch of a gopher on this case, and Matt did nothing to dispel that notion. As our meeting was wrapping up, Kylie handed me the file and said, "McKayla, I'll need you to make me one copy of the file and also scan a copy, so I can have the digital version as well."

I glanced at Matt, and he confirmed my worst suspicion. I was to do as Kylie asked because she was the big dog when it came to appellate matters.

I suppose the only saving grace to this week was that Matt did indeed give me two orgasms as he screwed my brains out against the wall of my office. When he was zipping himself up, I tried to bring up Kylie so that he could clarify the nature of our working relationship, but he brushed me off, telling me to "work it out" with her myself.

"Come on, Macy," I tell her as I grab the bottle of wine. "We're getting drunk tonight, and then we're going to talk shit about Matt and his new girlfriend, Kylie."

"Matt has a new girlfriend?" Macy asks, bewildered.

"Well… no, but she thinks she might be. I want to kill her. You can help me plot."

"Right on," Macy says. "I'm all in."

CHAPTER Three

When I get into work the next morning, sporting the mother of all hangover headaches, my mood plummets even further when I see the note on my desk. It's from Kylie, and it says, "Meet me in my office to discuss Pearson as soon as you get in."

Here's what sucks about Kylie.

She's just a contract attorney, here just to work on a single case for the firm, yet she gets one of the bigger offices with a window. Fine, I can deal with that, I suppose.

But that's not the only perk to being on contract

for a limited time. The thing that chaps my ass the most is that there are no rules or barriers between Kylie and Matt if they wanted to have a relationship. And I'm not saying that Matt wants to, but I've seen enough of Kylie to know that she's interested. She doesn't have the whole "he's my boss" sort of thing stopping her the way it should have stopped me.

Making my way to Kylie's office, I grab the copy of the Pearson file I had made for her and a legal pad to take notes on. Her door is open, and she's sitting behind her desk in a cherry red power suit. Her chocolate hair is pulled into a neat chignon, her makeup is flawless, and her nails are painted the same cherry red as her suit.

"McKayla, thanks for coming by. I wanted to get a head start on Pearson," she says as she stands up from the desk. When she walks around, I see the skirt is really short and she's wearing four-inch stiletto heels that are better designed as hooker ware than for a law firm.

Motioning me to take a seat at her small worktable, she says, "I brought you in a latte from Starbucks."

I stare at her open-mouthed for just a moment, and she seems to be giving me a genuine smile. Maybe she wasn't going to be so hard to work with.

"Thanks, Kylie. I really appreciate that."

I pick the cup up and take an appreciative sip, just as Kylie says, "Good. I took a chance you'd like that. I mean... you don't look like a girl that really cares if the calories go to her hips."

It's a good thing I was only taking a tiny sip of the scalding hot beverage. Otherwise, I may have sucked it down my windpipe over her completely catty remark. Instead, I just stare at her in shock, but she doesn't pay me any attention. She just sits at the table and starts flipping through the file.

I take my seat next to her and we work for about twenty minutes, getting familiar with the issues and formulating an outline for our game plan. I'm caught up in reading the jury instructions that had been given at trial when Kylie says, "McKayla... can I ask you something personal?"

My stomach sort of pitches sideways because I know—just know without a doubt—that she's getting ready to ask me about Matt.

I try to sound sincere when I say, "Sure."

She leans in toward me like she's afraid we'll be overheard, which doesn't seem plausible since we are in her office with the door closed. "I wanted to ask you about Matt. I mean, you've been working closely with him... but is he seeing anyone?"

What to do? What to do?

The truth? Yes, Kylie... He's seeing me, and I will cut you if you get near him.

A lie? Yes, Kylie... he's seeing someone... His name is Mark, and they make a really cute couple.

A semi-truth? Yes, Kylie... I heard he's seeing someone, and it seems to be fairly serious.

Instead, I opt for none of those options, because the last thing I want her thinking is that I know Matt personally enough to know about his love life.

"I'm sorry," I tell her. "I just don't know. He's a pretty private person."

Kylie nods in understanding. "Of course, you're just an associate after all. Just thought I'd try because maybe you had heard some gossip. No matter... I'll just figure it out myself."

And with that, she goes right back to working as if she never just told me that she has Matt in her sights. I sit there and stew over this, knowing that I should probably give Matt some type of warning.

After about an hour, Matt knocks on the door and Kylie makes a big deal about inviting him in. She lays her hand on his arm again while they talk, and I don't fail to notice Matt doesn't pull away. He is so going to get a piece of my mind over that.

I try to ignore them, intent on focusing on my work, but then Matt interrupts my thoughts. "Mac, can I see you in my office? I have a few things to go over with you on the Jackson case."

"Sure thing," I tell him as I gather up my stuff.

"Want to meet up later, Kylie?"

She gives me a dim smile and nods. "Tomorrow morning again—eight AM sharp. You're in charge of coffee next time. I like mine black."

With that, Kylie turns her back on me, dismissing me from her mind. I turn to look at Matt, and he actually has a smirk on his face, clearly enjoying our interplay. Glaring as hard as I can, I push my way past him. I reach his office before he does and head on in.

He's hot on my heels and when he closes the door, he steps up close, wrapping his arms around my waist. "I missed you last night," he rumbles near my ear, just before giving my earlobe a little bite.

The touch sends a jolt of lust through my body, and I can't help the little moan that comes out of my mouth.

That is all the encouragement Matt needs. His hands go down to the sides of my skirt and he starts pulling the material up, his knuckles grazing my skin. When the cool air hits my ass, I come to my senses and pull away.

"Wait... what are you doing?"

"Trying to get under your skirt," he says with a lecherous smile as he advances toward me.

Holding my palms out, I say, "Hold it, mister. We can't just keep having sex in your law firm. We're going to get caught."

His grin gets even wider as his hand goes behind my head to pull me closer. "That makes it all the more exciting, don't you think?"

His other hand palms my breast, softly squeezing it. My breath hitches and I'm about ready to capitulate, but then common sense takes hold again.

I step firmly out of his reach and give him a soft smile. "Sorry, baby... no can do. You'll just have to wait."

His eyes are dark and disappointed when he looks at me, but then he gives me a small smile and a nod of resignation. Turning from me, he says, "No worries. I have a meeting I need to get ready for anyway."

Matt's voice is a little aloof and a touch icy. It makes me uneasy. "Are you mad at me because I said 'no'?"

Turning his head to look at me, I'm relieved to see surprise on his face. "God, no. You can say no any time you want to me. I'm a little disappointed, but trust me... I'll get over it and try again with you."

The anxiety in my chest eases up a little, and I give him a smile before heading back to my office.

It's not until I sit back down at my desk that I realize I forgot to tell Matt about Kylie and her interest in him. Oh, well... I could tell him tonight when we get together.

CHAPTER Four

The yawn that overtakes me is a doozy and it's so deep and drawn out, I almost pass out from lack of oxygen. I glance over at the clock that sits on my desk and see it's close to seven PM. It's now the third day in a row that Matt has not meandered down to my office and tried to make plans to see me.

Not that he's the only one that has to do so, it's just... I went to him the last two nights and asked him if he wanted to do something, to which he said he couldn't because he was swamped with work.

So, do I just go ahead and go home, or do I make my way over to his office yet again to probably get shot down... yet again?

It's with a heavy heart that I decide to be a glutton for punishment, and I walk down to Matt's kingdom. His door is open. As I step inside, I see him putting his suit jacket on and picking up his briefcase as if he's ready to leave. Joy leaps in my heart that he's not going to work late tonight, so that I can finally have some alone time with him.

When he looks up and sees me standing there, he says, "Hey you... I was just getting ready to come down to your office, so it looks like you saved me a trip."

I shoot him a radiant grin and then immediately start thinking of how quickly I can get him naked once we step foot in either his apartment or mine. I hope my voice doesn't sound too salacious when I ask, "So, what do you want to do tonight?"

I expect Matt's eyes to start a slow burn and fill with lustful promise, but instead he blinks at me and gets a sheepish look on his face. "Um... actually, I was on my way down to your office to tell you that I'm going out with some of the guys to get some drinks."

Yes, it's like a wall of cold water hits me, almost knocking the breath out of me. But I'm Mac Dawson, and I have more fortitude than that. "Oh... okay. Well, do you want to come over to my place after?"

Matt's face turns slightly red, and his head hangs down. "I'm sorry, Mac... but this is kind of one of those nights that I'll probably be out all night with the boys."

"The boys?" I ask blankly.

"The boys. You know, Rob, Mike, and Joey from litigation, and Sam in estates. And I think that new guy... Bill's paralegal is going. The boys."

"But you never go out with the boys," I say lamely.

"Sure I do," he says with confidence.

"No, Matt... you don't. You even told me once that you couldn't stand being around a bunch of drunk guys acting like morons."

I can see the moment that Matt remembers making that statement to me, and he has the grace to look embarrassed. But just like with anyone who gets called on the carpet, he becomes a little defensive. "Look, Mac... if you don't want me to go, I won't."

The tone of his voice is really saying, I feel henpecked to death, and I'll really be pissed if you don't let me go out with the boys.

With a sigh, I tell him, "It's not that I don't want you to go. I do want you to go out and have fun. It's just... I haven't seen you in a while, and I miss you is all."

Giving me a lazy smile, Matt walks up and kisses

me. It's not deep, it's not seductive, but it is sweet and caring. "I know," is all he says, and then he picks up his briefcase.

What the fuck? I get an "I know"? There should have been something else. Maybe an, "I miss you, too," or even a half-assed attempt for him to cop a feel. But just an "I know," and he's walking out?

My eyes narrow in suspicion at him just as he reaches for his doorknob. "Are you doing this to punish me for not having sex with you today in your office?"

Matt turns slowly around to look at me. His face is impassive. "Absolutely not."

"You're sure?" I ask as I saunter toward him. "Because you looked a little peeved at me when I said no."

Smirking at me, Matt reaches out and tugs on a lock of my hair. Rubbing it between his fingers for a moment, he finally looks at me. "Don't fool yourself, Mac. If I really wanted to, I could have gotten you to change your mind today. So you see… there's nothing to be mad about."

Damn him and his confidence and yeah, his arrogance. He knows good and well I would have capitulated with a few more soft touches and hot words, and I know it, too. So it appears that he's not punishing me.

Which means that he would rather go get drunk with a bunch of guys than come home with me and attempt to break my headboard. The thought makes me feel utterly dejected and if my self-esteem had balls, they just took a swift kick there.

I'm not sure what expression my face is wearing because something softens in Matt's eyes. His hand comes up to tuck under my chin, and his thumb strokes my lower lip. "I promise… tomorrow you and I will do something special, okay?"

Blinking hard so the tears that have been threatening to expose me for a weak, puny, sissy girl don't fall, I nod. He leans in and gives me a light kiss, and then he's gone.

CHAPTER Five

As scheduled, I show up the next morning to Kylie's office with a cup of black coffee for her and another latte for me. When she calls me into her office, I find her rooting around her in her purse. She looks up and grimaces. "Oh, McKayla. Do you have an aspirin or something? I have a raging headache."

Actually, I do as I keep a supply in my briefcase because hello... nothing causes a headache like the law. Reaching in, I grab two and hand them to her along with her coffee.

She tosses them back, swigs the coffee, and

swallows with a groan. "Thank you."

"Sure. Are you okay, though? You look a little pale. Maybe you should go home."

Kylie gives me an indulgent smile. "A headache is no reason to leave work. Hell, I'd still work if I had the raging flu. Sick days are for pussies."

Oh-kay.

So she's a hard-core worker. Big fucking deal.

"Besides," she continues on, "it's my own damn fault. I shouldn't have drunk so much last night."

Sitting down at her table, I pull my file out of my briefcase and start pulling out the items I need to go over with her. I could really care less if she's a raging alcoholic or what, but she seems intent on continuing to talk.

"You would think I'd learn my lesson, right? I mean, I went out with a bunch of friends the night before that and got toasted. I was so miserable. But I guess the lure of Matt was just too much to pass up."

I had only been half listening to her but at the mention of Matt's name, I went on hyper alert. Every cell in my body sort of woke up and turned their antennas toward Kylie.

"Lure of Matt?" I ask, trying to sound like I'm only slightly interested when in truth, I want to water board the information out of her.

She gives me a tinkling laugh, and then grimaces

because it apparently hurts her head. "Yeah, I went out with him and a bunch of the other lawyers here last night. We closed the bar down. But now I'm paying for it."

Kylie actually goes on and says something more about her night out, but I don't hear a word. That's because a strange sort of buzzing has just filled my head. It gets louder and louder, until I can't hear a thing that Kylie is saying at all. All I can see is her mouth moving.

It occurs to me that this incessant buzzing sound is actually the blood that is pounding through my veins, and the tingling over my skin means that I am so angry right now that I may be on the verge of stroking out.

I mumble something to Kylie… I'm not sure exactly what I told her, but she nods at me, so I get up from the table and practically stumble out of her office.

Once outside, I lean back against the wall and try for some deep breathing exercises. I must calm myself down because otherwise, I am in very serious jeopardy of doing severe bodily harm to Matt.

The motherfucker told me it was a guy's night out, which is why I assumed I wasn't invited, and yet, he invited Kylie.

Motherfucker!

While I am brimming with anger, I'm also starting to notice a deep sadness start to well up inside of me because I knew something had been wrong for several days.

It went back to the day Marissa came to Matt's apartment to get Gabe. He has not been the same since. I've sensed the change in him, but I couldn't quite put a name to what was going on. But now I see it just as clear as day.

Matt is trying to sabotage our relationship.

Now, whether he's doing it intentionally because he doesn't want to be with me, or he's doing it subconsciously because he is still ruled and commanded by his bitter feelings of betrayal and hurt, I just don't know.

But I can tell you... I'm going to find out right now.

By the time I make it down to Matt's office, the buzzing in my head has waned and the only outward sign of my distress is the slight shake to my hand as I knock on his door. He calls softly for me to enter and, when I walk in, I can see that he's meeting with another attorney. It's Rob Something-or-Other from litigation... one of his drinking buddies from last night from what I remember Matt saying.

They were both clearly laughing about something when I walked in, both of them looking assured and relaxed.

"I need to talk to you," I manage to get out with a level voice while I look at Matt.

His smile stays in place even as his tone dismisses me. "Can this wait until later? Rob and I were just in the middle of something."

I close my eyes briefly and take in two deep breaths.

I will not kill him. I will not kill him.

Opening my eyes back up, I say, "I'm sorry. It's urgent."

Then I turn to Rob and say, "I'm sorry, Rob. I wouldn't ask if it weren't really important."

Rob stands with ease and says, "No problem. I'll catch you later, Matt."

Matt just nods his head toward Rob briefly and watches him walk out the door. As soon as we're alone, his gaze turns to me. I'm pleased to see he doesn't have such a smug look on his face now.

"What's wrong?" he asks with some hesitation. Apparently, whatever is on my face is giving him forewarning that this will not be a pleasant conversation.

His eyes are warm and shining like a tumbler of whiskey. His face is classically beautiful, and never fails to give me pause when I stare at it. But right now... right now, I'm seeing a whole lot of ugly when it comes to Matt.

I walk up to his desk, put my palms on the edge so they aren't shaking as badly, and say, "I want to know why you lied to me last night."

CHAPTER Six

Matt swallows hard once, but his eyes give away nothing. I don't see guilt, remorse, or even annoyance from my statement. "How exactly do you think I lied?"

No sense in beating around the bush. "You told me you were going out with the boys last night, and I get that. It's good to have a boy's night out, even if it did hurt my feelings a little that you wouldn't rather be with me. Still... I let it go. Except I come in this morning to find out that your boy's night wasn't such a boy's night after all. It appears you invited Kylie to go with you and from what I can tell, she doesn't have a dick swinging between her legs."

My last words are bordering on the shrill side as my anger threatens to overwhelm me again. I expect Matt to come raging at me with a fight. I can almost feel the tension vibrating off him.

Instead, he shows immense calm when he says, "I didn't invite her. One of the other guys did."

I knew he was going to say that. I have no clue if it's true or not because I didn't bother to ask Kylie the details. But it doesn't matter. "Then how come you didn't invite me once you realized she was coming? Once you realized it wasn't just a 'boy's night out'?"

Now Matt looks a little uncomfortable and I know, without a doubt, that he had in fact considered it, but for some reason, decided against it. "I couldn't invite you, Mac. People can't know we're together."

"Bullshit," I seethe. "I've been in your presence plenty of times around other members of this firm, and we both could have had fun last night without ever giving anything away. But the truth of the matter is—you just didn't want me there. You wanted space from me, and I want to know why."

"Mac," he says in a gentle voice, trying to talk my anger down. "It's not a big deal—"

"Tell me the truth," I beg.

"You're making this—"

"TELL. ME," I yell at him across the desk as I

slap my hands down.

"Calm down," he hisses at me. "Do you want everyone to know about us?"

My voice quiets, and it's so very sad when I say, "Know what, Matt? What is there exactly to know?"

Matt leans back in his chair with a heavy sigh, and I can see resignation fill his face. "I don't know what to tell you, Mac. I've been trying. I really have. But lately... it just seems like a lot of work."

"I seem like a lot of work?" I ask disbelieving. "You mean... it's a real chore for you to have to get it up for me?"

I know that's a ridiculous accusation but I'm feeling so hurt and attacked right now, I can't help myself.

"NO! That's not what I'm saying. I'm insanely attracted to you. You have to know that."

"Then why is it work?"

"Because... because you wanted more than just sex, and I tried to give it to you. But lately... it just seems too hard. Ever since..."

He trails off and doesn't finish his sentence, but I know what he was going to say. Because I had already thought the same thing. "You mean ever since Marissa came over to your apartment that day. That was the day she reminded you that you've been screwed over and all women must therefore be the same as her. Thus, none of us are good enough to get the great Matthew Fucking Connover's full attention. I mean, if we're lucky girls... he'll fuck us and fuck us good, but he'll never let us into his heart. No woman is apparently good enough to warrant that type of attention from you, right? Because poor little Matt had his feelings hurt, and now he wants to wallow in misery. Boo fucking hoo, Matt. Boo fucking hoo."

I finish my little rant and my chest is heaving, but apparently, I did a good job of pissing Matt off because now he stands up on the opposite side of his desk and leans over to snarl at me. "Don't you think you may be trivializing what I've been through just a bit? This isn't easy on me, you know."

I'm not sure if he's trying to get sympathy or trying to justify his actions, but neither course matters to me very much. I'm seeing clearly now that Matt is comfortable with the way things are in his life. He clearly only craves physicality and could do without emotional intimacy. So be it. I know I need more than that, and I'm not going to waste another minute trying to make him into something he has no desire to be.

Spinning away from him, I start to walk out, but then a thought strikes me. Turning back around, I decide to hit him hard with something I had been dying to say for weeks.

"Cal didn't initiate sex with Marissa."

Matt's eyebrows shoot straight up, and then his face goes red, his eyes stark. "I don't want to hear this."

I'm not about to shut up. "He was drunk at her party. I understand you were out of state and your plane got delayed, so you couldn't make it in. Marissa offered him the guest room, and he accepted."

"Enough, Mac," he says, his voice getting louder as he steps around the desk toward me.

"He was really, really drunk... on the verge of passing out. In fact, he thinks he did pass out for a little bit, but when he came too—"

"Get the fuck out," Matt yells at me. "I don't want to hear this."

I sidestep around the other side of his desk to buy myself time. "Tough titties, you chicken shit pansy. You're going to listen. Cal sort of woke up, and Marissa was in bed with him... giving him a blow job. He tried to push her off at first, but he admits... he didn't try hard. He was drunk and didn't have much control. She climbed on top of him, Matt. He let it happen, for a while. Then he came to his senses a bit and stopped it. I mean, the act had still been done... but he stopped it."

I expect Matt to yell at me again or advance on me further, but he just closes his eyes as if he's in pain and his head hangs down low. I keep going before he tries to stop me again.

"If you're honest with yourself, Matt, you know it's true. He didn't make the move. Otherwise, why would he have been the one to confess it to you? He came to you to let you know, and you never even gave him a chance to explain. You beat the crap out of him and kicked him out of your life, without even giving him a chance."

Matt turns away from me, walking back behind his desk. I decide to let him hear the last of my mind, and then it's over.

"I'm not justifying what he did, Matt. Cal doesn't try to do that either. He was wrong, and he knows it. But he did not instigate it and, although he was weak at first, he did stop it. But you already know that's true, because I understand Marissa wasn't stingy with her charms."

Out of breath and out of stamina, I watch Matt as he stares out the window over downtown Manhattan. His shoulders are hunched, and he looks defeated.

I turn and walk to the door, but before I leave, I swing back around. "I only told you this, Matt, because your pain and bitterness are holding you back. I only wanted to show you that it might be a little easier to forgive Cal than you originally thought.

Carrying that bitterness is not good. It's already turned you into someone that is destined to lead a lonely life, because you can't let it go. That's fine... that's your choice. But remember this... you teach Gabe by example. What is he learning from watching you? What are you teaching him about love and forgiveness?"

Matt doesn't respond. He just stares out the window, and it's clear he has nothing to say. Unfortunately, neither do I. I said my piece, and it's time to move on.

Opening the door, I walk out, hoping that Macy is at home with a huge carton of ice cream for me. I'm feeling a massive, crying meltdown coming on.

CHAPTER Seven

I'm slogging through every workday at Connover and Crown, and it's getting harder and harder to get through it because I'm depressed. I watch the clock constantly, waiting for it to be 5:30 PM so I can go home. I don't work late at the office anymore, preferring to work from home instead.

Anything to avoid seeing Matt.

It's been a week since we broke up. This past weekend was brutal. I spent countless hours obsessing over whether I did the right thing, or if I should have given Matt more time and patience. Now I obsess over whether I have already been replaced by another numerical match through One Night Only. I pull my phone out time and again with the intent to call him, or even to send a short text, just to see how he's doing.

But my common sense always prevails. I'm no dummy, and I'm not one to keep attempting the futile. My gut tells me that Matt doesn't have it in him for anything further, and it's time for me to move on.

The only way I know this is affecting Matt is because I'm getting daily ratings from Bea. She always greets me each morning with a Matt Report, and he hasn't dropped below a ten since we parted ways. I know this should give me some comfort, but it doesn't. Matt's not missing me. He's just missing the convenient and stellar sex. I've heard lack of those things will make men grumpy.

Fortuitously, Matt had been out of the office a great deal this week with court hearings, and I didn't really need his help on any of my stuff. We both were doing a great job of avoiding the other, and I was starting to believe that this might actually be workable. I'm sure with time, my hurt feelings and his surliness would just naturally ease, and then maybe we could have at least a polite working relationship. I mean, I might have some major issues with Matt, but I really love the type of work I'm doing for him.

Today, however, Matt makes it clear to me that

there's no room for a polite working relationship between the two of us. There is an email waiting for me as soon as I get in. It reads:

Mac,

In an effort to help with the burgeoning increase in complex business cases, you are being transferred into that division under the general supervision of Bill Crown. Obviously, you will still work on the Jackson case since the clients are attached to you, but John Casting will act as your co-counsel and immediate supervisor. You can direct any and all questions to him. Finally, with the addition of Kylie Wynn to the Pearson appeal, I will not need your help on that case further.

I wish you the best of luck with these new endeavors, and I'm sure you'll be a successful member of the complex business litigation team.

Sincerely,
Matthew Connover

Is he fucking kidding me?

Is he mother fucking kidding me?

He sends me a formal email telling me that I'm no longer going to be doing injury litigation, which is what I love doing? He's transferring me to the hell of business law? And more than that, he "wishes me the best of luck"?

What a fucking asshole coward.

I wait for the anger to well up further and overtake me, but it never gets above a low simmer. In fact, I feel sort of a cool calmness. I suppose the fact I have been telling myself over and over again that there is no hope of a relationship with Matt has led me to believe, deep down inside, that it would be impossible to go backward to just an employer/employee relationship.

There is no second-guessing, and I don't have even an ounce of doubt over my next actions.

I pull up a blank Word document, and I start typing.

When I'm finished, I print it, sign it, and put it in an envelope. I handwrite the words "Matthew Connover" and place it in my outbox. A gopher boy comes around several times a day and takes all the stuff from the attorneys' outboxes and distributes it. Matt will get my notice sometime soon, but I don't give it another thought.

Instead, I pick up the phone and call Cal. He knows Matt and I broke up, and we've talked a few times. He's been a very good friend to me and provided me with an open ear. He's not been judgmental, and he's been strangely quiet as to taking my side over Matt's or vice versa. I invite him for lunch the following day, and we make plans to meet in the cafeteria that's in our building.

I lose myself in the Jackson case, writing up a detailed summary memorandum of it so I can give it to Cal. His help is going to be instrumental to me.

The details of the memorandum are so engrossing that I don't even realize there is someone standing in my office doorway until he clears his throat.

It's Matt, and he's holding my letter of resignation in his hand.

Without invitation, he walks in, closes the door, and takes a seat. He throws the envelope on my desk. "What the hell is this?"

"Come on, Matt. You know what it is." My voice is gentle, without harshness or even bitter feelings. It doesn't mean those feelings aren't there, but I'm choosing not to bring them into this. I want to keep this professional.

"You're resigning?" he asks, as if he can't believe what my letter says.

"Yes. I'll give you two weeks' notice or, if you want me to leave immediately, I'll do that. I'm taking the Jackson case with me though, so please don't think about fighting me on that. My clients won't stay here if I'm not involved."

Matt looks at me with exasperation and waves an impatient hand at me. "I don't give a fuck if you take that case. I just can't believe you'd quit. I mean... I moved you out of my section so you wouldn't have to deal with me. I thought it would give you want you wanted."

Cocking my head, I try to gauge what Matt is really feeling. He looks agitated and nervous. He looks confused... lost. I'm not sure what it means, but none of it changes my decision to leave.

"I'm sorry. I appreciate you trying to make my work environment easier. It's just... it's just too hard for me to be here. Too many memories. Some right in this office," I say with a little smile, and I'm surprised when Matt even smiles a little over my reference to the times we'd gotten down and dirty in here.

"There's nothing I can do to change your mind?" he asks. His eyes peer hard into mine, trying to determine if there is a loophole he can work his way inside of.

If he could really read my thoughts, he'd see that my heart is screaming, Yes. You can tell me you've made a huge mistake—that you miss me, love me, and you'll die without me.

But that's too much wishful thinking. So I say, "I'm sorry. This is for the best."

He stares at me for a long moment. I can practically see the wheels and cogs spinning in his brain. But then I see the moment when resignation takes over his face, and he accepts what I say. "All right then. I'll accept your resignation, and I'll take the two weeks' notice. That's very professional of you to offer that. Since you'll only be here two more weeks, obviously I won't be transferring you over to Bill. You can help me wind up some stuff."

"Okay," I tell him, not sure if I'm relieved or sad that he didn't beg me to stay. "Sounds like a game plan."

Chapter Eight

"You resigned?" Cal asks with astonishment as we move through the cafeteria line. He pulls a turkey sub onto his tray, and I make a grab for one of the last Caesar salads left.

"Yup," I tell him, also grabbing a cupcake. I think I'm entitled since I'm eating rabbit food for lunch.

When we get to the cash register I open my wallet, but Cal beats me to it by handing his credit card over to the cashier.

"Hey," I say in exasperation. "I'm supposed to be buying. I invited you."

Cal glares at me, and I close my wallet. "I'm buying because you're getting ready to be a poor, unemployed lawyer. You need to be saving your money."

We take our food and easily find an empty table. The lunch rush is starting to wane, but that's because we didn't get here until about 1:30 PM because Cal was running late. The crowded nature of this cafeteria is one of the reasons I try to avoid it. Yes, it's super convenient having it in our building, but I hate having to battle for a table.

We sit down, and I pull my cupcake toward me. I love eating my dessert first, although, sometimes I feel self-conscious about it. I don't feel that way with Cal, which is again a testament to what a good friend he's become to me.

"I can't believe you just quit," he mutters. "You know the job market sucks out there for attorneys right now."

"I know. But I have an idea."

Raising his eyebrows at me, Cal takes a bite of his sub and waits for me to explain.

Licking a chunk of frosting off my finger, I say, "I'm going to open my own firm. And I want you to be my partner."

Cal pauses chewing and just stares at me. I hold his stare, so he knows I'm not kidding. He quickly swallows his food and wipes his mouth. Pushing his sandwich aside, he leans across the table toward me. "Are you serious?"

Okay, at least his tone isn't mocking me but he is in disbelief, so I need to convince him. "Yes. My mom was well insured when she died. I'm willing to put some of that money into opening up my own firm. And you are always telling me how you want to switch from doing defense work to plaintiff's work. So, now is your chance. Plus, I have a really huge case, and I need help with it. If we win it, it will be worth millions. And if we lose it... well, I'll need someone's shoulder to cry on."

Cal takes a deep breath and leans back in his chair, his lunch completely forgotten. "Let's say I even entertain this idea. When would you want to do this?"

"In two weeks... I'm ready to start as soon as I leave Connover and Crown."

"Jesus Christ," Cal mutters, scrubbing his hand through his hair. "This case you're talking about... tell me about it."

I do one even better. I hand over the typed memorandum and eat my cupcake while he reads it. When he's done, he looks up. "Well, the good news is, if I were to help you on this, at least my firm doesn't represent this particular insurance company so there would be no conflict of interest for me to be involved in this case."

Laying the memorandum down, he reaches over and picks his sub back up. "There's a lot to consider. I mean, what type of firm would we have, where would we locate it, what do we need to do to go about setting it up? I mean... we need bank accounts, office space, equipment..."

Reaching down into my briefcase, I calmly hand over a thick document that I stayed up all night working on. The cover says, "Business Plan, Carson and Dawson, LLC".

Cal glances down at it, and his eyes widen in disbelief. "You got to be kidding me. When did you do this?"

Shrugging my shoulders, I say, "It's just a little something I whipped up last night."

Giving a huge bark of laughter, Cal sets his sub back down again and picks up the business plan. He starts reading it and, because it will take a while, I go ahead and get to work on my salad.

I amuse myself by people watching, but amusement turns to sadness when I see Matt walk in... with Kylie Wynn right behind him. She's talking animatedly toward him, and yup... there goes the classic laying of her hand on his arm. Apparently, that move never gets old for her.

After they pay for their meals, which I take a small measure of glee in noting that they paid separately, I watch as Matt scans the room, looking for an open table. His eyes pass over Cal and me, not giving much of a glance since our table isn't empty.

But then his eyes snap back to me, and our gazes lock.

We stare at each other a moment and, for just a brief time, it's like nothing bad ever happened between us. There is still a palpable connection, and our eyes hold all of those secrets. But then Matt's gaze flicks over to Cal, and his face hardens a tiny bit.

I expect Matt to try to find a table as far away from us as he can, but he surprises me when he walks over to us. When he's only a few feet away, I kick Cal under the table. He looks at me, and I nod over his shoulder so he knows someone is approaching.

Cal turns slightly and sees Matt and Kylie.

"Matt," Cal says with a nod of his head.

Matt is ever polite, because he has to be since he and Cal deal with each other in the professional world. Matt nods back and introduces Kylie. While Cal makes small talk with Kylie for a few moments, I see Matt's eyes glance down at the business plan I had just handed Cal. He sees the words Carson and Dawson, LLC clear as day. I watch his face carefully so I can gauge how this will affect him. I mean, it's truly none of his business, but I imagine this would piss him off royally.

He does nothing more than bring his eyes up to mine though. They look sad for just a flash, and then he gives me a small smile.

I'm not sure if that is approval or just general acceptance, but he didn't react the way I expected him to.

After some quick goodbyes, Matt and Kylie seek out their own table and Cal and I return to talking about logistics.

CHAPTER *Nine*

Matt and I are flying back to New York from Atlanta. He had me, once again, attend some depositions with him so I could take notes, while he meticulously picked apart witness after witness. He sprung this trip on me at the beginning of the week, telling me three of the last four days of my employment would be spent with him in the Peach State on a medical malpractice case.

We just finished a long day of depositions and made it to the airport with a little bit of time to spare before we boarded the eight PM flight into JFK.

I'm not angry to be here. In fact, it gave me

another few days to observe the legal brilliance of Matthew Connover. And yes, I got to observe the hotness of him, too, which is always nice, although it made me a little nostalgic. Just looking at Matt in a custom-made, tailored suit was worth the trip.

While leaving his firm is truly the best decision for my own peace of mind, I am going to miss being able to see his gorgeous face.

And that magnificent body.

And that brilliant mind.

And fuck, that just makes me sad, but it is what it is.

Matt has been strange since I gave my notice. I expected him to be cold and aloof. Rather, he treats me with the utmost respect, and I even see flashes of his easygoing humor. Sometimes, there will be brief moments when we are talking about a case, and I will forget how badly I'm hurting. I can see he forgets it too, because sometimes I see warmth in his eyes. Sometimes, I've even seen lust, which affects me on a whole other level I'd rather not think about. It doesn't help that I have dirty dreams of him almost every night, and my poor vibrator is just not measuring up.

While we were in Atlanta, he was very professional. We worked each day together, spending seven to eight hours straight in depositions. We usually had dinner together at night in the hotel restaurant, where we would continue to work… going over my notes for the day and strategizing on how to best attack the next day's deponents. We would say goodnight in the elevator, and we both went to sleep alone.

It was truly the employer-employee relationship we should have had all along.

But I'm not gonna lie… it was extremely unsatisfying, knowing what I used to have.

Now, as wait for our flight to board, there is no work to prepare for the next day so we have to rely on general conversation to get us through. I'm nervous, because so far, Matt and I have been able to get along by keeping things on a professional level. I'm trying to think of something interesting to say when Matt takes the lead.

"I'm releasing Kylie Wynn from her contract on the Pearson appeal."

"Really?" I ask with extreme curiosity. "I thought she was an expert or something."

Matt sort of grunts and picks at an imaginary piece of lint on his dress pants. "I really just needed the extra pair of hands more than anything. I know as much about appellate law as she does. I was just short on time. Besides… she got a little, uh… too personal with me."

Now I'm surprised. Surprised that Matt admits

this to me, and I have to wonder why.

"I kind of saw that coming," I tell him. "What did she do?"

He shrugs his shoulders and sighs. "Just made a pass at me in my office. I mean... a really awkward pass."

The giggle that pops out is unintended. "What is it with you and female lawyers? First Lorraine... and now Kylie. You're like a magnet."

We both chuckle, and then Matt's gaze sort of focuses in on me with a somber look. "You were actually first... then Lorraine, and then Kylie. But you were in a different league than they were."

His words warm me—that he is at least validating that I was different. That I was more.

I just wasn't enough though.

Clearing his throat, he brings me back out of my rumination. "I brought up the thing about Kylie because I was wondering if you would like to contract with me to help me on the Pearson appeal?"

"What?" I ask, utterly shocked.

"I saw the business plan Cal was reading that day at lunch. I assume you two are going to start your own law firm together?"

Cal and I did indeed decide to go for it. We've met several times to iron out the details and, starting next week, we open the doors to Carson and

Dawson. We're each going to fund fifty percent of the startup costs and be equal partners. I'm excited but scared as shit, because I'm risking a lot of my inheritance on this.

Matt doesn't sound in the least bit perturbed by my new venture, which actually makes sense. He didn't want me to have anything to do with Cal when we were a couple. Now that we're not, he clearly doesn't care.

"Yes," I confirm to him. "We are starting up a firm. While I would need to talk to Cal about it first, I'd love to be able to do some contract work for you. As you know, I really only have one case to my name."

The smile that Matt gives me is surreal. It's reminiscent of the smiles I used to get when we were at our happiest, and it causes a tiny jolt of longing to shoot through my heart.

"Excellent," he says. "We can discuss the details tomorrow before you leave."

We're called to board and, after we take our seats, the conversation actually seems to flow as if there was never anything harsh, sad, or bitter between us. It seems Matt has made peace with the way things are, and while I'm still in mourning over my loss of him, it's amazing to me that we can be together like this... in a friendly manner.

I suppose that has to do with the fact that neither one of us really screwed the other over. We just came to a quick realization that neither one of us wanted the same thing. So, yes... I'm very, very sad that Matt isn't my lover anymore. But I also don't hold it against him. He tried for me. He tried to give me what I asked for, but he just wasn't very good at it.

How can you fault someone for at least trying?

Chapter Ten

Matt and I share a cab from JFK. It's just past midnight when it pulls up to my apartment building.

"Pop the trunk," Matt tells the cabbie, and he steps out to help me with my luggage.

After pulling my suitcase out, he shuts the trunk and turns to me. "I'll see you tomorrow morning."

I smile at him, and it takes everything in my power not to reach out and brush a lock of his hair from his forehead. "Okay. See you tomorrow."

I start to turn toward my building when Matt's hand reaches out and grabs my wrist. Turning to look at him, I'm almost knocked over by the look on his face. It's an arrangement of emotions that Matt never dares to share with me. There's confusion, loneliness, and uncertainty—everything that would make someone like Matt extremely vulnerable.

I raise my eyebrows at him, and he seems to be at a loss for words. But then he quickly recovers, because this is Matt Fucking Connover and he's never truly without his prose.

"Let me come in with you?" he asks in a low voice that is laced with sensual promise and just a hint of desperation.

"Matt..." I begin, intent on turning him down.

But his thumb strokes over the pulse on my wrist, and my body is deciding to weigh in on this decision. "We shouldn't. We can't. We're not together anymore."

He pulls me toward him until we are toe to toe, but he doesn't touch me anywhere else, except that continual stroking over my wrist. "I know. I know we're not, and I know we shouldn't. But... one last time?"

One last time? I mean... what could one more time hurt, right? It's to say good-bye.

To make peace.

To have closure.

All of these reasons sound so damn good. I

know that my heart is going to hurt worse tomorrow because I'll start my grieving all over again, but wouldn't that be worth one more night in Matt's arms?

"One last time?" I ask, just to make sure of what he's offering.

"Just tonight," he says softly. "But it will be all night."

Shivers race up and down my spine from the seduction in his voice, and any tiny thought of declining his offer completely evaporates.

"Okay," I whisper, almost afraid if I say it too loud that Matt and I will snap out of this stupidity we've talked ourselves in to.

"Let me pay the cab," he says as he releases his hold on me. I watch as he walks around to the driver's door and pays the fare. Then the trunk pops open again, and he pulls his suitcase out.

Now that he's not touching me anymore, I have a small kernel of doubt.

Okay, a huge kernel of doubt. This is dumb, dumb, dumb.

I'm giving in to Matt's desire for sex, and what do I get in return? I don't get a relationship, true love, or hell, I won't even get breakfast in the morning. I'm scratching his itch, and I'm telling him that I admit I was never good enough to be more than a good fuck for him.

Those thoughts alone almost have me telling Matt to get in the cab but, as he looks at me, with fire burning in his eyes… it's game over. My body is telling me that I have an itch to scratch just as much as Matt does. It's true that what I really want is the relationship. I want to be with the man I can tell all my secrets to, and who will love me through thick and thin. But the one thing Matt has taught me over the last few months is that I also need more than just the emotional bond. I need the physical as well. I crave the touch and the sounds. I relish gasps, moans, and grunts. I have to have the wild excitement that comes from dirty words and rough fingers.

While Matt can't give me all of what I want, he can give me part of what I need.

So, yeah… I'm going to have one more night with him before I close that door.

And I'm going to enjoy the hell out of it.

Turning away from Matt, I walk into my building with him following. We ride the elevator up in total silence, but there is a buzzing energy around us. I sneak a glance at him and he's staring down at his shoes, seemingly lost in thought. I sure hope he's giving serious analysis to all the ways he's going to make me come.

When I open the apartment door, Matt follows me in. Macy is sitting on the couch and, when she sees Matt, her eyebrows go through the roof. I shoot her a smile that says, I'll fill you in tomorrow but don't you dare say a word right now, because I'm getting ready to get fucked like a queen and I don't want you to ruin it.

She gives me a slight nod, and I march right past her. Matt follows along, and I'm sure we make quite the sight as we head down the hallway with our suitcases rolling along behind us. I can't even imagine what's going through Macy's head right now, but I have a feeling things are going to get loud before too long, so she'll be able to piece it together.

Entering my room, I push my suitcase up against my closet door. I turn on my bedside lamp, and the room is filled with a soft glow. Matt closes the door behind him and pushes his suitcase next to mine. Then he turns to look at me, and my breath catches as I watch his lazy perusal. He has run his hungry eyes over me more times than I can remember, but he's never done it with such exquisite care. He takes his time, checking out every part of me, now that he has the time and the permission to do so.

A lush heart swirls between my legs, and I hope to God it's Matt's plan to hit it hard and fast with me. At least for the first time.

Matt takes his suit jacket off and tosses it across his suitcase. He slowly undoes his cuffs while he continues to stare at me. I have no clue what to do but, even if I did, I don't think I could make a move. I'm mesmerized by the way Matt is watching me, and I think I'm better served to just let him direct me on what to do.

When he steps up to me, I watch as his hand slowly rises. I feel his fingertips at my temple, and then he's sifting through the long length of my hair. He seems to be mesmerized as he watches the dark locks filter through his fingers. When he reaches the end, his eyes return to mine.

"Where shall we start?" he asks.

I lick my lips and try to sound like I have some coherence left. "Anywhere you want."

The smile he gives me is wicked, and he pulls that bottom lip between his teeth as he contemplates. Finally, he says, "It's been too long since my face has been between those beautiful legs of yours."

Holy hell... said beautiful legs almost buckle under the sex that is dripping from those words. Matt can see how it affects me, and he chuckles.

"Yeah," he says, his voice rough with lust. "We'll start there."

CHAPTER Eleven

You've read enough of my story by now to know that sex with Matt is beyond stupendous. So I probably shouldn't take the time to tell you what happened next.

What? Was that cursing?

Okay, fine I'll tell you, but I'm not sure I can do it actual justice.

The minute he tells me he wants to go down on me, every muscle in my body seems to liquefy. I'm on the verge of collapsing, but Matt saves the day by pulling me into his arms so he can kiss me.

This kiss is something else. It's a combination of

every type of kiss that he's ever given me, and I'm assuming he's intent on making this night memorable. I feel lust, desire, heat, passion, tenderness, caring, kinkiness, flirtation, playfulness, savagery, and roughness. It's all there, hovering underneath those lips, coating his tongue, which in turn coats my tongue.

His hands get to work, shedding me of my clothes. He's a pro at this. He knows how to get my clothes off without even needing to break the kiss. He's a master at unsnapping my bra with just a flick of one hand.

When he has me naked, he pushes me onto my bed and then takes a step back so he can disrobe. I watch him boldly, and he gives me a show because he knows I like watching him.

And I know he likes me watching him.

His clothes drop to the floor, and he takes himself in his hand and starts stroking with long, fluid pulls. His eyes close and he tilts his head back, moaning slightly as he works himself into rock hardness.

That is so fucking hot, and I'm hypnotized by the sight of him masturbating. When I finally am able to look away from what he's doing to himself, I let my gaze wander to his face.

That beautiful face.

I see his eyes are no longer closed but watching me with intensity, the weight almost oppressive upon me.

"Spread your legs," he commands, and I don't even hesitate in my acquiescence. I'd do anything he told me to do tonight.

Anything.

His gaze moves down my body and stares at his intended destination. "Touch yourself," he says thickly.

And I do, causing his eyes to go so dark, that they look almost completely black. He just stares at my hand between my legs, his breaths getting shorter and shorter while he strokes his cock.

He doesn't even look back into my eyes when he releases himself and murmurs, "Enough. You're ready for my mouth, and I don't think I'll stop until I've made you come at least three times."

Fuck, but his dirty talk is like the best in the world. I bet if he tried, he could give me an orgasm just by talking to me. He's that good.

As Matt steps up to me, a thought crosses my mind. I'm on borrowed time with him, and I want to give to Matt as much as he wants to give to me.

"Wait," I say, because he starts to kneel between my legs.

His gaze snaps to mine, and I almost giggle at the impatience firing through his irises.

"Let's make this a little more balanced."

Impatience now turns to interest. "What did you have in mind?"

"We've done a lot of dirty things together, but I don't think we've ever done sixty-nine. Let's give that a try."

Matt's lips curve upward, and there are those dimples that I just haven't seen enough of lately.

"You are like the perfect fucking woman," he says reverently, but also with good cheer, because he's getting ready to feel really, really good too.

"No, I'm not," I remind him, because otherwise, this wouldn't be our last time together. "But I'm damn close, so get your ass on this bed and get into position."

I expect Matt to immediately hop on the bed and get our mouths and body parts aligned, but he surprises me by crawling in between my legs and right up my body until he's covering me completely, his lips hovering just above mine.

His gaze is soft, and it reminds me of the time he held me in his arms in Nashville the night before my mother died. I feel like he wants to say something, and I hold my breath. Because I see emotion on his face, I immediately start thinking that maybe he wants to confess his feelings to me. Maybe he realizes that while yes, the sex is smokin' hot and really can't be compared, there is something deeper between us. There always has been.

Matt's mouth even parts, words ready to tumble out of his lips. His breath stutters, and he takes a deep breath while closing his eyes. When he opens them back up again, the softness is gone and carnality reigns supreme. He gives me a smoldering kiss. He takes his time about it, even while grinding his erection between my legs.

By the time Matt is ready to give my idea of sixty-nine a try, he has made me completely delirious just from his kiss. I know it will not take long for me to find my happiest of places.

He arranges our bodies, a master of placing his leg here or my arm there. Then our mouths become occupied with each other and just as anticipated, it's just a matter of seconds before he kick-starts an orgasm in me. It's hard to scream out loud when your mouth is filled with yummy Matt goodness, but I'm sure he felt the vibrations of my gratification bubble up through my body, straight out of my mouth and onto his dick.

The way we pleasure each other at the same time… giving… receiving. Our hands eager to always touch the other's skin. The sounds we make that urge the other on, or even the acknowledgement we give because we are so very grateful how good something feels.

We are fucking perfect in bed together.

Absolutely perfect.

It just sucks that it's the only way we seem to be compatible.

Chapter Twelve

I stare at my computer monitor, trying to finish the last legal memo that Matt had assigned me. I have about fifteen minutes of work left on it if I can just concentrate.

But I haven't been able to concentrate for shit all day.

Thanks to Matt Fucking Connover.

Last night was unimaginable. It exceeded my expectations. If I had thought that our sex life was amazing before last night, I would tell you today that it sucked in comparison.

I'm not sure if it was the desperate nature of our

coupling, knowing that we were parting ways forever, or if it was merely the fact that we were just trying to outdo ourselves.

Regardless, I got a grand total of two hours of sleep between four and six AM, which was when my alarm went off. When I drifted off around four, Matt had me wrapped up in a tight embrace, spooning against me. When the alarm woke me, his side of the bed was cold, and just like that... Matt and I were officially done.

So what's a girl to do after a night of mind-blowing sex with the man she loves who doesn't love her in return, but still managed to still give her five orgasms last night?

She pines for him.

All fucking day.

Shaking my head, I focus back on my computer monitor. With a sigh, I poise my fingers to type but my cell phone rings, interrupting my one true effort at doing some actual work.

It's Cal calling. For a moment I consider not answering, because he'll know something's wrong. He'll dig and push at me until I spill my guts, and then I can sit on the phone and just imagine all the ways that he pities me. But it could be something important about our new firm, so I answer and try to sound as joyful as I can.

"If this about you wanting to lease that high-tech, super-duper copier, you can forget it. I won't change my mind," I joke with him as soon as I connect the call.

"You are not going to fucking believe this," he practically shouts into the phone with excitement.

"What?" I ask, thinking he just landed a multi-million dollar case to add to our pathetically small caseload of one.

"Matt just left my office."

"As in he had some type of meeting set over at your firm?"

"No, as in he showed up here at my firm and asked to see me... to talk to me."

"About what?" I ask.

"He wanted to talk to me about the night that... well, you know... the night Marissa and me..."

Cal's voice trails off in embarrassment, and my heartstrings start playing a sad tune for him.

"What did he say?" I ask, completely blown away that Matt would even approach Cal for something personal, much less give him an opportunity to talk about what happened.

"He told me straight up that you had told him some of the details, and that you had urged him to learn the entire truth and see if he had it in his heart to forgive me."

"Matt said all of that?"

"Word for word."

Oh my gosh. I can't believe Matt actually did that.

"So tell me everything that happened. Spare me no detail," I urge him.

Cal proceeds to lay out the entire story. He says Matt listened without any comment and no snide remarks as Cal embarrassingly recounted what happened that night. Cal says he didn't pull any punches with Matt, including telling him that he was drunk and that contributed to what happened, but it was no excuse and all the fault lay with him. He made sure Matt understood that he didn't "finish the job," but that he knew that didn't make it any better. Cal finished off by telling Matt that he could never begin to tell him how sorry he was, and although he really doesn't deserve it, he would do just about anything to get Matt's forgiveness.

"Then what happened?" I asked with bated breath. This was better than any Hallmark or Lifetime movie.

"Matt simply told me that he forgave me. He said that he had been doing a lot of soul searching, and he felt that he was not the man he had the potential to be if he was carrying around all of that bitterness. He also said he forgave Marissa, although that would be another conversation he'd have to have with her."

"Oh my God," I whisper, my heart swelling with joy that Matt opened himself up to forgiveness. "I just can't believe it. How do you feel?"

"I feel light, Mac. I feel fucking light. The weight has been lifted from my shoulders. I know Matt will still never be anything more to me than a professional acquaintance. The loss of his friendship will be the cross I'll always bear. But knowing that he's telling me to let it go... that means the fucking world."

Tears well up in my eyes because I'm so happy for Cal and so very damn proud of Matt. I wish he were here right this very moment, so I could give him a huge hug.

"So, there was one other thing," Cal says, interrupting my very own Hallmark moment. "Remember when I said I told Matt I'd do just about anything to get his forgiveness?"

"Yeah."

"Well, he already called that chip in."

Dread wells up inside of me. "What does he want you to do?"

"Well..." Cal says, hedging a little and clearly afraid that I might not like what he's getting ready to say.

"What did that asshole make you do, Cal?" I grit out, getting all incensed on Cal's behalf, before really even knowing what he will tell me.

"Calm down there, Annie Get Your Gun," Cal says with a laugh. "Actually... it's not much that he asked me to do. First, he said he had an idea he wanted to run by me and get my opinion on. And once I listened to him, and gave him my thoughts about his idea, the real favor he wanted had to do with you."

My breath seems to be caught somewhere between the top of my lungs and the bottom of my throat, so all I can do is whisper, "What's that?"

"Well... Matt is standing right outside of your office at this very moment, and all I need to do is convince you to give him ten minutes of your time and listen to what he has to say. So, what do you think... can you do that?"

My head starts spinning. I glance around my office to make sure I haven't fallen down the rabbit hole, but nope... still in my office.

"I'll talk to you later, Cal," I tell him and then disconnect.

Standing up, I walk to my office door and open it.

Chapter Thirteen

Just as Cal said, Matt is standing there, looking somber and slightly uncomfortable. I step back, making a sweeping gesture with my arm for him to come in. Turning, I head back to my desk, hoping that my racing heart won't cause coronary arrest. Matt doesn't move from the door but stands there with his hands in his pockets, watching me.

I start the conversation. "Cal said you forgave him."

Matt shrugs his shoulders as if it were nothing. "It needed to be done."

"Why is that?" I ask, completely fearful and yet

totally needing him to tell me.

But he doesn't. Instead, he reaches into his coat pocket and throws an envelope on my desk. I immediately recognize it as the envelope that had my letter of resignation in it. The words "Matthew Connover" are written in my completely messy handwriting.

I glance up to Matt, who returns my stare.

"Open it," he says.

Opening the flap, I reach inside and pull out a pile of paper, all torn up into itty-bitty pieces. I can see clearly enough that it's my letter of resignation, completely shredded.

"I don't accept your resignation," he says, his voice authoritative and commanding.

"Excuse me?" I say in shock.

"You heard me. You're not quitting. I need you."

Hmmmm. He needs me?

"You don't need me," I scoff at him. "You can put an ad in the paper and have a hundred attorneys lined up in the morning, all with better grades and references than I have."

"No," Matt says with equal authority. "You don't get it. I. Need. You."

He punctuates each word so that I hear him clearly.

I. Need. You.

And that's all it takes for my heart to start really hammering. Matt takes two steps until he is directly in front of me, and I have to lean my head back to look up at him from my chair. He doesn't make me strain my neck for long because he drops to his knees in front of me.

His eyes hold me. I see all the things I've been dying to see. Desire, care, nurturing, tenderness, and passion.

I also see something else.

Pleading.

His eyes plead with me to understand something, but I'm not sure what it is he wants me from me. Before I can even fathom a guess, he leans in, wraps his arms around my waist, and lays his head in my lap.

He squeezes me, gently, and I can't stop my hands from coming up and stroking his head.

He stays in that position for several minutes, just squeezing me, his head nestled in my lap. My mind is racing... I have no clue what this means.

Finally, he lifts his head and looks up at me. The pleading is still there, along with fear and uncertainty.

"I need you, Mac," he says with a shaky voice. "I need your smile, your touch, and your wit. I need your tenderness, your brilliance, and your common sense. I need you to be my champion, and I need you to want to come home to me every night. I need all of those things... desperately. I think I might die without them."

He stares at me... a storm of emotions brewing within those golden eyes, and my heart is thundering so hard right now, I'm surprised he can't hear it.

"You need me?" I ask, completely shell shocked over his proclamation.

He nods and his lips curve upward, his dimples just starting to pop. "You're usually not this dense, Mac."

I smile in return and push my hair behind one ear, leaning it slightly toward him. "It's just... I'm not sure I heard you correctly. You did say you need me?"

"Yes," he says as his hands come up to hold my head. He leans in and kisses me, so very sweetly. "I need you because I love you. When you love someone the way I love you, the need for that person is unquenchable."

"And when did you come to this realization?"

The smile he gives me is so loving, that my heart just turns over and kicks its little heart feet up in submission.

"I think I've always known it. I was just too filled with so many other things that I refused to acknowledge it. But last night... I held you while you slept, and I just laid there... the entire time, realizing how wonderful it felt to have your body next to mine.

When it got close to the time I needed to leave so I could get ready for work, I felt like my heart was being fucking pulled out of my chest. That's the moment I decided to acknowledge it."

"Why didn't you just stick around... tell me then?"

"Because I had to let my hatred of Cal go first. And Mac, I mean it with every breath in my body. I did hate him. But the minute I decided to forgive him, I became a different person. A better person."

My hand reaches out, and I stroke his cheek. His eyes close at my touch, and a serene smile lays over those sexy as fuck lips. "I'm so proud of you, Matt. You're really kind of amazing."

"And you love me?" he asks with a grin, as he stands up and pulls me from my chair.

"What makes you think that?" I tease him, just before he leans in and kisses me.

It's a kiss I'll never forget. It's our first true kiss, because it's being done after he proclaimed his love for me. When his lips finally leave mine, he answers, "Because you already told me you did."

I wrap my arms around his neck and step into his body. "Yeah, I guess I did."

"Say it again," he demands of me.

And because I'd give him anything he asked of me, I say, "I love you... so much."

CHAPTER Fourteen

We kiss again, and it starts out sweet but, before long, we're both pressing into each other hard and our breaths are choppy.

"Let's take the rest of the day off," he whispers urgently in my ear. "I need to be inside of you."

I groan over the thought but shake my head in denial. "I can't. I have to get this stuff finished. You know, today's my last day and all."

Matt laughs and kisses me again. "Didn't you understand me? I'm not accepting your resignation. There's no way I'm letting you out of my sight. And I sure as hell don't want you working around Cal unattended. I don't trust the bastard."

"Hey!" I exclaim and punch him on the shoulder. "I thought you forgave him?"

Matt looks at me in all seriousness. "I did, Mac. But I don't like him. We're not friends."

Sighing, I lay my head on his chest and squeeze him tight. "No, I don't suppose you are. You did more than enough by offering forgiveness. But I can't turn my back on him. I made a deal with him to open up a law firm."

"Yeah, well... I sort of might have changed his mind after I talked to him today."

I pull back and look at Matt. He has a sheepish expression on his face.

"What did you do?" I ask, already trying to shame him with my tone.

Matt holds his hands up in defense. "Nothing bad, I swear it. I just sort of offered him a job here, as long as you agreed to stay."

"What?" I ask, stunned beyond comprehension. "You asked Cal... your arch nemesis... to come work for you? I thought you said you didn't trust the bastard."

"I don't," Matt says smugly. "What better way to keep tabs on him than having him come work for me?"

I arch an eyebrow up in skepticism. He returns my stare, and we poker face each other.

Then he cracks.

"Fine," he says with a long-suffering sigh. "I want you to stay. You're a brilliant attorney, and you're going places. I want you on my team. I also want you within reach of me at all times because I love you to fucking death. So, the easiest thing seemed to be for me to get Cal on board. I knew you had committed to him, but if he came here, you'd stay."

"You're rotten," I scold him. "And completely selfish."

"When it comes to you, you're damn right I am. But talk to Cal... you both have a decision to make."

Wrapping my arms back around his neck, I stand on my tiptoes and give him a light kiss. "I'll talk to Cal, and we'll see. But for now... let's get out of here."

Matt doesn't need any more encouragement; the promise of our bodies coming together the minute we step over the threshold of his apartment... or mine... is almost too overwhelming.

He doesn't even let me log off my computer. Grabbing my purse to shove in my hands, he starts leading me out of the office. With his fingers laced through mine tightly, he pulls me through the firm in a hurry. We pass attorneys, paralegals, and secretaries, who all stare at us with mouths hanging open. There is no doubt by looking at us, and the impatience on Matt's face, that he's either dragging me out to murder me or fuck me, none of which matters to me because I'm officially not his employee anymore.

As he pulls me through the lobby, Bea looks up and I have to giggle at the stunned look on her face. As we pass her desk, Matt stops abruptly and looks at Bea.

"You need to redo your rating scale," he tells her.

Her jaw drops open, and her face goes red. "Rating scale?"

"Yeah… that scale that you and Mac use to judge my mood."

Bea turns to look at me, a pleading look on her face for me to step in and save her. I'm shocked as well and turn to Matt. "How in the hell do you know about that?"

Giving me a smile that seemingly melts the panties away from my body, he steps in and gives me a kiss. "I know everything that has to do with you. Let that be a word of warning."

Then he kisses me again, this time more deeply, and his hand even palms my ass to bring me closer. I can hear Bea choking behind us.

When Matt pulls away, my head is completely

fuzzed, but I'm able to watch as he turns to Bea again. His voice is authoritative, and this is Matt Connover, Supreme Boss and Litigation God Extraordinaire, talking to her. "Yeah... redo that scale. This is me at a fifteen on the 'one to ten happiness scale'. That's what you use as a baseline to judge my mood from now on. Clear?"

Bea just nods her head at him, fear and confusion in her eyes. He stares at her hard for a moment, and I'm just getting ready to slap him for being so rotten, when he levels a brilliant smile at her. "And Bea?"

"Yes, Mr. Connover?" she says timidly.

"Thanks for looking out for my girl here when I was being an asshole."

Bea's mouth drops open again, and then snaps quickly shut. "Yes, Mr. Connover."

Flashing her both dimples, which, if you're not quite ready for it, can cause pleasurable blindness on a temporary basis, he pulls me to the door. He lowers his voice so I hope to God only I can hear. "Let's go, baby. I'm dying to see how great our fucking is going to be now that love is involved."

Smiling, I follow behind him.

The man I love, who loves me back.

The great Matthew Fucking Connover.

I'm such a lucky girl.

Epilogue

"Listen... I'm not impressed by that offer. It's twenty-five and not a penny less. If you don't pay it, I'll drag your ass through the shit storm that is our legal system for so long, that you'll be ready to retire before this case is over. And I could care less if I win it. Just drowning you in legal expenses makes me all tingly inside."

I hear the voice on the other end give a sigh. Finally, he says, "Fine. Check is in the mail."

"Thank you," I say sincerely. "And have a nice day."

As I'm hanging up the phone, I hear clapping

from my office door. Turning, I see Matt standing there, smiling with pride, and giving me an exuberant round of applause.

"That was fantastic, baby," he says reverently.

Shrugging my shoulders, I say, "Well... I learned from the best."

"Twenty-five?" he says.

"Yup, twenty-five hundred dollars. I know it's not your twenty-five million, but baby steps," I say with a smile.

"I'm proud of you nonetheless. We should celebrate tonight."

I love Matt. He is my biggest supporter, my grand champion, and even though my victory is tiny compared to his legal prowess, he's just as proud of me as if I had just settled a case for twenty-five bazillion dollars.

Smirking at him, I say, "I'm not sure a twenty-five hundred dollar settlement is worth celebrating. But... if you want to give me an extra orgasm tonight, I wouldn't be opposed."

"I can arrange that," Matt tells me with a grin. "But how about we fly down to Florida for a weekend getaway?"

"That's a great idea. And let's ask Marissa if we can take Gabe."

"I'll give her a call and hopefully I'll catch her in a good mood."

Marissa and Matt's parenting relationship has changed somewhat in the last several months. Matt did indeed talk to Marissa and told her that he forgave her, and he even apologized for the times he was an asshole. While Matt did that more for himself rather than his ex-wife, it seemed to provide a balming effect on Marissa. She's become slightly easier to deal with, although it's a little hit or miss with her. She and Matt have had some serious discussions that they had to work together to provide a stable environment for Gabe. Since then, she's been a little more relaxed with Matt, and on an occasion or two, Marissa even managed to actually smile rather than sneer at me.

Matt walks all the way into my office and sits down on the edge of my desk. I try not to be distracted by the rock-hard thigh that is bulging through the material of his pants, which causes my gaze to run up the length of his leg to the bulge that is now becoming more prominent in the crotch area.

Flicking my gaze up to his, I see his eyes are dark and heavy. I swallow hard and try not to look back down again.

Matt chuckles and leans forward to kiss me. "You know you can't look at me like that and not make me hard. It's a hazard of having you in the same building as me during the day."

I kiss him back and make it hot. Because I want

him to know that it doesn't take much for him to get my motor running either.

Pulling away, Matt reaches into his pocket and takes out an envelope. Handing it to me, he says, "Actually... I thought we'd celebrate this."

I take the envelope. It's white linen with the Connover and Crown logo on the front. As I open it, I sneak a peek at Matt. He's smiling at me with love and warmth. It makes me go all gooey inside.

Reaching in, I pull a piece of paper out of the envelope. It's a check. It's made out to Carson and Dawson, and my eyes bug out. It's for an amount that has an insane amount of zeroes behind it. My legal fee for the Jackson case.

You see, approximately eight months ago when Matt proclaimed he loved me, I had a decision to make. Matt wanted me to continue to work for him, but Cal and I wanted to open our own firm. We ended up compromising. Carson and Dawson was formed so the employer-employee issue between Matt and me was gone. But we subleased space in Matt's office, and Matt hired Carson and Dawson to do contract work on some of his cases. This provided immediate income to Cal and me, and provided Matt the ability see me throughout the day, although I put a halt on his insistence that we could have discreet office sex. I was terrified we were going to get caught.

Plus, I was with Matt every night, so it's not like we were suffering.

The most awesome thing that has happened in my legal career is that, with Matt's presence on the Jackson case and his guidance and expertise, we managed to settle it for mega bucks. We were able to fund an amazing annuity for our clients after paying off all of their expenses, and they would never have to struggle with bills or healthcare again.

So yeah, my legal fee that Matt just handed me will ensure that my new law firm of Carson and Dawson will actually be in the black during its first year of operation. Most of it is going into savings though, so that we can rely on it during leaner months. I'm not falling into the same pitfall that Lorraine dropped into while trying to run a business.

I look at the check one more time, and then set it on my desk. Standing up, I walk into Matt's embrace. He has to shift his legs so I can step in between them, our arms coming up to mutually wrap around the other. He pulls me in close, and I can feel his erection pressed up against me and, as is usual the case, my brain goes a little wonky.

Giving myself a mental shake, I lean in to give my man a kiss before saying, "Thank you for helping me with this case. I could have never gotten that type of justice for the Jacksons without you."

He doesn't respond but resumes the kiss, pushing it hotter... gripping me tighter. His tongue is almost as magical as his dick, and I'm on the verge of begging him for desk sex when he pulls back.

I feel flushed and faint, and I can barely focus on Matt and his grinning face.

"I have something else for you," he says.

"Please, please, please... tell me it's an orgasm. I don't care how... mouth, fingers, dirty talk. Just give me one."

Matt busts out laughing and leans in to kiss my nose. "You never, ever fail to amuse me. I think I've laughed more since I've met you than in my entire life."

"And that's a good thing, right?" I tease him.

He pulls me back in and hugs me tight. "It's a very good thing," he murmurs, just before he pushes me away from him.

When I'm at arm's length, he reaches back into his suit jacket and pulls something else out. It's another envelope.

I take it from him, completely curious because it's fatter than the one with the check, clearly containing a thick packet of papers.

"What's this?" I ask curiously.

"Open it and find out."

The envelope is almost identical to the previous

one I just opened. White linen, but the logo on the left corner catches my attention. It says, "Connover and Dawson," and has a heart next to it. No address, no other information.

Weird.

I undo it up and pull out the thick packet. Opening it up, I'm first struck by the fact that the papers are blank.

I'm next struck by the fact that there is a ring taped to the middle of the first page. Even with opaque tape over it, I can see it's a stunner. Platinum... or is that white gold? I have no clue, but there is a square-cut diamond in the center with tiny diamonds surrounding the edge. More diamonds litter both sides of the band.

My hands start shaking.

I mean hard, and all I can see is the ring sort of bouncing around in my vision.

Matt's hands reach out and cover mine. They are calm and reassuring, which makes the shaking stop.

I glance up at him, and he's looking at me with such love that my heart actually hurts a tiny bit.

But in a good way. In a painfully, pleasurable way.

Matt nimbly plucks the ring from the packet and pulls the tape off. I watch like I'm in a dream as he pulls the papers from my hands and sets them down.

Then he takes my left hand and slides the ring on.

Neither of us has said a word, and the room is heavy with emotion.

I look down at my hand, at the ring sparkling and Matt's hand holding mine. Looking back up, I hold his gaze and his smile wraps around me like a blanket.

"Will you?" he asks simply.

The great Matthew Fucking Connover, the King of Prose and Wordsmith Genius has no great speech prepared for me. He just has a simple question, and I give him my simple answer.

"Yes."

If you enjoyed the Legal Affairs Serial Romance
Boxed Set as much as I enjoyed writing it,
it would mean a lot for you to give me a review.

NEWSLETTER SIGNUP!!!
Don't miss another new release by Sawyer Bennett!!!
Sign up for her newsletter and keep up to date on
new releases, giveaways, book reviews
and so much more.

Connect with Sawyer online:

Website: www.sawyerbennett.com
Twitter: www.twitter.com/bennettbooks
Facebook: www.facebook.com/bennettbooks

BOOKS BY Sawyer Bennett

The Off Series
Off Sides
Off Limits
Off The Record
Off Course
Off Chance

The Last Call Series
On The Rocks
Make It A Double
Sugar On The Edge (Coming Soon)
Shaken Not Stirred (Coming Soon)
With A Twist (Coming Soon)

The Legal Affairs Series
Objection
Stipulation
Violation
Mitigation
Reparation
Affirmation
Confessions of a Litigation God (Coming Soon)

The Forever Land Chronicles
Forever Young

Books of the Stone Veil
The Darkest of Blood Magicks
To Catch a Dark Thief

Stand Alone Titles
If I Return

ABOUT THE Author

USA Today Bestselling Author, Sawyer Bennett is a snarky southern woman and reformed trial lawyer who decided to finally start putting on paper all of the stories that were floating in her head. Her husband works for a Fortune 100 company which lets him fly all over the world while she stays at home with their daughter and three big, furry dogs who hog the bed. Sawyer would like to report she doesn't have many weaknesses but can be bribed with a nominal amount of milk chocolate.

Made in the USA
Middletown, DE
03 July 2017